HER DARK PAST

JANE HEAFIELD

First published in 2021 by Bloodhound Books.

www.bloodhoundbooks.com

Print ISBN 978-1-914614-53-8

ALSO BY JANE HEAFIELD

Dead Cold

Cold Blood

Don't Believe Her

1

It started with two phone calls.

The first was to a house in Sheffield at nine in the morning. Sara Yorston took the call. She was in the barn, a small, shed-like structure in the backyard where she worked, when the landline rang. She couldn't hear it from the barn, but her daughter yelled that someone was calling. Sara waited for her husband to get it, but Marcie shouted again a few seconds later. Sara got up, wiped clay off her hands, and trekked through the thin snow blanket smothering her backyard.

When she entered the kitchen, she heard the shower running upstairs – that answered the question of why her husband hadn't picked up the phone. She answered the call in her standard form, receptionist style: name and how could she help?

It was a male voice she didn't know: 'Mrs Yorston, my name is Oliver Elliot with Elliot and Harmon Solicitors. I'll get straight to the point. Mr Drake Mills wants to meet with you. Now, I understand this is–'

She hung up and stepped away from the phone as if it were radioactive.

It was Sara who made the second call, about thirty minutes later. Sixty-three miles almost directly south, at a house on the northern edge of Birmingham's Burbury Park, a man answered on the third ring. She asked for Jenny Pitchford.

A crack as the handset was put down. A shout of, 'Mum.' Extraneous noises as people moved about. The scrape of the handset being lifted once more.

'Hello?'

That voice: unmistakable, even though she'd last heard it almost twenty years ago. 'I need your help,' Sara blurted, tears washing down her cheeks. 'I need to see you. Please. That evil bastard, Drake, has reared his ugly head.'

2

Marcie wasn't an observant teenager, but nobody could have missed her mother's dour demeanour. Sara was quiet as she made breakfast, and although Marcie asked what was wrong, her mum couldn't even fake a smile. How could she after that phone call?

When Joe had showered and suited up and thumped downstairs to make a packed lunch, he paused, watching his wife. Sara knew he'd sensed something off with her, but as yet hadn't mentioned it. At the table, as the family ate, Marcie finally clocked that her mother had something worrying on her mind.

'You okay, Mum? What's wrong?'

'How's the research going?' Joe asked his daughter before Sara could respond.

Marcie had recently joined VolunteerLife and was due to jet off to South Africa. Learning about her placement had made her giddy and she was always eager to speak of it. As the teenager talked ten to the dozen, Sara glanced at Joe and saw him staring right back. She realised he'd distracted Marcie so Sara could fret in peace. She also knew he'd demand answers later.

After her breakfast, Marcie grabbed her bag and shoes, kissed her mother's brunette fringe, tickled her dad's thick, wiry beard, and left the table. Sara waited for Joe to ask about her mood, but he didn't. He left the table and headed out to work. Maybe he hadn't noticed her dour mood after all. She would have to tell him though.

Sara went to the living-room window to watch Marcie leave. Outside, the sky was as white as the skin of snow on the ground, but scaffolding at the front of the house cast gloom across the window. It matched her mood. As Marcie stood on the pavement, awaiting her ride, a grimy blue van pulled up at the kerb and ejected three men in coveralls: the roofers here to fix their tiling.

As the trio of men congregated outside the front window, Sara shut the curtains. She didn't want to hear their masculine chatter, or the radio they'd soon set blaring, and this time hoped that short, bald one had used the toilet before leaving his house. She trekked out the back door, using her existing footsteps to cross the snow and enter the barn.

She sat at her pottery table and began feeding clay into the roller to create flat pancakes for moulding. A shadow moved across her and she looked up. Joe was in the open doorway. He must have been impatient for answers and had turned his car around.

'Okay?' he said.

'Yes. Of course. I had the dream again, that's all.'

He didn't buy this and she knew why. That terrible dream had invaded her sleep for thousands of nights, and she had learned to manage its effects. Sometimes it resulted in a sleepless night, but it had been a long time since it had caused a black attitude the next day. He knew this was about more than that.

'Anything I can do to help?'

She shook her head. 'I'm fine. Just a bit of a headache.'

No lie here. There *was* a headache, but she wasn't yet ready to explain the phone call that had caused it. Joe looked unconvinced. 'Anything else I should know about?'

Yes, she almost blurted. But she held her tongue. She wouldn't tell him a thing until after she'd made a journey.

So, here a lie: 'No, I'm fine. Just this freezing weather, I guess.'

Despite spending half her life with Joe, from the age of nineteen, she could still find his expressionless face hard to read. If he accepted her words, or didn't but chose not to push, she couldn't tell. He bid her a good day and left. She felt guilty, but he would know everything soon.

She went to the tall fence between their backyard and the driveway, poking her nose over until she saw his car peel away from the kerb. Then she rushed upstairs to get changed. For the journey that would change her entire life.

3

Little Riders was a riding school where kids could try out horses at five pounds for ten minutes. Sara saw a school party in the muddy car park as she arrived. The arena was alongside, with young women in high-vis jackets walking children on horses. There was a static caravan that had been turned into a café with tables out front and a small petting zoo by the livery. The place was very busy for a wintry school day. She waited for the throng of schoolkids to clear and parked.

A path led from the car park and through high conifer hedging to a lake of gravel, in the centre of which stood a two-storey Georgian farmhouse with a modern annex. The stone archway in the hedge was barred by a gate with a keypad, but she'd been given the code during her phone call that morning. The house was set next to the main road but shielded by more high hedging. Behind the building, a long lawn laid with smooth snow sloped down. Sara was instantly jealous. Jenny hadn't managed her dream of a house in the country, but this was an adequate runner-up.

The front door was a massive slab of oak, like something from a Gothic castle. Sara slammed the knocker against it and waited. Curiously, there was a ramp rather than a doorstep. She wondered if Jenny lived with an elderly, infirm relative.

The handsome young man who answered the door wore a shirt and trousers, but had marred his smart appearance with sturdy safety boots. Earlier, when she'd phoned Jenny and a male had called for 'Mum', Sara had been too worked up to understand. Twenty years ago when Sara knew her, Jenny had never mentioned a son. The man looked about thirty – which would have made him about ten back then.

Before Sara could state her business, he stepped past her and said, 'Hey up. In you go. Living room on the right.'

He left her there as he crossed the gravel, headed wherever. She entered the foyer and closed the heavy door, which automatically electronically locked. To her left was a wide staircase with a lift next to it. A door at the far end led to a kitchen with long windows displaying the distant, snowy landscape.

The first doorway on the right led to the living room, which was smaller than she'd imagined from the exterior of the house. A bay window had a deep sill with framed photos vying for space. There was a corner sofa, a three-seater sofa and an armchair, and the entire back wall was a bookcase with a doorway cut into it.

Jenny was sat on the corner sofa, doing paperwork. Sara was shocked to see a wheelchair by the older woman's legs. And she looked tired and worn out, older than her years. Noticing her guest, Jenny put her arms out for a hug, which Sara gave. She then took the armchair, but Jenny patted the sofa.

'You've aged well,' Jenny said as Sara sat by her. 'Still a pretty girl. And now you have a grown-up daughter. How is she? How's Joe? I assume you're still with him.' She pointed at Sara's neck, where a yin-and-yang charm with faded black hung on old string. It had been a gift from Joe to celebrate a... new dawn, she liked to call it.

Sara had come here to discuss Drake, but that monster was a subject she was happy to avoid at the moment. She told the older woman all about her family. Joe was manager of an events venue in Barnsley and sometimes played gigs at pubs with his rock band. Marcie was studying humanities at college, keen to dedicate her life to charity; with VolunteerLife's Blue Ocean Research and Conservation, she would be helping the needy in Plettenberg Bay, South Africa's major beach resort.

'She's under eighteen, so I had to give my permission for her to go. I did that with a heavy heart. She goes in a few weeks. I don't want to lose her for a year, but she'd probably move out and never speak to me again if I refused.'

'And you? You had those dreams of teaching football to kids...'

'Long gone,' Sara told her. 'My new love is pottery. I've got a Facebook business page and I sell through some shops around Sheffield. Speaking of dreams, I see you got your wish to own a horse stable.'

Jenny explained that she'd met a man called Raymond, a music producer, on a day trip to Birmingham. A year to the day, he asked her to marry him. His wedding gift to her: this house and the stables. Jenny caught Sara's glance down at where a finger should have held a wedding ring. There wasn't one.

'He died nine years ago,' Jenny said. 'Car crash.'

'I'm sorry.'

Jenny waved it off, but there was sadness in her eyes. 'A long time ago now. Let's not talk about it. That wound is scabbed over and no longer painful.'

'The young man who answered the door. Is he...'

'My son, yes. I know what you're thinking. He's too old. I had no children when I knew you. Raymond already had a son when

I met him. Christian and his wife bought this house and land off me after Raymond died. The stables were just a hobby for me, really, but since they took over it's become a pretty successful business.'

'You still live here though?'

Her room was the new annex, she explained. She didn't want to live alone, so Christian let her stay on, and she made a wage by cleaning the house, running the café, and managing the staff. But Jenny would be alone again in a few weeks because Christian and his wife were going backpacking for six months. 'So, we're a couple of gossips moaning that our kids are about to abandon us. Anyway, that's my history since we last met. Except for one thing, which I know you're dying to ask about. The wheelchair.'

Embarrassed, Sara shook her head. 'Oh, no, I wasn't going to...' She saw Jenny's smile and deflated. 'Okay, yes, I was. What happened?'

'I'll tell you another time. Now we've broken the ice, let's get down to why you're here. Let's talk as I show you around.'

Jenny climbed into her wheelchair and escorted Sara from the house via the back door. A rubber mulch pathway, ideal for the wheelchair and clear of snow, led around the back edge of the land, with offshoots spearing to the arena, the café and the other outbuildings. They took the path to the closed café, entered through the rear, and took a table in the back corner, by a window overlooking the arena.

While Sara watched two young girls have the time of their lives riding horses, Jenny rolled behind the counter to make tea. When they were both at the table, sipping, Jenny said, 'Okay. In your own time, Sara. You said Drake has reared his ugly head.'

Sara had to put her cup down before her shaking hand sploshed tea everywhere. 'Drake wants to meet me. I don't know why. I can't think what to do. I hope he doesn't think he can... I fear he wants to... I'm scared he'll come for me.'

Jenny took Sara's hand in both her own. 'He can't, you know that. That bastard can't hurt you or anyone else who matters, ever again.'

4

With Jenny watching, Sara knew she couldn't back out at the last second. But her old friend's presence also gave her confidence. She paced up and down an aisle of the café as the phone rang.

'Elliot and Harmon Solicitors, how can I help?' answered a female.

'Mr Elliot, please.'

The secretary's happy tone continued, even though she imparted bad news. 'Mr Elliot is out at the present time, I'm afraid. He also doesn't take unsolicited calls. Is he expecting yours?'

'No, but he'll take it, I guarantee that. Give him a message. My name is Sara Yorston and I'll be at the office at seven tonight.'

'I'm afraid office hours are nine until five, and neither Mr Elliot nor Mr Harmon ever–'

'Seven o'clock,' Sara cut in. 'And if he's not there, tell him never to call me again.'

She hung up and looked at Jenny. 'I sounded rude. I should call her back and apologise.'

'No. Solicitors deal with all manner of scum and you're probably the most respectful call they've had all week. Just remember that they need you, you don't need them. So this will all happen on your terms.'

Sara sat at the table and cradled her tea, now as cold as her hands. Jenny said, 'Are you sure you don't want to bring the solicitor here? I don't mind.'

'No. I want to be able to walk out at a second's notice.'

'Of course. What if Joe doesn't want you to go?'

Sara had picked the evening so she could talk to Joe beforehand. She would steadfastly refuse if he demanded to accompany her to the solicitors' office, but part of her almost hoped he'd try to talk her out of going altogether. She couldn't imagine any outcome to the meeting that benefitted her. 'Joe will understand. As long as you're there. He might have a problem with it if I go alone. You really don't mind?'

'Sara, mind or not, I'll be there. Those horses out there couldn't drag me away. I can't wait to hear what that monster, Drake, wants.'

'He won't be there, will he?'

Jenny laughed, which surprised Sara. 'At the office? You think they'd let him out for that? Relax, Sara. The only time that animal is getting out of his cell is when they drag his corpse to an unmarked grave.'

5

When Joe returned home after work, he was in his usual inert mood, until his *Waltons*-like shout of 'Hey, I'm back!' received no reply except Marcie's. She was upstairs, washing her hair over the bathroom sink, and he appeared in the doorway with a rare frown.

'Where's your mum?'

'I got a text saying she'd be late. She said your phone was dead.'

'Battery went. Where is she? You're dripping water.'

Marcie turned away from him to lean over the sink again. 'Dunno. Didn't say.'

It was uncommon for her mum to be out when Dad got home from work, so his puzzled face was warranted. He made a curious grunt and vanished. A few minutes later, while towelling her hair dry in her bedroom, she heard the landline ring. Her dad answered it, listened for a moment, and yelled, 'What?'

Her dad was the most chilled man she knew, so this outburst drew her to the top of the stairs to eavesdrop. She only got his half of the conversation, but filling in the gaps was easy.

'Well, I hope you told those fools to get lost,' he said next, again loud. She'd never seen her father angry. None of her friends would believe it; they all thought he had no personality.

'Why would that bastard, Drake, suddenly have anything profound to say?'

Drake? That was a name she had heard before. Someone bad from her mother's past – an old boyfriend, she suspected. Marcie was so eager to learn more, she leaned too far over the stairs and almost overbalanced; only a fist around the banister prevented a thudding tumble downwards.

'Meet? The hell do you mean, meet?'

This Drake man wanted to meet her mother? Why? And how could he? The man had been in prison for years and years. No wonder her dad was angry – what man would want his wife's old lover back in contact?

'Well, I'm going to be there when it happens. No way you're meeting that bastard on his own. Look, where are you?'

Marcie learned little from the rest of the conversation, except that her mother wouldn't be back until later in the evening. But there had surely been more juicy information, because when her father got off the phone, he fell into a thoughtful trance. Marcie bounded down the stairs like someone who hadn't just overheard a scary conversation and was desperate for news. She adopted a fake smile as she entered the living room.

'Did I hear the phone? Was it for me?'

He barely seemed to hear. He was in the armchair, erect and stiff, staring off into the distance. Marcie had to break his line of sight with her body to get a response. He blinked rapidly, as if exiting hypnosis.

'What?'

'I said was that phone call for me?'

'No, nothing to do with you. It was your mum. Just to say she's shopping and won't be back until after eight. Look, I'm going to go out. You'll be okay on your own, right?'

'Fully grown woman, Dad.'

The moment he was gone, Marcie went upstairs. She stood on the upper landing, eyes raised to the ceiling. To the attic trapdoor. Only now did the gravity of the situation with her parents hit her.

They had never spoken to her about this Drake, but she knew a little because of her grandmother. He was a former boyfriend or husband of her mother's and he'd gone to prison, many years ago, for murder. Which made the secrecy obvious – how embarrassing to have been romantically involved with a killer. For a long time now Marcie had respectfully refrained from using the internet to research Drake, knowing her parents would tell the story when the time was right.

But things had suddenly changed. For some reason, somehow, a man long locked up and forgotten had entered the picture, and Marcie was desperate to know why. She knew those answers lay just feet away, above her head, in that dusty attic.

6

The centre of Sheffield could be hell for parking, but there was a private car park behind the long building containing Elliot & Harmon Solicitors. The gate opened by a code number Oliver Elliot had sent by text after his receptionist had relayed Sara's message. Jenny's Mitsubishi Outlander pulled in at two minutes to seven, but the two women decided to take five minutes to chat. There was no need for punctuality. The solicitors needed her, not the other way around.

'You're sure you don't mind coming in?' Sara asked.

'Nobody is keeping me out of that office. But one thing. Only give them my first name, no other details. If they don't know who I am, they won't be guarded and I'll get a better read on what's going on.'

Sara nodded. She stared out the window, summoning the will to do this. With every mile closer to ground zero, she'd had to fight against telling Jenny to turn the car around and take her home. Now, this was her last chance to back out. If she opened her door, this was happening all the way.

'Are you ready?' Jenny asked.

'No, but let's do it.' Sara threw open her door and got out.

And it was done. Knowing there was no going back, a calmness overcame her. But it quickly eroded as she felt the darkness of the car park close around her, as if weighted and tangible. She had hated dark and lonely places for a long, long time.

Once Jenny was in her wheelchair, the women set off. The office was situated in a row of commercial establishments, just past a funeral home. Sara wondered how many of the solicitors' clients had created work for the neighbour. This late, all the businesses bar a betting shop were closed. The front window of Elliot & Harmon had a shutter across it, but the one for the front door was rolled up and the light was on.

As they moved into the oblong glow across the dark pavement, the door immediately opened. Someone had clearly been very eager for Sara's arrival.

He was a man of about sixty in shirt and trousers with a loose tie. He looked at both women, but his longest glare was for Jenny. He clearly recognised Sara, but hadn't expected her to arrive with an unknown. It gave Sara another sliver of confidence.

He introduced himself – Oliver Elliot – and put out a hand, but Sara didn't shake. 'Let's just get this over with,' she told him.

He asked both women to step inside, where they found a man already seated to one side of the desk. He was more dapper, tie knotted tightly, jacket buttoned, and younger by at least fifteen years. Elliot introduced him as Raymond Harmon. So, both partners, the big dogs, were here for this. Sara felt that rising confidence hit its peak and start to descend the other side.

Harmon didn't stand, but he stiffened at the sight of an unexpected guest. 'Who are you?' he asked, surprise giving him bluntness.

'This is Jenny,' Sara said. 'She's my friend and she's staying, so don't even go there.'

Despite being the elder and having the lead name, Elliot

looked at his partner for a response. Harmon simply nodded at the women. Both solicitors were clearly unhappy, but they were smart men and knew they had no veto.

Sara was offered one of the chairs before the desk. She didn't want to sit, but complied only to be at Jenny's level. Elliot sat behind the desk. Harmon's position almost made him seem like a spectator who could watch both parties. Perhaps the intention. Elliot said, 'Thank you for coming, Mrs Yorston–'

'Don't bother,' Sara snapped. 'I don't want to be here, and for sure no longer than is absolutely necessary. So, excuse my rudeness, but just get on with it. You have a psychotic monster as a client and for some reason he wants to meet me. Just tell me why so we can rush to the point where I say no way and get up and leave.'

7

By self-admittance, her father was the 'anal-retentive one' of the family, so Marcie played Sherlock Holmes and chose to ignore the neatly packaged items in the attic. And it was a smart decision.

Using the torch on her phone, Marcie crawled across the dusty floor, worming around elegantly taped-up boxes. Unwilling to display brand names and logos, her father had turned all the boxes inside out so their faces were blank, and upon each was his neat writing. She paused at one labelled MARCIE'S BABY CLOTHES and thought about opening it to have a giggle at some of the items she'd worn as a rug rat. But she moved past, eager to get out of the attic as soon as possible.

Sure enough, she found an anomaly amongst the neatly arranged boxes: a crisps box messily bound with tape, no label of its contents. Her mother's doing, for sure. She opened it to expose a mishmash of unwrapped items. Now, she recalled an event she witnessed when she was about eight: her mother emptying the bottom of a wardrobe and tossing everything into a box. This box. But one item *was* wrapped, albeit in a carrier bag gone yellow with age. An oblong artefact. She tore away the tape, ripped open the bag, and was presented with the jackpot. This was what she'd come for.

That day when her mum had been clearing out the wardrobe, she had jumped back in horror when the book fell out. She had quickly scooped it up and hidden it when Marcie had asked what it was. Her mother had refused to show or discuss the book, and it had been relegated to the attic for years to come.

But for a long time, Marcie, eight and inquisitive, had been intrigued by the hardback that seemed to scare her mother. And she remembered when, a few weeks later, her grandmother had tried to tell her about a man called Drake... a man who was featured in a book... Plus, there had been an event at school a few years later.

In time, though, Marcie relegated the knowledge of that book to a dusty mental alcove. But she had never forgotten about it. And now, finally, it was in her hands.

But only for a second. As Marcie looked at the front cover, her hands shook and the old hardback fell from her grasp. She blinked hard, as if to vanquish a dream. But this nightmare was real. There, on the dust jacket, was her mother's face, just a year older than her own, and her original name: Sara Tasker. But it was the title that held Marcie's attention.

Oh, how stupid and foolish and naïve she had been. She wished she had never hidden her head in the sand, because then she would have known the truth all along, and would have long ago accepted it. Instead, it had just hit her like a juggernaut, and from today forward life was going to be tougher.

She didn't recall why she had assumed Drake was her mother's former boyfriend or husband, but it had been about as wrong as possible. Her mother hadn't hidden this book and the story and the memories because of simple shame at being a killer's lover. She had done it to prevent the disintegration of her sanity and lock out a nightmare.

The book was called *Her Dark Past: How I Survived a Serial Killer*.

8

Sara's outburst didn't seem to faze Elliot or Harmon, as if they'd expected this meeting to become a fight. Calmly, Elliot leaned his elbows on his desk. 'Sara, I must tell you I have no idea why my client wants to speak to you. But it is my theory that he wishes to...' He gave a quick glance at his partner, Harmon, as if for permission. 'To atone.'

Sara laughed before she could stop it. But Jenny almost hissed in anger. 'Atone? A joke, right? Is he hoping to get a cushy transfer?'

The solicitors looked at Jenny. Then each other. If the claim about Sara and Jenny being simple friends had been bought, it just got refunded. Neither man made a comment about this, but Harmon pulled out his phone and started tapping away. Elliot remained on track. 'We doubt that's Drake's reason. Are you aware he has bowel cancer?'

Sara felt a warm glow at this news, but it would be a step too far to show it. 'No. I ignore the bastard. You think I spend my time looking him up on the internet or something? Why would I?'

Elliot said, 'Mr Mills hasn't exactly outright told me he wishes to apologise to the people he's hurt, but–'

'He can't, they're dead,' Jenny cut in.

Elliot ignored her. 'He asked to see you, Mrs Yorston, and he mentioned that it's soon the twentieth anniversary of his first crime. Some, I admit, see it as a cause for celebration, but I've known the opposite to occur too. So I'll be honest and tell you it's an assumption of mine, but I do believe he might want to repent.'

Sara was ready to leap on the solicitor, Elliot, but Jenny got there first. 'First crime? Well, a rat-faced monster like him doesn't just jump in at the deep end. There was animal cruelty, and God knows how many dry runs for murder. And using the word *crime* for the brutal slaughter and rape of young women doesn't really cut it.'

Sara said, 'Do you mean he wants to apologise? To unburden himself because he's dying? Is he worried about going to Hell? Is he getting abused too many times a day by prisoners? Too late. He should have thought of that before he chose to kill people.'

Elliot seemed unfazed by the tag-team attack. 'My feeling is that he wishes to make amends in the only way he can.'

'I have my life,' Sara said. 'I'm over what he did to me, I and my family don't care anymore, so it would be a waste of words. Let him say sorry to the people who are still suffering the effects of his evil. The people he took most from. The next time you have a little friendly chat with him, tell him I'm not interested, okay?'

'Mrs Yorston, you seem to be under the impression that I'm directly dealing with Drake Mills, as if he's my long-term client. Let me explain something...'

According to Elliot, he had never met Drake and their conversations thus far numbered one, by phone. Elliot didn't know why Drake had contacted their offices – perhaps he randomly picked a Sheffield solicitor – but the call had come out of the blue, yesterday evening. In it, Drake had offered to hire Elliot & Harmon for a single task: find Sara Tasker and inform her he wanted to meet. No further details.

Elliot was to call Drake back as soon as he had an answer. Because Sara had moved across the city and changed her name, it had taken Elliot most of the evening to locate her.

'I had about half an hour spare last night to research this man and his crimes. And yourself. I knew nothing about you until my research. I did manage to get hold of a copy of your book, but it was photographed pages uploaded onto an obscure true crime website. I haven't read more than a couple of chapters as yet.'

'Well, stop reading. I want that book erased from history. I took back the rights and it's never been reprinted since that first edition. And never will be. I wish I'd never written it, but I was forced to. I'll hunt down and burn every last copy if I have to.'

'My point, Mrs Yorston, is that Drake is a relative unknown today, which is uncommon for a British serial killer. He's made no moves to appeal to the European Court of Human Rights to quash his whole life tariff in favour of a minimum term to serve, or any other appeals. He's refused to talk to anyone about his crimes since he was convicted. Because of this, there's been nothing newsworthy and Drake has been largely forgotten over the years. Neither my partner nor I have an interest in or connection to him. His original defence was nothing to do with this office – in fact, we've only been trading five years. We're not on his side or yours, but simply playing the middleman. He called, he asked, we responded.'

'So that would make this all about money,' Jenny said. 'You're willing to participate in a murderer's vile game, or whatever he's up to, just for some cash?'

Elliot and Harmon exchanged a glance, and Sara caught a

soft nod from the younger, more elegant, and far quieter man: permission to continue. Then he went straight back to his phone.

Elliot said, 'Not quite. During the phone call, Mr Mills made a reference to *making things right*. That was what gave me the impression he wishes to atone. We feel this might mean more than just admitting his remorse.'

Sara didn't understand, but she saw Jenny sit up straight. The older woman said, 'Drake was always suspected of other crimes. Are you saying you think he might be ready to admit additional attacks?'

'I can't say for sure.' He turned to Sara. 'There could be other victims, unknown. Families still seeking answers, and–'

Sara slapped the table hard enough to hurt her hand. 'No, don't try to guilt trip me. I refuse to meet this bastard. I won't have anything to do with him unless I know why. If he *is* willing to admit trying to kill other women, then let him write a confession and you can tell him I'll read it.'

'He was quite specific about a face-to-face meeting. He mentioned possibly informing the media. As in, if you don't meet with him, he'll talk to a newspaper. That could be something not in your interests. I should also add that he gave me no other names. No police officer, no journalist, no talk-show host or priest or anyone else. You, Mrs Yorston, are the only person he wishes to speak to.'

His sales pitch fell flat. Sara stood up, angry. 'No, no, no. How do you know this man isn't lying to you? Why are you so sure he's not after a trophy?'

Elliot looked puzzled.

'He wants to atone, but only wants to meet me, his one surviving victim? Bullshit, Mr Elliot. I know what's going on here. Some killers, they have keepsakes, or photos, trophies they can obsess over and stroke in order to recapture those glorious moments when they drove the knife in or tightened the garrotte. But he's got nothing, has he? He's rotting in a cell, masturbating over memories of stabbing women. Now he thinks he's got a chance to sit across from the one that got away? It's not going to happen. I won't help that animal get a sick sexual thrill. We're done here.'

Elliot made no reply; oddly, it was Jenny who tried to convince her to reconsider. 'Let's just think about this, Sara.'

Sara was shocked at this sudden about-face from a woman who had her own reasons to hate Drake Mills. She didn't know what to say, yet everyone was awaiting her response. Into that awkward silence came a tiny murmur, which turned all eyes towards Harmon. Something on his phone had amused him.

He looked up from the screen, directly at Jenny. 'My suspicions about you were correct.'

Harmon held out his phone for all to see. Sara leaned close. It was an old newspaper story that Sara knew well, for she had been close to the site when photographers, dozens of them, had snapped away.

The headline was: BODY FOUND IN ACADEMY GROUNDS. The photo showed a crime scene loaded with police and media and gawkers, police tape cordoning off the area around a plastic tent. It was obvious that something bad had happened right there. In the foreground was a suited female. The photo's caption said *Detective Inspector Jenny Pitchford at the murder scene.*

HER DARK PAST

CHAPTER ONE

The nightmare begins on the same day I first see the police officer leading the case, Detective Chief Inspector Jennifer Pitchford. It is a hot Sunday morning, 27 August 2000. Jenny is months away from knowing my name, but I will learn hers later that day, when the news sweeps across the city of Sheffield.

Back then I lived in Aughton, Sheffield. My house overlooks St Mary's Catholic primary school and, next door, Arkwood Academy. It is the grounds of the latter that the police invade that morning, as I am preparing to leave for my part-time job.

The school has a playing field and the academy has a football pitch, tennis courts and a large field of its own. Beyond are yet more fields stretching north to Ulley Reservoir, and west to Treeton Dyke. So there is a lot of open space surrounding my home, empty and dark at night, and perfect for a predator to lurk about unseen.

Because of the easy access into the fields for vehicles and an escape route onto a main road at the far end, the academy's open space is used after hours by teenagers. At night they congregate to smoke, chat, and race quad bikes. The police, if called, will make a routine pass to dissuade the youngsters, but usually the quads are hidden in the trees by the time a patrol car arrives.

The entry and exit roads into the academy's grounds bookend the row of houses I live on. The police block these with cars and tape to help preserve the crime scene. Only when I head out to work and see this cordon, and a throng of gawkers, do I realise something has happened.

The last time more than a single police car had business here, it was because a shed filled with argon gas canisters caught fire and neighbours had to be evacuated. That was two years ago and it's still talked about today, so whatever happened last night is going to be big gossip. And I want my information first-hand.

So I rush inside and to my bedroom window, which will give a great view of the academy grounds. And what a shock I get. The school-bus park is behind our house and it's full of police vehicles. Further past, I can see crime-scene vans and more police cars near the academy's main building. I am young, only eighteen, and naïve, and I think the activity is because someone got hurt in a quad bike accident last night. I don't yet realise the crime-scene vans mean something else.

But even those in the know have no clue that last night's event is the start of a terror campaign by a serial killer called the Slasher. But he's not quite here yet.

Information comes in slowly, but even as I watch from my window, my mum comes upstairs to tell me there's been a murder. A local girl has been found dead in the academy grounds. I really want to stay and watch, but my boss arrives to take me to work. I usually work evenings, but, annoyingly, Sunday is my morning/afternoon shift. While there, I stay in contact with my mum and friends by text.

At lunchtime, my mum calls. The police have been knocking on doors to speak to everyone in the area. Those not present – like me – can expect a return visit. I don't know if that scares me or not.

Some of those texts from friends relay all sorts of crazy stories that are doing the rounds. A woman was mauled to death by a local man's dog, later upgraded to a tiger, unbelievably, although the closest zoo is miles away. A prostitute was decapitated – never have I known the grounds of the academy to host such activities. A woman was sacrificed by members of the Anglican group the Nine O'Clock Service, even though the cult was never suspected of anything so radical and was disbanded five years ago, but facts can ruin a good theory.

There are also rumours of two victims done by one killer and two victims of a suicide pact. But when I get home from work, my mum has a more reliable and less fantastical story, apparently confirmed by a rookie police officer manning the cordon.

The victim was a young woman who had been quad-biking on the sports field with a female friend. They had argued and the friend had gone home around ten pm, leaving the victim alone with the quad. The friend is not a suspect and was unable to give any details about an attacker, since no one else was around when she left. Neighbours have made statements to the police that they heard the quad bike until roughly half past ten, so an additional thirty minutes after the two girls parted company.

As for the identity of the victim, no one has yet heard a

name. Actually, there was one bandied around, when a mother tried to call her daughter, who'd been out partying all night, and got a dead tone. But that girl came home, flat battery, hangover and all, an hour later.

The activity at the crime scene is ongoing and when I look out my window, I see neighbours down by the fence running along the end of our back gardens. Just beyond is the school-bus park, which has been overtaken by police vehicles. Milling about here are a throng of uniformed police and a handful of people in suits that I assume are detectives.

The tall, middle-aged woman I later learn is DCI Jenny Pitchford stands with two males in suits, all smoking, just a few metres from the fence. Now I know why my neighbours are in their gardens: to hear something exciting. I rush downstairs.

Behind our brick shed and close to the fence is an old, metal-and-wood bench set in concrete. It is out of sight from my bedroom window, so I get a shock when I walk past the shed and see my dad already sitting. He raises a finger to his lips. I sit by him and we both act as if we're chilling in the hot August sun, while straining to hear the detectives just fifteen feet away. But they're careful and we catch only single words here and there, and nothing that fills in any blanks.

All I manage to ascertain is that Jenny Pitchford seems to be the one in charge. She's got a slightly masculine headmistress look to her, perhaps because of the trouser suit, but she's very handsome and has an athletic musculature to her neck. She just looks like the sort who would be uncomfortable as anything but a team leader.

I get her name from a public appeal later that evening. In front of dozens of cameras and microphones, DCI Jenny Pitchford tells the country that the victim is nineteen-year-old Kymm Dymock, a beautiful blonde university student. Her address is just half a mile from mine, but I don't know her. That morning, the academy's caretaker found her naked body. It was hidden between a small toolshed on the edge of the sports field and a low bush border. None of her clothing has been found.

Jenny doesn't go into specifics about Kymm's injuries, only mentioning stabbings to various parts of her body, hands cable-tied behind her back, and sexual assault. But what she leaves out is leaked by whoever over the coming weeks. Kymm wasn't entirely naked – chillingly, a pink rubber swimming cap was stretched right down over her blonde head, covering her eyes, nose and mouth. The sexual assault was actually anal and vaginal rape. The stab wounds numbered about fifteen and were located in the neck, torso, abdomen, groin and thighs.

The theory is that she was subdued, raped, and stabbed while suffocating. For the first time, it scares me how close this crime was to my home. While I wrapped up warm, watched TV and ate supper, a hundred metres away someone my age got brutalised and butchered in the freezing dark.

Around nine pm on the evening of the discovery, the police return to question me. My mum sits with me, prompting me when I stumble over words or get brain-freeze, but I don't have much for them. I saw nothing, heard nothing, know nothing.

They reassure me that there is no evidence that the killer is local or still in the area. It's a claim they bandy around, but nobody really buys it and the streets are quite quiet of young females that evening, and for many to come. I for one act as if the darkness is a burning, toxic entity and determine to get behind locked doors before it makes an appearance.

But soon the initial explosion of horror dissipates. As

night after night passes with no new bodies appearing, more and more young women take to the streets at night. Confidence, or ignorance, takes the place of fear. Life moves on. Routine returns. The killing of Kymm Dymock, it appears, was just one of those unfortunate chance-in-a-million things, and is soon pushed aside for fresher gossip. The Slasher is here, but we're not quite ready for him yet.

By 31 December 2000, the country has forgotten about Kymm Dymock, the teenaged girl found naked and murdered in the grounds of Arkwood Academy. Not forgotten by her family, of course, who still grieve and hope for justice.

And not by the police, who are still investigating, although they're not really giving us updates. They don't have any. In late November, a paper reported that the hundred-strong team that hunted her killer months before had been reduced. Other crimes dipped into that team until the number of detectives working full-time on Kymm's killing is now in single digits.

As the weeks after the murder dragged by, evidence that could have paid a jackpot failed to deliver and new evidence had trickled to a standstill. House-to-house enquiries came up short. Witnesses couldn't help. CCTV unmasked no killer. The police admit they have no fingerprints or DNA or anything else of worth. It's no secret they'll need a lucky break to slot this file in the SOLVED cabinet.

On a radio interview in mid-December, the senior investigating officer, Jenny Pitchford, had stacked nasty news upon bad. She admitted that there might not be a breakthrough in the case unless the killer gave them more clues. Short of walking into a police station to confess, his only method of imparting such evidence was at another crime scene.

In other words, the police were unlikely to catch this monster unless he killed again. And criminal psychologists agreed that a murderer like this was highly likely to reoffend. A community that had worked hard to overcome its fear suddenly regressed, and once more the big question on everyone's lips was: when will this madman strike again?

On the last day of the first year of the new millennium, the killer answers that question.

That Sunday evening, he strikes just four miles east of his first victim, in Dinnington. Bluewood Court is an industrial estate with its right flank nestled against woodland, which Church Lane passes through to reach the housing estate where twenty-year-old Sheila McGirr lives. It is a meagre three-minute straight blast from her parking space outside Farsome Ceramics, through the woods, and to her driveway on Apple Crescent.

So within ten minutes of finishing her cleaning job at ten pm that evening, Sheila should have been home. She isn't. Her mother calls Sheila's mobile to see what is taking so long. She expects to get a car-broke-down or bumped-into-a-friend story. But she gets only a dead line.

Worried, Sheila's mother sends her teenaged son out on his bike to Bluewood Court, to see if his sister might have had trouble starting her car. He doesn't get that far. Halfway along Church Lane, he stops upon spotting a car in a lay-by. Not just any vehicle though. Sheila's Ford Escort.

The driver's door is open a few inches, so the interior light is on, but Sheila is nowhere to be seen. He calls her name, waits a minute or so, then walks into the woods. Forty feet in there's a chain-link fence barring access to private property, and here he stops. Not because of the barrier though.

Through the fence, he can see his sister. She lies in the thin undergrowth, naked, bloodied. He stumbles to his bike, pedals it home as fast as possible, and tells his mum.

Minutes later, the police are at the scene, and word gets out that it's the handiwork of the same man who killed Kymm Dymock a few months earlier. Sheila is almost a carbon copy of victim number one. Another beautiful blonde girl, stabbed all over her body, entire head squeezed into a swimming cap, none of her clothing around.

This time, though, there are new aspects. Her throat has been slashed. And her hands were not tied, which leads some to a theory. A tied victim does not struggle, and this killer gets off on seeing his victim thrash and fight for her life. Indeed, her hands and forearms are covered in defensive wounds. There is evidence of extra frenzy to the stabbing, with thirty-seven wounds, which is more than twice the number inflicted on Kymm Dymock.

The police hide these details at first and mention no connection between the murders. Even when they do finally admit the similarities – the swimming caps, method of murder and closeness of the two crime scenes – they lean more towards the notion of a copycat.

But two victims just four miles apart is enough for the media and public to cry 'serial killer', and sod the Federal Bureau of Investigation's criteria of three victims to achieve this moniker. The story jumps through the masses like a virus.

The reaction of the public is a little different this time. Kymm Dymock's death garnered nothing but sympathy, but Sheila doesn't get such treatment once her personal life is laid bare. It is reported that she had two boyfriends and a profile on a sex website, where she offered intimate massages and 'more'. To some, the slashed throat is evidence of this: such anger and overkill suggests a slighted punter. Overnight, dead girl Sheila turns from innocent victim to someone who had been 'asking for it'.

The scorn for this poor murdered girl is a terrible attitude that Sheila's family, and even her two beaus, strive hard to dispel. Unfortunately, the flames are fanned by a police assertion that her killer couldn't have hoisted her body over the fence.

Now, the police do explain what they meant by this: coercion, perhaps at the point of a knife. But the woods near Bluewood Court were once a place where prostitutes serviced drivers delivering to the industrial estate, and to some people this fact overrides everything else. Never mind that this activity ceased years ago, after the woodland lane was thinned, and now a truck can't park there without blocking passage. Who cares that no deliveries take place on a Sunday evening because the businesses are shut? Doesn't matter that it rained that night and the ground was a muddy hell for anyone wishing to have sex.

A primeval prejudice prevails: Sheila McGirr serviced men for money and she climbed that fence of her own free will, and she should have known the danger of going off with strange men. So sod her.

Because of this lack of sympathy for Sheila, one newspaper sees fit to call the killer the Barbie Doll Slasher. The newspaper's claimed reason is that both victims were very pretty and blonde, just like Barbie dolls, but a portion of the public condemns the title. Barbie doll is generally used as an insult, and it doesn't go down well with the families of either victim.

As the father of Kymm Dymock responded, 'You idiots might as well call this guy the Bimbo Butcher.' His complaint results in an apology from the newspaper, but the damage is done. Serial killers need a nickname and this one sticks. For a while.

The police don't buy the random-trucker theory, but high-ranking heads will roll if it turns out to be correct. So detectives start tracing drivers in the area on Sunday evening. But the idea of a sex-for-sale transaction gone wrong isn't entirely discarded. Her activity on the adult website is analysed, leading to the questioning of nine men who'd paid for Sheila's services.

One is even arrested when it is discovered he lied about being at his friend's house that night and cannot provide a checkable alibi. This man later does prison time, but not for murder. He's eliminated from the enquiry when linked to a burglary thirty miles away during the period when Sheila was attacked.

And on to Sheila's two long-term sexual partners. Neither man knew about a second boyfriend, but that becomes a possible motive. What if one found out about the other and was overcome by rage? Cause of many a bloody attack across the world for sure, but not here. Both men are genuinely distraught at losing Sheila, and their alibis are solid.

Evidence, as with Kymm's murder, is scarce. No CCTV in that remote slice of urbanity. No witnesses except a few other cleaners and janitors working late at Bluewood Court, but they know nothing of Sheila's actions after she drove away from the industrial estate. Heavy rain has cleaned the crime scene of possible fingerprints and DNA and other forensic clues.

Except for footprints: the police get a beautiful impression from a left running shoe, with enough idiosyncrasies on the worn sole to make a certain match. But that's only good news if they have the shoe, and it's an untraceable, mass-produced, big-brand item.

Another angle gives the police big hope early on: the swimming caps. Detectives contact swimming pools to try to track cap sales, but these items, like the running shoes, are sold in all sorts of places, including the internet. They also scrutinise the pools' member records, seeking the parents of children who attend classes. I know some fathers were investigated and I heard they put surveillance on a man, but it all proves fruitless. By the end of January the trail goes the way of the Dymock investigation: cold.

The lack of updates and refusal by the police to admit the connection between both killings, twinned with the public's lack of sympathy towards Sheila because she was a secret sex worker, soon ejects the murder from the news. Like Kymm's death, it is deemed just another standalone, random, senseless, mundane instance of man hunting his favourite prey.

It seems we must wait a while longer for the Barbie Doll Slasher.

9

Back in the Outlander, in the car park behind the solicitors' office, Jenny started the engine but made no move to drive away.

'Are you sure about this?' she said.

'You think I made the wrong decision, don't you?' Sara replied.

'It's not that. It's your choice. I know it will be hard for you. But we don't know what Drake wants to say to you.'

'Do you think he really wants to apologise to me? Do you believe an apology will do me good? Should I face this man as a kind of aversion therapy? If I face the man, I'll suddenly find peace? Is that it?'

'I'm not saying that's the reason to do it. But who knows, right? And, like the solicitor said, there could be some answers for Drake's other victims.'

Sara stared at Jenny for what seemed like a long time. 'You're not here as my friend, are you?'

'What? What does that mean?'

'You're here as Detective Pitchford.'

'I retired eight years ago, Sara.'

'But not by choice. I looked you up while we were driving from Birmingham. You didn't want to quit the police, but you were forced to. I read about the attack that put you in that wheelchair.'

The story had made the news. Jenny had accompanied an arrest team to Sheffield's Parson Cross to apprehend a convicted rapist, who'd attacked another woman just days after his release from prison. Jenny had been his original arresting officer for the prior offence and wanted her face to be the one he saw locking him up again. He'd been detained without fuss and led quietly from his house, out to a car.

But at the kerb he'd suddenly launched himself at Jenny, knocking her into the road. His timing had been precise: a delivery van was racing by at that moment.

Seven months later, she was released from hospital and eager to return to work. Four months after that, with her rehabilitation going well, she had turned up for her first day back on the job. In the wheelchair she was to spend the rest of her life confined to. Her mental outlook had been fairly rosy.

Until two days later. An attempted murder in a second-floor flat landed on her team's desk, but Jenny had not been able to attend. She had had to view the crime scene by video. This had not only hurt her pride, it had forced home the ugly truth that the best part of the job – working out in the field – was forever gone.

She quit the police following the resolution of that investigation, three days later.

'Yes,' Jenny admitted, staring at the steering wheel. 'I won't hide it. I'd love to still be a police officer, although I'm nearly retirement age. I admit that when I heard Drake wanted to meet you, my first thought was that he might be willing to admit some secrets. My team always suspected there could be other victims, as you well know.'

'But he's never said a thing since he was convicted. And you saw a chance to use me to get to him. You want me to get Drake to admit further crimes so you can show the police that you're still the great detective.'

Before Jenny could respond, Sara threw her hands to her face: 'God, I'm sorry, I didn't mean that. I...'

'It's fine,' Jenny said, rubbing Sara's back. 'This whole Drake thing hit you like a free kick, and you're allowed to be angry. And you're not entirely wrong, except that I never did this job for the glory. And it wasn't for praise. I did it to help people.'

'I know. Of course I know that, and this could help. I know I might be able to help those poor families with missing daughters or sisters. I just don't know if I can meet him. I'm sorry. I got that man out of my life twenty years ago, and I don't want him back in it. He should have been dead already. I know he was getting abused from the first day he went into prison. Other prisoners don't like men who hurt women. I remember you telling me that. So in a just world, he'd be dead already.'

'You've done nothing wrong, Sara. I know facing Drake will upset you very badly, and nobody wants that. Nor is anyone forcing you to meet him. If you feel you can't, don't.'

Sara tried to read Jenny's eyes, to see if there was honesty in her statement, but the interior of the car was too dark. 'Those solicitors also think I should do it though.'

'They're not in charge and they don't care about you. I do. And let's be realistic, Sara. Even if you did meet Drake, there's no guarantee that monster will suddenly clear up a file cabinet full of unsolved cases. Like you said, he could be playing some kind of game or seeking a kick. We said no back there in the office, and let's leave it at that.'

'Do you really mean that? It's okay if I don't do it?'

'If Drake truly is ready to cleanse his soul, he'll do it whether or not you're involved. And if not, then nothing has changed over the last two decades. Either way, if he really has bowel cancer, he'll be dead soon, and that will go some way to appeasing all the people he hurt. Maybe it will help you stop having that terrible dream. Come on, let's get you home.'

'Thank you.'

Jenny started driving. She watched the road, but Sara watched her. There had been a glow about the former detective ever since she learned there was a chance Drake might unload his dark secrets, but now it had gone. Because of Sara's ineptitude and fear. Jenny had sounded sincere, but Sara hadn't missed a direct accusation under the surface. *If you don't face Drake, the terrible dream will haunt you for the rest of your days.*

10

The final five minutes of the journey to Sara's house was in silence. After pulling up, Jenny said, 'I guess we've got no need to stay in contact now. So have a good life, Sara Yorston. If you need anything, call me. In fact, just call me.'

Before today, Sara had barely thought about the former detective, even though Drake had been in her head daily, but their time together way back had meant something. She didn't want to part from her for another twenty years, or even forever. 'I'll call. I'll also call if I just want a natter about something. We should stay in touch. If that's okay?'

Even as Jenny said it would be absolutely okay, Sara wasn't sure she *would* call. Jenny was part of that old world Sara was desperate to forget. And maybe, subliminally, Jenny felt the same: *have a good life* was another suggestive remark.

They parted with a wave. Sara watched the Outlander turn off her street before she headed for the house.

Marcie was exercising in front of music videos on the living-room TV. The volume was so loud she hadn't heard her mother enter, evidenced by the shriek she gave when Sara tapped her on the shoulder.

'You and Dad were supposed to be going out,' the teenager said when over her shock.

Sara grabbed the TV remote and sliced the volume in half. She was in no mood for an evening out, but Marcie's use of the past tense was intriguing. 'What makes you think we're not?'

'Dad's not here. He went out, said he'd be back later this evening. But he left you those.' She pointed to a pair of expensive-looking wine bottles on the fireplace cornice. The gifts were no clue to Joe's mood because he was always bringing home items left over from functions at his workplace. Sara had no doubt he'd gone out because he was upset about Drake's reappearance in her life.

'Did he say where he went?'

'No. But I reckon he went bombing. I know you two had a falling out on the phone.'

Joe rarely got angry, and even when he did it was hard to tell. Mostly he would play music through headphones and ignore everyone, but another habit was aimlessly driving around the housing estate – 'bombing', as he called it.

Sara returned to the living room to pull her mobile and call him, but at the window she saw headlights cut through the dark. She watched Joe park his car and get out. Because the living-room light was on, he saw her and stopped. She waved, but his reply was a beckoning finger.

'Marcie, stay here, I'm just popping out for ten minutes.'

Sometimes, if a serious discussion was needed, she and Joe would bomb together. Neither of them uttered a word until the car was zipping down the road.

'Drake. Explain, please,' Joe said.

On the phone earlier, Sara had already told him most of the tale. He knew she planned to meet Drake's solicitor, with Jenny in tow, to discuss why Drake was suddenly interested in her after two decades. Now, she detailed the conversation that had taken place in the solicitors' office and her decision to have nothing to do with the man who'd once tried to kill her.

She expected Joe to ask why she hadn't taken him as moral support, instead of a police officer she hadn't been in touch with for years. But that wasn't the question he put to her.

'Why did you say no to meeting Drake?'

She was surprised. 'Why would I meet with that bastard? I'm shocked you think I should. Did you want me to? Jenny seemed to want that as well. What good could come from it?'

'Well, you still have that dream. Maybe facing him would help you get over it. And if you go, I'll be going.'

She threw her arms up in frustration. 'Did you two confer on this or something? You both act as if this is the same as getting over a fear of heights. Confront and control and all that crap.'

He gave a lazy shrug. It seemed like an emotionless gesture, but one hand fiddled with his beard, and those in the know would recognise frustration bubbling below the surface. 'How do you know it won't help?'

'I don't, Joe, I don't. But I've spent twenty years trying to forget that man, and slowly it's been working. How do you and Jenny know facing that bastard won't knock me back to square one and start the process all over again?'

Another invisible giveaway that Joe was worked up occurred: the car increased speed as he took a corner. But his tone, again, was bland. 'Forget him? But he'll be with us forever, won't he? We made it that way when we named our daughter after his third murder victim.'

HER DARK PAST

CHAPTER THREE

On Saturday the twenty-fourth of March of 2001, three months after his second kill, the man known as the Barbie Doll Slasher officially meets the FBI's criteria defining a serial killer.

His third victim is Marcie Whitecotton, twenty-two, again pretty and blonde, and this time the police can't deny that a dangerous maniac is stalking the streets of Sheffield.

Marcie Whitecotton is found on Lady Field Road, a country lane passing through farmland just north of the civil parish of Thorpe Salvin. Her corpse lies over a low stone wall, tightly pressed up against the bricks and hidden from view from the road. Early on the morning after her murder, a dog walker steps over the wall and plants his foot directly onto Whitecotton's abdomen. She had been raped, stabbed fifty-nine times, had her throat slashed and her skull battered into pieces. Her dumped body was naked except for a swimming cap covering her entire head.

Her hands, like those of the second victim, were not tied. But unlike victim two, Whitecotton has no defensive wounds, although high blood loss indicates she was alive when the stabbing started. That mystery will never be unravelled.

Whitecotton's bicycle is found an hour later by police, deeper into the field. By then they know she was a cleaner for a rich couple in Thorpe Salvin and had been on her way to their home the previous evening. The owners were away and had allowed their employee to stay the night so she could spend Sunday morning preparing the house for their return that afternoon. When police visit the house, statements are taken in the garden because the elderly couple are embarrassed by their untidy living quarters.

As before, news of a local murder billows outwards from ground zero like a shockwave, stunning everybody in the blast radius. Three similar, bloody murders in little more than half a year sends the entire region into a frenzy. The public can't talk about anything else, journalists can't type fast enough, and pressure drops upon the police like a lead blanket. Whitecotton has nothing in her history to give her a bad name, so the press start to dump the word Barbie from the Barbie Doll Slasher. Thankfully, the new title is adopted by all. Later still, perhaps to save ink and breath, he'll simply become the Slasher.

This one hits me particularly hard, even worse than when the serial killer's first victim was butchered and dumped a hundred metres from my house. In a sense, this murder is even closer to home.

Marcie Whitecotton was my work colleague and good friend.

When I left school, I got a part-time job at The Ball Centre in Loxley, about ten miles east of my home. It boasts five indoor football pitches and a café, and is run by girls about my age, although the boss is older. We do everything from coaching kids to cooking bacon.

Marcie Whitecotton had worked there about a month longer than me. She lived a little south in Stannington and rode her bike everywhere. It gave her strong, athletic legs I was jealous of. By the time of her murder, I'd followed her lead and had been cycling to work for a few weeks. My parents had met Whitecotton a couple of times, once when she came to my house for dinner, and they liked her. I think Dad was a fan because he no longer had to drop me at work when my boss couldn't pick me up.

Whitecotton's murder was in Thorpe Salvin so this time their door-to-door canvassing didn't include my address, but I expected an interview because of our work relationship.

They hit my doorstep on Tuesday evening, two days after Whitecotton's body was found. This time it isn't a pair of uniforms with a routine script and a feeling that they're wasting their time. I get Jenny Pitchford, the lead detective, and a younger man. I know this isn't down to a lucky draw or because Jenny is the kind of boss who likes to muck in. I have a much deeper connection to this murder series than Whitecotton's other friends. They don't live a stone's throw from the murder site of victim number one.

This in mind, I sit down for the interview a little bit apprehensive. No, fearful. The big gun has come to personally talk to me: what if they think I'm involved in some way?

My dad is out, so my mum sits with me as I answer the questions. Jenny takes the lead, sitting on an armchair directly across from me. She leans forward, which might have appeared menacing if not for her reassuring smile. She talks slowly, gives me time to answer, and nods a lot.

I like her and even start to wish my mum was as cool as this detective. I bet outside of work she has lots of friends. The young male stands behind her chair and takes notes as I describe my relationship with Whitecotton. We cover what I know of her history, her conduct at work, personality, family, likes and dislikes.

It is very easy to answer Jenny's questions and at no time do I feel that the police suspect me of anything untoward. I am totally forthcoming, eager to help, so much so that I start to feel guilty when I'm asked something I don't have an adequate answer to. So easy-going is this seemingly friendly chat that at first I don't notice we've breached a boundary, moving from the mundane to the serious.

'And will this boy's name be in the records?' Jenny asks. That's the point where I stop and take stock of the corner this conversation has taken.

I had just described an incident that occurred about a week ago. A team of six lads rented a pitch to play three-a-side football, and the ball popped when it hit the latch on the gate in the pitch wall. All considered a hoot, until Whitecotton said they'd have to pay for the ball. One of the lads said no way, we shouldn't have had sharp edges on the latches. Whitecotton insisted and an argument ensued. The angry lad called Whitecotton a bitch and the group left.

And then I realise where we're going with this. Jenny has asked me about Whitecotton's brother, who is known to the police for burglary. She's asked about Whitecotton's current and former boyfriends. And now we're talking about people she's had run-ins with at work. Jenny is pumping for clues as to who might have wanted to hurt my dead friend.

'But it's a serial killer, isn't it?' I ask. 'How could she have been targeted?'

My mum jumps in here. 'There's no evidence of that yet,

Sara. Serial killers are so rare. Most people are killed by someone they know, isn't that right, Detective Pitchford?'

'As terrible as it sounds, that's right, Mrs Tasker. Now, Sara, can–'

'I mean the police would have said if the killings were connected,' my mum jumps in. She's got this tone I recognise, only ever employed when she's had dangled bait snatched. I know she's trying to play the detectives, and here it comes: 'They haven't said that, so they're not connected. You can promise that for our peace of mind, can't you, detective? Promise that these three murders aren't the work of a serial killer?'

Mum's sly, but it seems Jenny is just as sharp. She gives a smile that tells me she knows exactly what game my mum is playing. The whole city is waiting for the police to conclude it's one man out there, butchering young women. Mum wants to be the bearer of this magnificent piece of gossip.

'We're still investigating,' is all Jenny will say before returning her attention to me. But now that I know I'm being evaluated for highly important information, it sends my nerves fluttering. The interview, despite its laid-back tenor, starts to feel like an interrogation, and I'm glad when it's over and the two detectives prepare to leave.

But I'm not done yet. I offer to walk the pair out to their car, to which Jenny agrees. I leave my mum standing there on edge – she probably wants to perform her own interrogation of me – and head out behind Jenny. At the car, she faces me, and I know she's aware that I planned to ask her something away from my mother.

Like I said, I didn't get Jenny today because of a lucky draw, but a loose connection to two of the victims. It has just sparked a terrible thought.

'Will I be next?'

The question doesn't take her by surprise and her response is instant.

'The reason I'm not yet willing to connect these three murders is that there's no going back from that. We have to be sure, and to do that we have to rule out the chances of coincidence. And that's what we could still have here, Sara. A plain and simple unhappy coincidence that you knew Marcie Whitecotton and live close to where Kymm Dymock was found.' Her eyes flick to my house, as if seeing through it, to the Arkwood Academy sports field beyond. I make the same look.

'If you're worried, Sara, you can do something about it. At night, try not to find yourself alone in remote areas. Don't talk to strange men. Make night-time journeys with friends. But I'm sure all of this is common sense to a pretty young female. Take care, but don't let worry overtake you. You can't live in constant fear.'

'What about my hair? He kills blonde girls.'

'A possible further unhappy coincidence.'

She spends another minute trying to convince me I'll be safe. But I'm not convinced and half an hour later, as it's getting dark, I see my dad's car pull up. I rush outside to catch him before he can enter the house.

'I need you to drive me to the shop, Dad,' I tell him.

He laughs and continues coming up the garden path. 'Snowball's chance in hell, little one. Just got back. Wrestling is on the telly in five minutes.'

'Fine, I'll go on my bike. Alone in the dark through the academy fields.'

He knows from my grin that I'm winding him up. His response is typical of the cheeky banter we have, but he's a father and no wild gambler. 'No, I'll drive you. They find another body there they'll block off our road with cop cars again. Get in.'

I kiss his cheek when we're in the car. 'Thanks, Dad. You saved my life.'

He grunts. 'Doubt it. That killer guy will be indoors tonight. Won't be missing the wrestling, unlike some of us. He's sick, not daft.'

Later, I sit in my room with the dye I bought from Superdrug and darken my hair. Dad's joke comes back to me, creating food for thought: can psycho serial killers really sit and watch TV like normal people? On my pillow, next to the empty dye box, is a hammer I took from Dad's toolbox. I plan to carry it in my handbag whenever I go out at night, until the day they announce the capture of the sick bastard out there.

Brunette and armed. I feel safer already.

11

'Marcie will have to be told about Drake. All of it.'

Joe had drawn the car to a halt at the kerb in order to deliver that bombshell. Sara shook her head.

'No way. I know we've put off telling her the truth for years now, probably far longer than we should have. But until she needs to know, why say it? She could go her whole life without knowing, and that's fine with me.'

Across the road, two yobbish-looking teenagers were trying to coax a cat out from under a car, doubtless for a callous reason. Joe was watching them, but Sara watched Joe.

'It would be fine with me, too, Sara, but you said Drake plans to talk to the media if you don't meet him.'

The solicitor, Elliot, had made this same warning.

'I doubt he will. He's been silent since he got arrested, not a word spoken to anyone who's tried to interview him, not for twenty years. And he'll suddenly talk to them just because he's had a whim to meet with me and I said no? I don't believe it.'

Joe gave a slow shrug. 'Seems like a big risk. Because if he does start talking, then the story is big again. The last time I remember it being in the news was when his first victim's mother died. Marcie was, what, ten? She didn't have Facebook or Twitter or watch YouTube back then. Hell, for all we know, she knows everything already. You remember my mother's input?'

Neither of them could forget.

Joe's mother had always had a problem with alcohol – it had killed her four years ago – and liked to stir trouble when drunk. At a barbeque, she had pulled eight-year-old Marcie aside and mentioned Drake. Joe managed to jump in, but not before his little daughter had heard enough to make her curious. Later, she asked her parents: who is Drake and why did he kill someone and why is he in a book?

Both parents had sat down with Marcie that night, and they had given her a stern warning. *That name Drake you heard? Never speak of it. Never ask who Drake is. Drake is not part of our lives, and you must forget such a man exists. Promise us now.*

Sara understood Joe's point. She said, 'You think she might know about Drake, but also knows not to talk about it to us? Do you think Marcie is that good an actress? That she could know the full story and never show it? Never bring it up? I can't accept that. It's not like Drake is in the news every day. I believe she doesn't know.'

'Let's say she doesn't know a thing. And let's say the last thing Drake wants is to talk to the media. And then let's say he really is terminal and croaks it. Get where I'm going with this?'

Sara nodded.

Just a year and a half or so ago, in May 2018, the serial killer Dennis Nilsen died in prison. It had been thirty-five years since he was captured and imprisoned, yet his passing was big news. Drake Mills didn't have even close to the same level of infamy, but when he died, his killing spree would certainly be relived, rehashed, at least in his home city. Her city. And her name, as the one who narrowly got away, would be on everyone's lips once more.

As Joe had said, the last time a newspaper had mentioned Sara's name was about seven years ago, following the death of victim number one's mother. It hadn't been a big story, but a reporter had tried, and failed, to get an interview with Sara. It was solid proof that she was eternally connected to Drake's notoriety and she had no doubt the microphones would return when Drake died.

Sara had easily managed to hide the event from a ten-year-old girl absorbed by cartoons. But Marcie was grown up and plugged into the internet, and that wouldn't be possible again. Joe could even be right that Marcie knew everything but had sworn herself to secrecy.

It wasn't just her brain talking. Her heart had an opinion too. It was silly and selfish to continue to keep the truth from their own flesh and blood. Maybe Drake's resurfacing after all these years was a sign that it was time to sit Marcie down and change her life. She also deserved to know the truth about her father.

Still, Sara had worries: 'She's an adult now. She doesn't need us. If we tell her the truth, and she hates us for keeping such a secret, she could move out, never speak to us again.'

Joe said, 'Or she could hug us, treat us like heroes. And if not, then I get her room for my music gear.'

A rare joke from Joe, but she was in no mood for laughing. 'Jenny told me about some of the abuse Drake suffered in prison, and I was happy. I wanted him to suffer every day, and die a hundred years old as a broken wreck. But that was back then, and it's different now. Now I wish he'd died in prison on day one.'

'Understandable. Drake's mum died years ago, so I guess there's no one left on the planet who'd have a different opinion.' He paused. 'So, what's our next move?'

She didn't need to think any more on the subject. 'Let's go find out exactly how Marcie will react.'

12

Marcie gave Sara all the prompt she needed. When they got home, Marcie was on the sofa and immediately said, 'So where did you two go? You're both acting strange.'

'Nowhere special,' was Sara's reply. She sat on the armchair. Joe remained standing, arms folded, waiting. 'I could do with a tea, Marcie.'

Marcie didn't look convinced, but she gave no argument. When she'd vanished into the kitchen, Joe said, 'Cold feet at the last second? I can tell her.'

'I don't want her to know until it is absolutely necessary.'

'I thought it was.'

'If I get wind that Drake is dead, we can tell Marcie before she hears the story on the news. I don't want to fall out with her and start somehow hating Drake any more. I won't be pushed into this by him.'

'You're the boss.'

'No, I'm not, Joe. We should both have a say here. I shouldn't just take control. I'm sorry. Look, if you think it's best to tell her right now, we can.'

Joe gave that slow shrug of his. Sometimes it was his way of saying *It is what it is*, which on this occasion meant he was bowing to her wishes. But it annoyed her. Sometimes she just wanted him to assert himself and decide for her.

They sat in silence. When Marcie brought tea for them both, she couldn't miss the tension and excused herself to go to her room.

'See, she knows something's up,' Joe said.

'Teenagers, that's all. They don't like sitting alone with their parents. She might think we'll want to discuss the birds and the bees with her.'

Joe either missed the joke or found it unfunny. It was hard to read when Joe was annoyed because the emotion rarely found outlet on his face. She only realised a short time later. He said he was going to have a shower, but it wasn't the shower she heard after he'd left the room. It was the front door.

'Drake, you bastard,' Sara hissed.

HER DARK PAST

CHAPTER FIVE

The dream makes the first of myriad appearances on the Tuesday when police interview me at my home. I know I'll have trouble sleeping, so I drink wine and stay up late, hoping to be ambushed by tiredness. It works and I drift off in the armchair, but my sleep isn't unbroken.

In the dream, I find myself on a busy high street, sunshine on my face. But I am not here for shopping. I am here for a killer. I am here to hunt the hunter, although I have no clue why I chose a street full of shoppers in the middle of Sheffield city centre. I know I will find him. I also don't know why I believe that. Dreams don't deliver exposition. But I know it will happen.

My brisk pace becomes sluggish suddenly, as if I just walked into a powerful headwind. But there isn't even breeze enough to rustle my clothing. I push on, but the invisible force against me increases. I fight to move ahead, but I become locked in place. Then, I start to move backwards. It's like being dragged on a dog lead. I don't know how this works either, but I know I've found him.

I turn to face the way I'm moving in order not to fall, eyes scanning ahead. There is no dog lead or anything else pulling me, at least that I can see or feel, but I feel a physical yank. And then I see him, just fifteen feet or so ahead of me.

I know it's him because I *don't* know him, do I? Nobody does, because he's just a faceless monster hiding in the dark. So my sleeping, refusing to guess, paints him as a humanoid silhouette, shimmering like a heatwave. He's real, though, because he stops to wait for a gap in traffic to cross the road, and people sidestep to avoid him on the busy pavement. I stop too.

When he crosses the road, I follow. I can't not. Now, instead of a lead connecting us, it feels as if there are hands pushing me from behind, guiding me onto the far pavement and down a side street. I match his speed, unable to slow and, most surprising, unable to move any closer to him. I no longer want to hunt him, but the invisible hands, or the lead, or whatever controls me, won't allow escape.

If I try to grab a lamp post to stop myself, my hand passes straight through, ghost-like; if I call out for help, it's as if my voice operates on a frequency inaudible to human ears. Desperate, I lift my legs to dump myself on the ground and snap the bond between us. This trick fails miserably as I literally float, like his little toy kite.

And there is pain now when I resist, which forces me to regain my feet and stride. The powers in control here must be punishing me for making them exert themselves, or they are eager to have me make this journey by choice. And so it will be. We're bound forever.

He walks for a little over a hundred metres before entering an alleyway by a line of shops, and here climbs a fire escape to a flat above a laundrette. I desperately hope the – ghost? – rules covering me haven't taken elevated trajectories into account, but it's my dream and it won't be foiled. I can touch if necessary and the metal steps take my feet, albeit silently. It beats being dragged up the brick wall. The killer closes the door in front of me, but, of course, that slab of wood might as well be a mirage.

His flat is grimy, messy, foul. The hallway carpet looks a thousand years old. Wallpaper peels in great tongues in the living room. Here, he kicks off shoes that I notice for the first time. They're actual branded training shoes, clear as day. And I know why. Police found prints from this brand of footwear at a murder scene: it is the only thing they know about him.

I just watch from across the room as the shimmering black humanoid sits on a worn sofa and eats from crisps in a bowl. He plays on a games console. And he masturbates. I don't want to see the latter, obviously, it appears my mind has ironed out all bugs and glitches.

Sidestep into another room so I can't see? Now the walls won't allow me to exit, probably not until he leaves.

Turn away? Now my body and head are locked facing his constantly, like a compass pointing north.

Close my eyes? The eyelids turn transparent if I do that.

So I do as I am fated to: watch.

The day grows long. I stand around as he potters about in the living room. I follow into the kitchen as he makes more food. I stand in the bathroom and listen to him defecate. In his nasty bedroom, I watch his shimmering black form tug strips of itself away before absorbing new pieces. It reminds me of working with clay at my pottery wheel. I assume he's just undressed and put on fresh clothing.

As the night becomes thick and heavy, he picks up two items, but these are not just dark blots. We know he uses a knife and a swimming cap, so the items in his hand are the real deal. With his murder tools and – probably – dark clothing, he is ready to hunt. And I have to follow.

My dream also controls the geography of this world; now the land at the end of his alleyway has switched from city centre highway to woodland. He treks along a dirt path through the trees, with his little pet always just behind. He picks a spot and hides. In later versions of this dream, he will string electrical cable between two trees to cut girls off their bikes. But this is not a tool the real Slasher has employed at this stage. More on that later.

My gaze suddenly unlocks from him and the invisible hands turn me. Now my eyes attach to a girl on a bike, approaching us. Ah, I am to watch his victim. Her shock as she is caught in his trap. Her pain as he has his way with her. And then her death.

The leash between us allows me to step onto the dirt path, where I wave and shout. Of course, she cannot hear me. I try to block her path, already knowing it's fruitless, and there is no surprise when her body and bike pass straight through me. I spin around to continue watching and see her catch the cable. She flips off the back of the bike and lands hard on the path. Her bike rolls a fair distance before veering into the undergrowth.

The girl is about my age, pretty, and, of course, she's got long blonde hair. She sits up, shocked, and doesn't see the black blob leap out of the darkness. He is upon her before she can scream.

I expect to wake here, but it does not happen. I watch as he works with his swimming cap and knife. With his penis. When it is over, and the killer stands over a naked, bloodied corpse, he turns to me, and I see a crescent of white appear in the featureless black face. A mouth.

It says to me, 'Did you enjoy that? We'll do it again soon.'

It is here that I usually wake, sweating, face buried in my pillow so I am as airless as his victim while her heart still beat. Perhaps, subconsciously, I have tried to suffocate myself in order to escape the nightmare.

But it visits me nightly, for two years now as I write this. The same dream, playing out the same way every single time. I will never escape it.

13

'Hey, it's okay, it's okay, calm down.'

Sara woke to find someone standing over her, shrouded in darkness. Loaded with sleepy shock, she tried to move, but her hands were clasped in that other person's.

'Mum, it's okay, just a nightmare.'

Every muscle had been locked tight, but only when they relaxed did Sara realise this. In the same moment that her body seemed to deflate, her waking mind connected all the dots. Marcie. It was Marcie standing by her, holding her hands tight. There could only be one reason why: the dream.

From Joe, she knew her reaction during the dream: she would punch and claw and scratch at the air above her, but make no noise. Early into their relationship her thrashing would wake him, but he'd soon learned to sleep through it. As now. The dream always came a single time each night, not always waking her, and thereafter her sleep would be unbroken. If she did wake, she would always be gone again within seconds, often never recalling the break in sleep. This was different: Marcie had dragged her out.

Sara knew Marcie was aware that she suffered nightmares,

although not their content or the reason they existed. It was the first time Marcie had intervened, but how had she known? Sara's reaction to the nightmare was noiseless and the bedroom door was always shut. Had she entered for another reason and witnessed her mother's unconscious outburst? Or had Sara made noises after all?

If the latter, did that mean the dream had been more potent tonight? Had Drake's reappearance in her life, twenty years later, changed the format of her recurring nightmare?

No. The way Marcie now clutched her mother's hands... something was different... Marcie knew...

Sara staggered out of bed, took her daughter's hand, and they left the room. In Marcie's bedroom, Sara shut the door and sat on the bed. She fiddled with the yin-and-yang necklace. 'You know about my nightmare, don't you?'

She saw Marcie's eyes flick to the bed, and hers followed. There, on the quilt, sat an item she hadn't seen in years. Not since the same day Marcie first saw it, as an eight-year-old, minutes before it was wrapped up and abandoned in the attic.

Her book, *Her Dark Past*. The story she had foolishly written twenty years ago and regretted to this day. Sara wanted to slap it off the bed like a foul insect. 'So you know everything?'

'No. Not yet.' Marcie knelt before her mother. 'I just finished chapter five. About your dream. It was why I came into the room. And you were in the middle of it.'

Sara's tension lifted a little. So Marcie hadn't yet read about... the attack. Or chapter seven, which featured Joe, and which would change her life forever.

'I already knew some of the story from when I was ten,' Marcie continued. 'But I stayed away from it. For years. You told me to.'

Sara remembered the warning she and Joe had given Marcie when she was just a little girl: *That name Drake you heard? Never speak of it. Never ask who Drake is.* 'You were eight, not ten. So small and innocent.'

Marcie shook her head. 'I don't mean when my grandmother tried to tell me. There was someone else.'

Marcie sat by her mother and told the tale, and it was terrible to hear. Seven years ago, when the Drake story got a boost with the death of his first victim's mother... that reporter who'd tried to secure an interview with Sara...

Having a door slammed in his face, and subsequently failing to rouse words from Sara's parents and friends, hadn't deterred him. He went to Marcie's school, figuring he could coax answers from a ten-year-old girl.

Marcie's teacher had confronted the reporter at the security gate and got rid of him, but she might as well have invited him in given her subsequent actions. She told Marcie that reporters might come to see her many times over the next few days. Because of an evil man called Drake, who was in prison for murder.

Sara was shocked, and angry. 'Your teachers never told me about the reporter coming to your school. Or that one of them had foolishly blurted out everything.'

'Not everything, Mum. I didn't let her. I remembered the warning. I shouted at her not to say any more. I don't know if she got a few more words out or if I filled in the blanks afterwards. But I believed you were hiding something about a killer from your past and somehow I concluded that you'd been his girlfriend or wife. I knew it was a dark secret and I guess my assumption was based on that. I don't know. But I do know now that I was wrong.'

Sara picked up the book. It had been out of print since first publication but copies were out there, somewhere. She wondered how many remained of that two thousand copy first run. And who had read it. Had Drake?

She looked at Marcie. 'I'm sorry for keeping such a secret. It's my past, your own flesh and blood, and it must have been hard for you to avoid going digging.'

'My own curiosity wasn't the problem, Mum. It was tempting at times, but I promised you and Dad. So not going digging up the past was the easy part. Staying out of its way, that was the hard part.'

Sara understood. She and Joe had talked about exactly what Marcie was referring to. Sara was locked in to Drake's celebrity, and her name would surface with his. Avoiding the story of their relationship wasn't just about willpower. You would also need blind luck or an existence in the shadows.

Marcie told her all about the great efforts she'd had to go to in order to hide from the story, unaware of when it might rear its head. She avoided libraries, or made a beeline directly to whatever books she needed. At university, people were studying law and criminal psychology, so certain words – prison, murder, evil – would often crop up. The moment she heard one, Marcie would step away. She never watched the news.

It was a daily challenge. About a year ago one of her friends had begun dating a boy called Drake, and it wasn't easy to hear his name constantly mentioned. But thankfully, the friend dumped that loser soon after.

And of her friends? If one of them heard the story, they would surely mention it to Marcie, so they had to be informed that this was a no-go zone. Marcie got her closest pals together one day and laid it out.

'My mother was once the girlfriend of a man in prison for murder. I don't ever want it mentioned around me. I know you'll all now be too intrigued to avoid looking it up, so go ahead, read up, learn the shocking history of your friend's family. Just don't tell anyone, and don't ever bring it up to me. You are my forcefield. Help protect me.'

Marcie had also had to be extra nice to all her friends, knowing an argument might prompt someone to employ a certain weapon.

'I'm sorry you had to go through that,' Sara said. 'It must have been hard on you. And it was all my fault. All because your mother is a coward.'

'You're not a coward for wanting to move on from the past. But I know moving on is hard, especially right now. Something's happened, hasn't it? Something to do with Drake.'

'That's why you got the book out of the attic. What have you heard?'

'Nothing, really. I heard you and Dad on the phone. Drake's name was mentioned. And you've been down in the dumps for a while. You wanted to tell me earlier today, I felt it. But you changed your mind. I guess that got me intrigued. So has something happened? Is he being released or something?'

'I should tell you the truth, Marcie. About what happened back then and how things stand today. You deserve it. I just don't know if I can.'

Marcie pointed at the book. 'You can tell me this way.'

Sara opened the book, found the end of chapter seven, and tore the paperback down the spine. She handed the first part to her daughter.

'Things were clearer in my mind when I wrote that. Go read it, and I'll answer any questions you have afterwards.'

Marcie stared at the half-book. 'Not all of it?'

Sitting Marcie down for a chat, right now, was the correct way to do this. But she was scared to. And she had the sudden urge to do something a long time in the making. She stood up. 'Not yet. We need to talk first. All three of us. But soon you can read the whole thing.'

'Dad knows everything, doesn't he?'

Sara nodded. 'We'll both talk to you about it tomorrow. Stay here. Read tonight if you want. I have to go out.'

'Out? It's past midnight.'

'I can't say why. Please just stay here.'

Marcie didn't protest and Sara left her clutching the half-book. God, this whole situation was bizarre. What Marcie had been through in the last ten minutes had shown what a tough girl she was. But was she ready for learning the whole truth? Sara had a horrible fear her daughter was going to start suffering her own recurring nightmare.

But Sara had to put these worries to the back of her mind, at least for tonight. She entered her bedroom and got her phone, and made a call. Joe was still asleep. For a brief moment, as a phone rang at the other end, she was annoyed at him for being able to sleep through her nightmare, condemning her to suffer alone. But he had helped her in so many other ways.

A sleepy voice answered. 'Jenny, I need your help,' Sara said. 'Can you meet me.'

'What's wrong?'

'I know how to help myself.'

'You're willing to meet with Drake?'

'No. But I know something that will help me get that monster out of my nightmares. Can you come here? Tonight?'

Jenny didn't even take time to think. 'I'll be there as quick as I can.'

'I need a bike. I don't have one.'

Now Jenny paused. Sara knew the reference to a bike had told the former detective all she needed to know. 'Of course. I'll bring my son's.'

After the call, and before she got dressed, Sara sat on the edge of the bed, staring at the back half of the book still clutched in her hand. Page one of chapter nine was facing her.

That ninth chapter of *Her Dark Past* was going to reveal the biggest secret they had kept from Marcie. The truth was, she was scared. Scared to sit face to face with her daughter and unload such shocking information. That was why she'd taken the cowardly and insensible route of handing over the book. It had nothing to do with things being clearer in her mind back then – everything was as fresh and terrifying as it had been twenty years ago.

14

As they drove along Loxley Road, Sara's eyes were glued to the houses on the right. Or rather, beyond them. Poking over their roofs was the spire of a much larger building, atop which was a pram. Today, apparently, the building housed a retailer of baby merchandise. Two decades ago, when she worked there, the spire had boasted a giant plastic football.

That building, this road, these houses, all had been around much longer than twenty years. Apart from the pram logo and a handful of other changes, everything was just as Sara remembered it. Already her gut was churning at the memories of riding her bike down this road in the evenings, headed to or from work.

'Stop here,' she said a few seconds later, but Jenny was already slowing the car. She knew as well as Sara did exactly where their destination lay. Directly ahead, bright in the headlights, was a break in the houses on the left side: the entrance to Black Lane. Dark, remote, scary at night.

'Are you okay?' Jenny asked, and put a hand on Sara's chest just below the throat. Sara looked down at it and saw her chest rising and falling, fast. Her breathing was like machine-gun fire.

She couldn't get a grip on her emotions. There was shame, there was anger, there was fear, and the mishmash was making her head spin.

'I'm okay,' Sara lied. Her breathing slowed as she looked at her wedding ring, and at a flashy new car in one of the driveways. She'd been acting as if she'd transported back in time, to that fateful night, to once more suffer the event that had changed her life. Foolish girl. This place was different now. She was different now. There were still human monsters out there, but her human monster was safely locked away.

So, when Jenny asked if she was ready to do this, Sara's answer was to open the door and get out.

HER DARK PAST

CHAPTER SEVEN

Black Lane: dark, remote, scary at night. Am I worried?

My new dark hair impresses all my friends, some of whom also erased their blonde. In fact, the number of young blondes everywhere seems to have dwindled recently. My parents don't see the attraction. Dad thinks it's stage one in my becoming a goth. He makes a semi-joke that when I get a nose ring, I can 'hang the keys to the new home I'll need from it'. Mum's a little sad to see my natural blonde locks go, but well aware of my motive.

'Perhaps I should do mine,' she says a few days later, stroking her own dark blonde. 'Just to be safe.'

Dad laughs. 'If he goes for your type, he'll definitely get an insanity defence.' Mum takes the joke on the chin, as always.

I guess it's hard for Dad to understand the fear some of us women feel at knowing a madman is out there and we could be his target. And, despite Dad's joke, age is no reason for confidence. Mum was a youngster back when the Yorkshire Ripper was active just over twenty years ago. She told me how much more terrifying the night had become when the Ripper moved on from killing prostitutes to targeting all women. You can't assume you're safe because of type. No woman wants to be the one to make people say, 'Oh, look, everyone, the Slasher isn't just killing blondes after all.'

This conversation takes place not long after the Slasher's third kill, when it's fresh and still major gossip. But by Saturday, 5 May 2001, it has been almost two months since an attack and the atmosphere is different. There was a psychologist on TV talking about the Slasher. He said some serial killers increase their output as the obsession becomes uncontrollable. Lack of capture adds to their perception of immortality, and the time frame between kills shortens.

He was basically saying: the longer the Slasher goes without taking a victim, the more we should expect one soon, like the eruption of a volcano.

But people read this as positive. If a lunatic like the Slasher hasn't killed for eight weeks, that volcano will never erupt again. A dangerous opinion to have, but it seems to sweep the city. The police are still warning us to travel in groups, avoid late journeys if possible, and talk to no strange men, but they're being ignored. Women have stopped dyeing their hair, sales of personal alarms have steadied, and young females are hanging out on the streets at night again. Even I stop worrying when I'm out after dark. The dyed hair stays only because I like it. Dad's hammer goes back into the toolbox.

On that Saturday in May, one of the girls from work is having a birthday party and we are all invited. Marcie Whitecotton's name might not be on everyone's lips now the story has died away, but it's on ours. She was our good work friend and the birthday party is in part to celebrate her. All the boys and girls who work at The Ball Centre went to her funeral, where we released helium balloons with her photograph taped on them.

The talk at the wake afterwards was not about our dear friend, but the police. They had been to the funerals of the Slasher's previous victims, in the hope that a strange face there might turn out to be the killer. Apparently it's common for killers to attend the funerals of those they've killed. They like the power of alone knowing the truth. They like the grief at their handiwork. Like a psycho's version of an actor attending a movie premiere.

The officers had been undercover and those present at Whitecotton's funeral were similarly dressed to blend in. But blend in they didn't. One male officer had such a bad poker face that he actually got challenged by Whitecotton's dad and had to present his warrant card. I think I spotted all four of them, including one secretly filming. But their presence there had been expected and reporters had also turned up to run a story about it.

Ultimately no suspicious characters were identified, but the newspapers nonetheless got something spicy to make money off. Whitecotton's mother fainted onto the coffin as it was being lowered into the ground. Her brother screamed deadly revenge to the skies. Photographs of both events made the front page of a local rag.

Anyway, I digress. I plan to go to the party, but had offered to work Petra's shift that evening because she is hosting the party. The boss can see I'm itchy and lets me go half an hour early. I call Petra and tell her to start pouring me some wine, I'll be there soon. She lives just minutes away, down Black Lane, off Loxley Road.

Black Lane: dark, remote, scary. Am I worried?

My boss is and wants me to call a taxi. On a Saturday night, when it could be an hour's wait? Pay for a three-quarter-mile journey? My plan was always to take my bike and I almost laugh at his concern. Pretty young girls are back on the streets late at night, but dodgy men, the rapists and robbers and flashers, seem to be staying indoors. No one wants to be confused for the Slasher. The police are pulling them up, and vigilante gangs are beating them up.

And the Slasher himself, in my stupid head, has given up killing or moved somewhere else to do it or been locked up for another crime. So, am I worried about Black Lane? No.

Around ten pm, I set off on my pushbike. I have been down Black Lane many times so, even in the dark, I knew where all the potholes were. I cut into the dark abyss between two houses and the ground aims downwards, adding to my momentum. Trees rise on either side, bloating the darkness. There is no fear. The Slasher could be here, waiting for me, but I will zip past before he knows it…

15

'Are you sure you want to do this?' Jenny asked for the second time. Sara, standing in the road by the driver's open window, gave her a smile.

'It's funny you ask that now. You virtually gave me no choice last time.'

After Sara's attack, the police had tried to get her to the crime scene, hoping to jar additional memories loose from her. Jenny, leading the investigation, had offered to ease the pressure by doing it in daytime and filling the area with officers, but still Sara had refused. She would undergo hypnosis, or she would take a special drug, or anything else that could help her remember something important about the attack.

But she was not going back there. Never. Jenny had been very understanding, although she'd slyly tried to foster guilt in Sara by hinting that the key to catching a serial killer might remain forever locked in Sara's head.

'Well, now you have a choice,' Jenny said.

Sara's answer was to get the pushbike out of the back of Jenny's car. She wheeled it to the driver's window.

'Shall we be in contact by phone throughout?' Jenny asked. 'It might help if you hear my voice.'

It *would* help, but Sara shook her head. 'I need it to be like before. I need the dark and the silence for this to work.'

But would it ever work? Over the years, she had asked herself that question myriad times. She remembered her comment to Joe, who thought a meeting between her and Drake might repair her fractured confidence. *You both act as if this is the same as getting over a fear of heights. Confront and control and all that crap.* How many times had she wondered if returning to Black Lane could provide healing? Confront the place where a man had tried to kill her, and control her fear of it.

She had imagined a Shangri-La state of increased confidence, an end to bad dreams, an eroded obsession with hiding her past and pretending it never happened. A brittle and emotionally wrecked Sara had been carried out of Black Lane on that night all those years ago. But in just a few minutes from now, could a new, self-assured, optimistic phoenix emerge from the flames?

She had doubts it was that easy, but she'd accept even the smallest step in the right direction. She wanted the nightmares and the timidity to end, but if her reward was only a decreased fear of the dark, it would suffice.

She'd get no answers standing here. She rolled the bike to the mouth of the lane. Here, high hedges on the left blocked the light from the headlamps and created a stark line on the road. One side light, one side dark. Like a doorway.

She heard Jenny's car rolling forward, so put up a stop hand. 'I have to do this alone,' Sara called out. The engine shut off. Then the lights.

Sara stiffened. The moment the headlamps shut off, the light/dark threshold vanished and the mass of darkness down

Black Lane leaped forward like a pouncing predator and swallowed her.

But she felt fine.

She climbed onto the bike. Black Lane dipped downwards at first, so it would take just one push. One press of the pedal, and gravity would suck her towards the source of all her anguish.

'We can do this in the daytime if you're not ready,' Jenny called over.

For the second time, Sara answered with actions instead of words. She lifted her feet off the ground, and pushed on one pedal, and the bike moved. Through the invisible doorway, and down the slope. Gravity had her, and she willingly let herself be drawn. Into the blackness.

...My cruising speed starts to slow as the lane levels out. The ground below me is so dark I might be rocketing through space. I fire dead straight, laser-like, except for where I remember there's a bump or hole, which needs only a slight jerk this way or that to avoid.

Ahead is the small stone bridge, my target. I've visited Petra's home many times on my bike, and on each occasion I've attempted to ride the lane and cross that bridge without touching the pedals. I've never made it, my best attempt just feet from the top of the arch before the bike slows to a stall. I duck low, determined this time because I feel a tailwind.

But as I reach the spot between two stone posts at the end of the parapets, it all goes wrong. I hit a pothole and the bike stops dead, sending me sailing over the handlebars. At least, that is my atomic clock reaction to what happens. The truth, learned from the police later, is that our roles are reversed. It is my body that stops dead, while the bike continues the journey without me. And I did not hit a pothole.

I hit a booby trap.

~

Sara stopped at the foot of the bridge and laid the bike on the ground. It was bitterly cold, but was that the reason for her shivering? The trees broke for the bridge over the train tracks, so it wasn't as dark here. But the dark wasn't a problem, surprisingly. Perhaps because she knew Jenny was back there, or knew the likelihood of lightning striking the same spot twice was remote.

She looked at the ground, at the very spot where she had violently parted from her bike all those years ago. She had known the location of every hole, bump and fissure in the road and could have traversed Black Lane blindfolded. Below her feet the ground was smooth, albeit aged and cracked, just as she remembered. No pothole or evidence that one had been repaired. How foolish she had been to not realise she had hit a trap.

Once she knew the truth, she had been ashamed, and that feeling returned now. Falling for the killer's trick had made her somehow feel in part responsible for what had happened to her, as if with a little more common sense she could have escaped. But she would never forget the words of one of Jenny's detectives, who had used a blunt tactic to try to offer her a modicum of comfort:

There was nothing you could have done. He was here, and he was determined to have a victim.

What a thing to say. Believing you became a killer's victim by your own mistake was a lot easier to accept than the idea of being chosen by the hand of fate. Thankfully, she'd been no believer in all that predetermination stuff.

Now, she looked at the stone posts, and her mind went

back again. The killer's trap had been black insulated electrical cable strung between those posts at waist-height, designed to clothes-line a victim right off her bike. It would give the man hiding in the dark the second or two he'd need to pounce.

How many times had she replayed the event in her mind? Seeing herself with a smile as she bombed through the dark, towards the trap? Seeing Drake, lurking behind the hedge, also smiling as he watched his prey come right towards him?

Afterwards, Drake had had the savvy to take his trap with him, but he'd made a mistake. Panicked, rushing, he'd cut the cable instead of untying it and had left behind a loop around each post. It was how the police had worked out how he captured Sara. In the early days she had wished Drake had removed every piece of his trap and left everyone bewildered. That way she could have believed in the pothole, and lived her life without blaming herself.

Her hands went to her chest, where the cable had caught her. The mark was long gone, of course. She had sat up straight on her bike at the last moment, which had been lucky. If she'd still been bent over to aid aerodynamics, the cord would have been level with her face. The cord had propelled her backwards off the bike in a half-somersault, and she had landed head first on the tarmac, stunned. And then, out of the darkness, he had approached...

~

...Before I can rise, something hits my head. I have no idea at the time, of course, and certainly no clue that I will wear the scar of that strike forever. In the moment, I am aware only of terrible fiery pain on the left side and sudden blurry vision. Then something scrapes down my face, and all goes black. But not the blackness of

unconsciousness, rather something blotting out all light. And I can get no air. I can't breathe.

Hands. I feel hands on me. At first I think he's covered my mouth and eyes with those hands. I only realise my error as I'm flipped onto my front and something is tied tightly around my wrists, securing my arms behind my back. Something else bars my sight and my breathing.

Right then I am lucid enough to know the man assaulting me is the Slasher, and I remember his other victims. I know the thing blotting out all light, and suffocating my lungs is a swimming cap pulled down over my entire head. Later, police will show me that swimming cap in a clear plastic bag. I will want to touch it, to keep it, like a soldier who owns the bullet that shot him. But I am not allowed. It is evidence.

I begin to panic as I feel my shoes scrape the ground. My chest is hurting from the lack of air. He's dragging me, I realise. In the next second, the ground is gone. I know he's lifted me into the air, and I know why. Black Lane is dark, remote, scary, but this doesn't mean someone won't come along and catch the Slasher red-handed. He wants an even more secluded place nearby, and none beats the train tracks below us. He plans to throw me off the bridge.

As I feel my legs scrape what I know is the stone parapet, I welcome the fall. I want to land hard on my head and break my neck. I don't want to be alive for what he has planned next for me. I want him to scramble down the embankment, salivating at the thought of torturing me, and then curse as he finds his victim already dead.

Suddenly, I feel no more stone and no more hands. I am falling. It takes only a half second, but in that time I have a strange thought:

Oh, look, everyone, the Slasher isn't just killing blondes after all.

Sara had told Jenny she would ride to the bridge. She would stand at the parapet. She would gaze down at the railway. And that would be enough. If that *confront* didn't *control*, there was no more she could do.

Fifteen feet below, she saw the train tracks, just a pair of glinting lines in the dark. And it was done. She felt warm even against the chill air. She had refused to look at the crime-scene photos, or even pictures of the area in newspapers, yet now, live, in the flesh, she had faced the most terrifying sliver of the entire universe. Her legs were not weak, her heart was not thumping. Confronted. Controlled. What curative effect this experience would have on her future was yet to be determined, but the mission was over. She could now go home and live the rest of her life.

But she did not turn from the stone parapet. Instead, she moved along it, to one of the end posts, where the embankment on the other side was highest. There, she climbed over. She stepped down the grassy slope, eyes never leaving the railway. Soon, those parallel twin lines were no longer below her but directly in front. Eight feet away. Four feet. Then beneath her feet.

This was it, exactly. The spot where human hands had tried to end her life. For the first few days after the attack, while bruises and lacerations were fresh and she tried to come to terms with it all, she had wondered why the fall hadn't killed her. Now, that fact amazed her.

She tried to remind herself her work here was over, but the voice was weak. A louder one was all pessimism: what if she hadn't done enough to dispel the demons? Here, now, was her one chance to make sure.

She sat down, swept a few stones off the sleeper behind her, and lay back. She stared up at the bridge, and the black sky beyond. The warmth of achievement she'd felt on the bridge was gone. Something wasn't quite right. So she shifted here and there, trying to minutely replicate how she'd laid here two decades before.

Nothing seemed to hit the spot, because her recollection of the event was shot through, hazy. Some parts weren't even memory but filler applied by law and medical personnel. All she could remember for certain was pain and terror as she'd fallen and landed.

But the real horror had been yet to come...

It is the pain that proves it. I am alive. No longer falling. I think I swim in and out of consciousness because the pain vibrates on and off, like morse code. But in those fiery moments of lucidity, I push the pain aside to focus on listening. The world is still black, so it is all I have.

I hope to hear nothing. It is late and I am alone, and without air because of the swimming cap over my head, and I cannot expect help or help myself. But the alternative is a far more horrendous finale. The order of the killer's method is unclear because nobody ever found the victims' clothing. But if the police theory is correct, he will cut off everything I wear, then thrust his knife in and out of my chest and abdomen and groin and thighs. So I want to suffocate in silence before then. However, the police also say the victims were still alive when the stabbing started.

'Hush now,' a voice says, startlingly close. He is here, alone with me where no one will interrupt us. Where he can carry out his plan. There's rape in his arsenal, too, and here there exists another unknown in the killer's procedure. Police are unsure if rape occurs just after death. They say it's possible that he takes his time to lift the swimming cap away from the mouth periodically, allowing a victim just enough air to grab a handhold on life. Suffering is prolonged, and

he can watch the body below him thrash against his weight and his touch.

If the latter, it could be a long time before he replaces the rubber mask firmly against my face one last time and lifts his knife. For all I know, he plans a duet between penis and blade. I can't stop it.

The truth is I do not recall if I had these thoughts during the attack, or if I rewrote events later while recovering in hospital. Did the killer even speak to me? But one certainty is that I hear a yell, a bellow, from high above, as if God himself, despite all he has allowed to pass before, cannot abide this.

HEY...

~

HEY.

The shout didn't make her jump to her feet: it froze her in place. Laying on the cold train tracks, Sara saw movement above, at the bridge. A black shape, blotting out a portion of the dark sky. A human figure there. A man.

She could only stare, locked in place by this echo from the past. A logical part of her brain screamed that she was wrong, because Drake was in prison, unable to hurt her ever again. But how could she deny an obvious truth: there were other monsters out there, in the dark, on the hunt for women, that most endangered of God's species.

'*What the hell are you playing at?*'

The figure vanished and she heard the patter of racing footsteps. Then something else – a scraping sound? Still, she couldn't move.

The figure returned, carrying something that it heaved over the parapet. Now, she found the will to shatter the invisible bonds of fear, but all she could do was throw her arms across her face as something plummeted towards her. She screamed in expectation of pain.

There was no pain. Her bike crashed to the ground ten feet away. Following the thud, she heard a car engine revving. She scrambled to her feet, backed away, eyes this time not on the bike or the bridge but the grass bank, which Drake had used to approach her that night as she lay bound and injured.

She heard a screech of tyres, then a voice. Not male this time. It was Jenny. She was calling Sara's name.

Sara rushed for the grass bank, and up, stumbling to her knees twice. At the top she flung herself over the parapet so ungracefully that she couldn't gather her feet and landed hard on her side. She saw bright headlights at the foot of the bridge and knew it was Jenny's car.

The shape, the figure, the man, whoever he was, had gone.

16

It wasn't until Jenny's car pulled up outside the house that Sara felt her air begin to flow properly.

'I'm sorry about your bike,' Sara said. It was the third time she'd apologised.

Jenny cut the engine. 'I told you. There's no need to say sorry. What happened out there was very unfortunate.'

Indeed. Black Lane was a road used by drivers and one had chosen an inopportune moment. Angry at seeing the road blocked by Sara's bike, he'd exited his car and peered over the bridge. Seeing Sara, he'd yelled out at her, then, without giving her a chance to move the obstacle, he'd flung her bike over the parapet. Jenny had heard his shout from two hundred metres away and raced to the scene, and had even had to slow in order to pass the stranger's vehicle coming the other way.

'It proves something, though, doesn't it?' Sara said.

'It proved you could face your fears. In twenty years, you never had the courage to go back to that scene. And you did it alone, at night.'

At the front bedroom window of the house there was movement. Sara watched Marcie close the curtains. 'No, it proves I wasn't ready, even after twenty years. Look at the state I got in. The nightmare will never leave me. Tonight proves I'll never come to terms with what happened to me. Unless...'

'Unless what?'

'I think you know. The thing everybody seems to want me to do. Can you arrange it for me?'

'Of course. If you're sure.'

Sara didn't answer for a moment. Marcie's bedroom light flicked off and the first floor of the house was cast into darkness. She stared at the skeletal frame of the scaffolding on the front of the building. She had never liked the scaffolding. It gave criminals easy access to the bedroom windows, and at night the area around the front door was so dark an intruder could stand there unseen.

Was that a natural fear, or a symptom of her long-ago ordeal? She would have to get a light installed above the front door. And make sure Marcie always kept her window locked. And tell those damn roofers to work faster.

'Sara? Are you okay?'

'Yes,' Sara said, snapping back to the moment. 'And yes, I'm sure. Confront and control. So I'll do what everyone wants. I'll sit face to face with Drake, and I'll once and for all get that monster out of my system.'

17

Sara had barely shut the front door before Marcie bombed downstairs and straight into her arms. The shock made Sara laugh, because Marcie hadn't hugged her like that for years.

'What's this for?' Sara said, hugging Marcie back just as tightly. But she suspected the answer, didn't she? And when she felt Marcie's fingers in the back of her head, seeking and then delving into an ancient depression in her skull, she knew for sure. And hadn't she permitted Marcie to know the truth by giving her that book? 'You read about my attack, didn't you?'

She felt Marcie's head nod against her shoulder. 'That evil bastard. I want him dead. He should be hung upside down and be given death by a thousand cuts.'

Sara made no reply, although she absolutely agreed. She could have spent the entire evening with her daughter, inventing clever and intricate and gruesome ways Drake could spend his final breathing moments. But she didn't want to fill Marcie's head with hate.

When the teenager broke the hug, she looked into her mother's eyes. 'Something's happened. He's back in your life all of a sudden. Why?'

Sara grabbed Marcie's hand and replaced it on her head, pushing the fingers once more into the spot where Drake's weapon had broken her skull. Fresh, the wound had itched like crazy; today that urge to scratch was long dead but, bizarrely, Sara still felt comfort in having the area massaged by others. Joe aside, Marcie was the first to do so in years.

Marcie stroked the healed wound for a moment longer, saying nothing, giving her mother time. But she was awaiting an answer.

'Living room,' Sara said. 'With your father.'

Marcie waited in the living room while Sara went upstairs to wake Joe. He'd been dead to the world the whole time she was gone and was groggy. 'We need to talk to Marcie now,' she said, and went back downstairs.

He came down a minute later, topless but wearing tracksuit bottoms, hair wild, eyes sleepy. Marcie was standing by the front window, Sara on the sofa. He sat by his wife. 'I gave Marcie part of my book to read,' she told him. 'She knows who Drake is. She knows a lot already. But she only read to chapter seven.'

Sara saw Joe's whole body tense, then relax. Chapter seven. He understood that Marcie knew the details of the attack on her mother. But not her father's role in the whole fiasco, which was detailed later in the book.

'I know something's happened that's brought Drake back into your lives,' Marcie said. 'I deserve to know what it is and how it affects me. I need to know everything.'

She looked at her father as if for his blessing. He gave it with a slow nod. But he still looked very uncomfortable, clearly worried about his daughter's reaction when she learned the truth about him. He said, 'Drake wants to meet your mother. We don't know why. He might want to apologise.'

Marcie almost spat. 'What a joke. The bastard can't just

apologise after all this time. Has he got a parole hearing coming up or something? Does he want to give a good impression?'

'He was ordered to serve a minimum of thirty years, so he's not getting out,' Joe answered. 'But he might be dying. So I guess it's a deathbed confession. If that's actually his plan. Nobody knows because he's saying nothing.'

'Let him. Let him die right there on the floor of his cell.' She looked at her mother. 'You're not going to go see him, are you?'

Joe seemed just as intent on hearing the answer to this.

'To answer that, you both deserve to know where I was tonight.' She outlined the evening's events, and held nothing back. To understand her motivation to confront Drake, they had to know of the malfunction of her attempt to cleanse her mind of his poison by another means. After the tale was told, her daughter and husband displayed contrasting emotions. Marcie: sadness – her mother had been forced into a desperate action. Joe: disappointment – because of her failure, or that she'd withheld her plan from him? She couldn't tell.

'So you're going to see this man?' Marcie said. 'You have that nightmare, and it won't go away. Now you think meeting him face to face will help.'

Sara didn't miss the contempt in her tone. 'You think I'm being stupid?'

'No, I think you believe it will work. And maybe it will? But I don't like the idea of you seeing that man. He might just want to get a sick thrill out of being close to someone he tried to kill.'

Sara wanted to wrap Marcie in a great big hug. She could be teenager-naïve at times, yet genius at others.

'I think she has to go,' Joe said. 'Drake has threatened to talk to the media. If he does, the spotlight's on this family. That's nationwide scrutiny. Especially if Drake lies and says we refused to help him clear the air about other crimes. The door won't stop knocking.'

That annoyed Sara. 'Joe, we don't have to try scaring her like this.'

Marcie indeed looked a little horrified, but it didn't change her stance. 'No, you can't go, Mum. You shouldn't go. It could mess with your head more than that bastard's done already. Don't give him the satisfaction.'

'I've already decided,' Sara said. 'I'm going. You don't fully understand everything yet, Marcie. But you will one day.'

'Today,' the teenager snapped. 'Give me the rest of the book. Maybe I'll see things your way.'

'Soon. After I've met with Drake. You deserve the whole story. I want to wait until we know exactly what Drake wants from me. It might be nothing, you know. Maybe he'll just apologise.'

'I doubt it,' Marcie said, sharply. She started for the door. 'It's late and I need sleep.'

She fled, ignoring Sara's plea to wait, sit, talk. Sara jumped up, wanted to chase after her daughter, but Joe told her to give Marcie time. Sara reluctantly flopped back onto the sofa.

'After I've met with him, we'll tell her everything,' she said. 'Then this will finally all be past us and we can forget about what happened to me and have a happy, trouble-free life.'

Joe nodded, but he didn't look sold on the promise of this rosy future. And why should he? She hadn't even convinced herself.

18

Early that morning, while the world was still black, the incessant dream woke Sara. Nothing new there, but this time she was sweating enough to soak the sheet underneath her. Not since the early days had she experienced that, and it was a terrifying modification.

If it was a one-off based on her ordeal the previous evening, fine, understandable. But what if something deep inside her mind had loosened or broken, and this was now the shape of things? What if it got worse, night after night, until she couldn't sleep at all?

And what if facing Drake didn't help? What would she do then?

The worry guaranteed sleep was a no-go for the rest of the night. She went into the bathroom and sat on the toilet. There, she ran her fingers through her hair, into the depression above and behind her left ear. She hadn't intentionally touched the old wound in years, but right now she felt the urge. Fingering the depression was like scratching an itch.

She returned to the bedroom and grabbed her phone, planning to send Jenny a text, and was pleased to see the former detective had already dispatched one of her own, about half an hour earlier. It said simply CALL ME.

'I got hold of Oliver Elliot at home,' Jenny answered. 'I figured you wouldn't sleep tonight, so why should he enjoy a nice night of dreams? I got his address and banged on his door at three this morning. He's agreed to meet us tomorrow, soon as we're ready. At his house this time. I say we do it as early as possible. Come on out when you're ready.'

'Come on out? Are you...?' Sara went to the window and poked her head through the curtains. There, on the street, was Jenny's car. 'I see you, Jenny. You didn't find a hotel?'

A shape inside the car moved closer to the driver's side window, then waved. 'I did book one, but it was so late after I'd spoken with Elliot that I didn't bother. It was easier to just come here. I'm fine. Just come out when you're ready and we'll go. Have your breakfast and everything. We're not rushing for these people.'

'I'm coming down to you. You're coming in. You're not sleeping outside.'

Sara hung up the phone so she couldn't hear further argument. She threw on a bathrobe and trekked outside. But when she tried to open the car door, it was locked. On the other side of the window, Jenny shook her head.

'Not a good idea, Sara. You'd have to explain who I am to your daughter. I don't even know how Joe would react to seeing me. Go back inside, go back to sleep, go through your morning routine, say nothing about what we're doing today, make up a reason for leaving the house, and come out when you're ready. Once we have a date set for the meeting and everything is arranged and it's definitely happening, then you can tell them everything.'

Sara wanted to argue, but everything Jenny had just said sounded logical. 'At least let me bring you a blanket.'

When that task was done, Sara returned to her bedroom. There was no chance of sleep, so she lay next to her snoring husband and opened a book. Surprisingly she immediately felt her eyelids trying to close. Perhaps the long day was catching up with her, but she had another theory. Jenny was out there, watching the house. It gave Sara a sense of safety that she hadn't felt for a long time.

19

Staring out the window through a chink in the curtains, Marcie watched her parents get into a car. But not their own, surprisingly. They climbed into an SUV she'd never seen before, with a woman at the wheel she also didn't recognise.

Whoever she was, if the woman was driving Mum to see Drake's solicitors, then she knew the story. But why Mum hadn't mentioned her before and how she knew about Drake were unimportant questions right now. The house was empty, and her search could begin.

She started in her own room, just in case her mum had thought it would be the last place Marcie would look. She checked under the bed, in all her drawers, the basket for dirty laundry, and everywhere else that the item could fit. No luck, so she moved into the bathroom. It wasn't behind the toilet or folded under a towel on the rail or even in a waterproof bag in the cistern.

The back bedroom was next, but the item wasn't under the exercise bike or in the drawers of her dad's desk or any of the vacuum-packed bags of old clothing. She was halfway downstairs, to start in the living room, when she stopped.

Her room, bathroom, back bedroom and all the rooms downstairs were places Marcie was allowed. But her parents' bedroom? While not strictly off-limits, parents' bedrooms were sacrosanct, weren't they? Kids never liked to go rooting in such places, in case they got caught doing so, or found something they'd never unsee. So Mum must have hidden it there.

A minute later, she found it, and it hadn't really been hidden at all. Perhaps subscribing to the sacrosanct theory, Mum had simply placed it under her pillow.

Marcie scuttled from the room and checked at her window to make sure the stranger's SUV hadn't returned. She would have rather been caught with one of her mum's sex toys than this item. No car. She sat on her bed, hands shaking as she looked at the item. Or the half that remained. The portion her mother had decided was too much for Marcie.

Nervous, Marcie started to read the first page of chapter nine of *Her Dark Past: How I Survived a Serial Killer.*

20

Oliver Elliot's detached home was next to The Richmond, a pub on a main road in Richmond in the east of Sheffield. Jenny stopped her car in the car park, by the chest-high wall running alongside Elliot's house.

From here, they could see past the back corner of the house, into a rear veranda with a thatched roof and ornate furniture. Elliot, suited as if for a day at work, sat at a tiny round table, eating breakfast with a female about his age.

Even before Jenny had killed the engine, Sara was out of the car, at the wall, calling for him. The dining couple almost jumped out of their skin and Elliot, alien to such an approach from a client, didn't know how to react. He chose to apologise to his wife and, still chewing toast, rushed for the back door. Sara, Joe and Jenny met him at the front.

By this time he'd swapped shock for outrage, but it was regulated to his eyes only as he adopted a fake smile to greet his guests.

'This is a friend,' Sara said, pointing to her husband. Elliot gave her and Joe a wary look; last time, Sara's 'friend' had turned out to be the detective who arrested Drake Mills. But Elliot didn't question this and invited his guests inside.

Sara helped Jenny get her wheelchair over the threshold and the trio were led down a hall and into a study. The books on shelves and on his oak aluminium desk were law and non-fiction tomes befitting his work, but it was clear he enjoyed to relax here too. There was a large flat-screen TV, a beanbag, a small fridge, and where there was space on the walls he'd pinned American football merchandise.

Elliot left them standing alone as he left the room. When he returned, he carried two stacked plastic chairs.

'I'm sorry, I expected a phone call first. I don't normally see people at my home.'

Sara caught the admonishment in his tone, but didn't care. 'Life is full of unexpected surprises. And we won't be here long enough to need chairs. Just tell me when and where we're supposed to meet your murdering friend.'

Elliot put the chairs down. He looked at each person in turn. 'We? All three of you? I'm not sure Mr Mills will agree to that.'

'I'll be at the prison, but I won't be in the room,' Jenny said.

'I'll be there,' Joe said. 'Moral support. I'm afraid he can like it or lump it.'

Elliot stared at Joe and his eyes narrowed. 'Joseph Yorston?'

Joe just shrugged in that carefree way of his. *It is what it is.* Not really an answer, so Sara provided one. 'Yes, I brought my husband. Is that a problem?'

'And you wish to meet Mr Mills with your husband alongside? I can probably say with a high degree of certainty that Mr Mills will definitely not be willing to see Mr Yorston. I hope this isn't going to cause a problem.'

'Well, that's a problem for Drake and you. Joe goes or no one goes. Should we just leave now?'

'It's just... I mean, you understand why Mr Mills wouldn't want to have your husband present, don't you?'

'I get it totally,' Sara said. 'If not for my husband, your evil bastard friend might still be out there, gutting young women.'

HER DARK PAST

CHAPTER NINE

Somehow, I don't just survive the fall off the bridge on Black Lane, I make it out almost uninjured. According to the neurosurgeon who works on me, I was 'super lucky' I didn't break more bones when I hit the train tracks. There's a few lacerations from the stones between the sleepers and sprained wrists because my bound hands were behind my back and were crushed beneath me, but little else.

The term 'more bones' applies because one did suffer: my skull. A depressed fracture. There's a dent in my head that looks like a moon crater in the X-rays.

Initially, I am rushed to the nearest A&E. I am awake when staff swarm around me to analyse my injuries, and they offer smiles and words of encouragement, but nobody mentions serial killers or police. I make nothing of this at that moment because I assume the doctors and nurses are prioritising and we'll get to my attack once the life-saving business is done.

I'm soon moved to the neurosurgery unit at Royal Hallamshire Hospital, where a surgeon works on my fracture and a brain scan gives good news. It doesn't even hurt by the time I'm out of surgery and into my own room.

By this time it's somewhere around six am on Sunday and the story has had time to travel. I wonder how the world is dealing with it. I'm still out of sorts and don't pick up on the significance of the hospital staff, after congratulating me for my falling technique, telling me that I should be more careful in future.

More careful in future?

Soon after, when I'm with a nurse who's working on my minor cuts and abrasions, I ask if the police have arrested anyone.

She looks a little puzzled. And alarmed. 'Arrested? Because of your fall? Did someone push you?'

'He tried to kill me,' I say. She rushes off, probably to report this. About two minutes later, a different nurse enters the cubicle. By this point I've started to wonder if I imagined the attack. Did I fall after all? Over that parapet somehow?

But no.

The new nurse tells me the police wish to interview me and Jenny is invited into the cubicle with another man I recognise as one of her team. There's no way they just got a call from the other nurse and arrived this quickly, which means they were here all along. Waiting for the hospital staff to finish and leave me alone.

By this time I'm conflicted because the atmosphere doesn't seem to suggest I was the victim of a serial killer, yet Jenny is here.

Jenny shuts the curtain and sits by my bed. The male stands near the curtain, like a security guard. She asks how I'm feeling, but I'm too worked up for small talk.

'I was attacked by the Slasher,' I say. I expect scorn, and I hope for Jenny to give me a rational reason why my claim is preposterous. I want to be wrong.

But I'm not: 'We know,' she says. 'What do you remember?'

'Someone saved me. I think.'

True, she explains. A local boy on his way to a party – the same one I planned to attend – was driving down Black Lane when he saw what looked like someone climbing over the bridge. His theory was a glue sniffer needing a quiet spot, and he would have driven past, but a bike blocking the lane made him stop.

He got out to move the bike and that was when he heard a scream – I don't recall screaming and didn't think it was possible because of the swimming cap – and he ran to the bridge. He saw electrical cable strung tightly across the road and figured he knew what had happened.

Here Jenny pauses at seeing my confused face. 'It's how you were caught,' she says. 'I know you said something to a nurse about a pothole, and I'd like you to stick with that story until we're ready to release the truth.' Which she promptly outlines: cable across the bridge to chop a rider right off her bike.

This is shock enough to make my head spin all over again. 'Was he after me all along?'

Jenny takes my bruised hand carefully. 'No, we don't think so–'

'Don't say that. You can't know that yet. A walker wouldn't be caught by cable across the road. They'd see it. A car would cut right through it. It's something that would only work on a girl on a bike.' Talking fast, I insist that she looks into all the men living in that area, and male members of the football club I work at. I'm in the process of starting to name shifty males living on my estate when she interrupts to tell me to calm down and stop talking.

'Your attacker probably watched the lane's elevated entrance for the right kind of victim,' she says. 'If one end was already tied, he could have placed the cable in the time it took you to ride down to the bridge. Even if you'd seen it, it would have given him time to launch his attack.'

I'm not convinced and she has to almost beg me not to assume I was a planned target. I try, but it will be a long time until I can accept I was just in the wrong place at the wrong time.

She continues her story. My saviour peered over the bridge and saw two figures below. One male, one female, who was laying on the train tracks, her head clearly covered by some kind of hood. He yelled out and the male fled. My saviour then headed down to me and yanked off the swimming cap, just in time. I sucked air in and started screaming again, but I also don't recall this. He called 999 on his mobile phone and waited with me until help arrived.

'We got there before the ambulance,' Jenny says, 'because this had all the hallmarks of being another Slasher attack. We had a team ready to deploy at a moment's notice.'

She explains that the man who found me had left the cable tie securing my hands because he knew it was evidence. The cable tie and the swimming cap all pointed towards the Slasher, but by the time the ambulance arrived, this evidence had already been photographed, bagged and removed. Nothing was said to the paramedics about a serial killer.

With no explanation from Joe, who'd been told by the police to say nothing just yet, the paramedics assumed I'd fallen off the bridge, thus clearing up how that theory got round the hospital. They had not seen the electrical cord trap on the bridge. Why? Because, shockingly, at some point while my saviour sat with me, the killer had circled around to retrieve the cable. He hadn't had time to untie both ends and had cut it. We're lucky he didn't kill us both.

The upshot: 'As yet nobody here knows you might have been attacked by the Slasher. I'd like to keep it that way so this place doesn't fill up with reporters.'

I am happy with that. I do not want the media hounding me. The thought of reporters camping outside my house appals me. I tell her this, but she warns me that word will come out eventually. I should prepare for that.

After this, my attention turns to the man who saved me. I want to know his name.

She tells me, and if I hadn't been lying down, I would have fallen. I know him.

My saviour and I attended the same school, Alderman Jones Comprehensive in Sheffield. He was a couple of years above me, but I always knew who he was. He was a mythical figure to the fresh Year Seven kids' influx, like me. His father was a head teacher at another school, so the kids in the years above him gave him respect. Maybe they worried his father and our head were good friends and Joe could make life hell for bullies.

He was also a very good-looking boy and many girls liked him, me included. He was popular, good at sports, funny and intelligent, and he would also stick up for the bullied kids. There was only ever one kid he didn't like at school, a weirdo boy in his class who I'll provisionally call Peanut. I know I just said my saviour defended the bullied, but even Peanut was beyond redemption. I didn't know him. But I would come to. In the most terrible way.

I never really got to speak to my saviour at school

because he was an older boy and there were prettier girls in his orbit. Once he'd left after his final year, I forgot about him, until the day he joined The Ball Centre.

I was working there and he came in with seven friends to play four-a-side football. I filled out his membership with a shaking hand and allocated myself as his helper if he needed anything. Every Tuesday evening he'd come in to play for an hour, but although I tried, I really didn't get much opportunity to strike up a meaningful conversation.

Until one day when I overheard him telling a friend that he had nothing to do that coming Saturday. I did have plans, and I got my friend Petra to ask him and a couple of his pals along. She called me a wimp, but went straight over and did it, and they accepted.

So, I would get to meet my saviour that night. And I did, but not in the way I expected.

It was 5 May 2001, and my saviour's name was Joe Yorston.

Joe had scared the Slasher away, removed the swimming cap that would have suffocated me, and he held my hand until the police arrived. The man was a hero in the eyes of many, but the police needed time to jump on that bandwagon. By the time I was told his name, the hero was at a police station, still giving his statement.

I have noted that Jenny continually uses the term 'according to'. Everything Joe has said about that night is 'according to' him, as if Jenny doubts the veracity of his story. Maybe this is just police-speak, but I read more into it.

'Is he a suspect?' I ask.

Now she's the one who appears shocked. 'A suspect? I didn't say that. We don't make judgements until we know everyone's version. We have to verify everybody's stories.'

No, she didn't say he was a suspect, but she doesn't refute the notion either. However, I have no time for getting into this further because now Jenny wants a full statement from me and a description of my attacker.

It is at this point my parents return; they have been hanging around the hospital all night, but gracefully waited until the hospital staff were done attending to me. I want to put my mind on things other than the Slasher so seeing my parents takes priority. Jenny leaves for the moment and my mum and dad take her place by my bedside.

It's an emotional reunion, and my mum cries at seeing the bandage on my head, underneath which part of my scalp is shaved. They don't yet know someone tried to kill me – the story they were told was the one given to the hospital staff by police, who need more information before they attribute it to the Slasher.

I decide I'm too nervous to tell my parents right then. Once they leave and Jenny returns, I will ask her to tell them the tale. When they've got over the shock, then I'll talk with them about it.

Jenny is eager to strike gold with what I know, but I don't have much for her. I didn't see my attacker's face, or his clothing, and although I think he spoke to me, I can't recall the voice. But I do offer something that she's very grateful for.

The police already know the killer rapes his victim before death. They know the stabbing occurs at the same time as the suffocation. Now I was able to educate them on a very important detail of the killer's modus operandi that had been eluding them. Because I survived to tell the tale, they know he subdues his victim by slamming the swimming cap over her head. With breathing cut off, death is minutes away, and this can only mean one thing.

While the killer is raping his victim, he plunges a sharpened weapon into her flesh and watches her suffocate.

21

As Joe was reaching for the front door, it opened. Marcie stood there, and she'd clearly been crying.

'Marcie, what wrong?' Sara said.

Marcie grabbed her father and hugged him tightly. He laughed, puzzled by this abrupt act of love from his daughter. Before Sara could ask, Marcie released her father and disappeared into the house. And that was where Sara got her answer.

They found her in the living room, standing in the centre of the floor, clutching something she obviously wanted them to see. Sara had told her husband that she'd given Marcie the first half to read. Their daughter clutched the second half, and now her parents knew she knew everything.

Joe shrugged. 'At least we don't have to sit her down and tell her.'

'My father is a hero,' Marcie said, more to herself. She took the sofa. Her fingers squeezed the book like a stress ball.

'Yes, he is,' Sara said. 'And we both–'

'And if not for Drake, I wouldn't be here.'

Sara sat by her. Joe just watched. 'Don't think like that,

Marcie,' Sara told her. 'Don't think of that man's life as a positive.'

'Or at least know that his existence wasn't purely negative,' Joe offered.

'Your father knew I gave you the first part of the book. He thinks it was the wrong way to do this. He said we should have sat you down together and told you. So we could answer any questions.'

'Well, we're all here now,' Marcie said. 'And my main question is: what happens next? Are you going to meet Drake?'

'Yes. We decided we need to know what he has to say. There's a chance he committed other crimes that he wants to admit. It would help other families.'

'I know about some of the other crimes he was suspected of. I've also been reading about him on the internet. But this is also about you. If you stare him down and you're not scared, maybe you can finally move on from him.'

God, she hoped so. It was starting to seem more likely. Now that she knew her daughter had the whole story, she had already felt a weight lifted.

'So what happens next, Mum?'

'We wait. The solicitor will try to get in contact with Drake today. We have to see if the prison will allow the visit, and when. But they shouldn't really deny permission, especially if they think that bastard might give up something. Then Elliot will contact me with a time. He thinks we could arrange it for tomorrow.'

'I want to go.'

'No,' Joe said with uncharacteristic assertion. 'I knew you'd say that. The answer is no.'

'If you're worried about him attacking me, don't. He's in prison. There will be guards everywhere.'

'It's too risky. Guards don't mean he's not a danger. It would only take him a second to get hold of you. Do you know what he could do in one second? Girls like you are exactly what he craves.'

'Joe!' Sara snapped. 'Don't say such things. My God, what's up with you?'

Joe immediately apologised, aware that he'd overstepped a line. But Marcie seemed unfazed. 'I saw that fool's picture. He's a weedy little man. He looks like a castaway. He only got those other women because he jumped them in the dark. I'd batter him before he could grab a breast.'

Sara's wrath shifted to her daughter. 'Shut your stupid mouth, Marcie. This weedy little man you speak of managed to kill three women and he nearly killed me. My God, both of you are so...'

She took a breath, long and deep. 'Look, I'm sorry for snapping at you, Marcie. But you can't come, okay? Drake will want to see me alone, for a start. Second, the prison isn't going to let other people in. They have all sorts of policies and security protocols. Even your father might not be allowed to go, so they're hardly going to let a seventeen-year-old girl inside. But we've discussed this, your dad and me. We'll allow you to have friends round while we're gone. The house to yourselves. A party, if you like. And when this whole silly mess is over, I won't keep anything from you. I'll tell you everything. No more secrets.'

Sara hadn't realised one of her hands had raised to her head, her fingers digging hard into the old dent in her skull.

'How about no more secrets starting right now?' Marcie waved the book. 'This story is twenty years old. It ends with you pregnant with me. I want to know about everything that happened after you wrote it.'

'Well, why don't we go upstairs to talk? Your father can make lunch.'

Marcie liked this idea. As the two women headed from the room, Joe gave Sara a look that passed a message. She told Marcie she'd be up in a moment. When the parents were alone, Joe said, 'Why did you tell her I'm not going to the prison? I'm going, I told you that. No one said I can't.'

'But Drake might.'

'So he's in charge now? He wants to see you, not the other way round.'

'But I have to do it, don't I? If he's got information about additional crimes, we have to get it. So you could say that evil bastard *is* in charge.'

'Have to? Is that what Jenny told you? She's still got a police brain, or she's hoping to win brownie points with her old colleagues by solving some old crime.'

'That's a bit unfair. Jenny just wants to help. I approached her about this, not the other way round. She hasn't thought about Drake for years.'

He shrugged. 'I'm going, and that's that. I'm not letting the man who tried to kill my wife be alone in a room with her.'

22

Two phone calls.

The first was to a typical house in Walkley, a suburb of Sheffield, at nine in the evening. Nervous, Sara forwent her standard form – name and how could she help – and said, 'Hello.'

It was Oliver Elliot: 'Mrs Yorston, I've spoken to Drake Mills...'

It was Sara who made the second call, immediately after she hung up. Sixty-three miles almost directly south, at a house on the northern edge of Birmingham's Burbury Park, a man answered. He patched her through to an extension and Jenny Pitchford picked up.

'Tomorrow morning,' Sara blurted. 'I need you there. Please.'

She gave the older woman the details. The governor at Her Majesty's Prison Orrell had arranged for Sara and Joe to be escorted into the facility via a rear delivery door at 8.30. By then the prisoners would have had breakfast and been returned to their cells, so the corridors would be empty. At 9am, Sara would meet with Drake in the visiting room. Face to face, as Drake had insisted.

There would be a pair of guards also in the room. Drake would be thoroughly searched before entering. The tables and chairs were bolted to the floor. Nothing he might employ as a weapon would be allowed within reach. Sara was promised her safety was paramount. It didn't make her feel much better.

Drake had allowed Joe to be present. Elliot, the solicitor, would be at the prison in case Drake wanted to see him afterwards, but he wouldn't be at the meeting. One hour maximum had been allotted in order to have the visitors in and out of the prison before the convicts were released from their cells for 10.30 association.

'Do you want the meeting tomorrow morning?' Jenny said. 'Or is that too soon?'

'It's a million years too early to see that bastard again. But I want this over and done with. I don't want an extra night thinking about that bastard. Can you come? I told Elliot you have to be there, even if it's not at the meeting.'

'I'm already getting my shoes on. I'll sleep on your sofa so we're not rushing about in the morning.'

Jenny was at Sara's home ninety minutes later. When she pulled up, Sara and Joe appeared at the door. With shoes and coat. Jenny watched them hug their daughter, as if they were leaving on a long holiday.

'Are we going somewhere?' Jenny asked when Joe and Sara got into her vehicle.

Sara said, 'If I wake up nice and comfy in my own bed tomorrow morning, I'll end up backing out of the meeting. So I've booked us two hotel rooms close to the prison for tonight. I think I'll need that push. We'll count the whole horrible experience as starting right now.'

Jenny was game and at forty minutes to midnight they entered the reception of the Seven Oranges Hotel in Orrell, situated between the train station and the Methodist church. It was half a mile south of the prison, which gave Sara an itchy feeling even though she hadn't yet seen the building. Jenny insisted on collecting the room keys. Joe and Sara waited by an open-plan lobby restaurant in the foyer.

Sara could see that Joe was nervous: the giveaway was fidgety hands inside his trouser pockets. She wanted to crack a joke and tell him to stop because someone might think he was playing with himself. Instead, she apologised.

'For what?'

Ever since they'd learned that Drake was back in their lives, he'd kept his emotions mostly in check, as much for her benefit as it was his passive demeanour. But it was clear from his restless hands that he was suffering, perhaps as badly as she was, and he'd had no one to soothe him. 'For being a pain in the arse these last few days.'

'It's fine.'

The entrance to the restaurant was simply a gap between two six-feet-tall artificial dragon trees. She ran the back of her hand across one of the tricolour leaves. 'Don't go blind, will you?'

He gave a smirk of understanding. 'We should get a table. Replay everything over the last nineteen years. Although I wouldn't change a thing.'

'I would,' Sara said before she could stop herself. She moved into Joe's arms and they hugged. 'I'm sorry. You know what I meant.'

He nodded against her head. She clutched him tightly, staring at the restaurant and thinking about her first date with Joe, so long ago now. But she was disgusted with herself. Over the years, she had often told herself that if not for Drake, she wouldn't have her awesome husband or magnificent daughter. It was a way of attaching a positive tint to the whole thing.

But it hadn't stopped the *what if* thoughts. *What if Drake had never attacked me? What would life be like now?*

Each time, she mentally slapped herself and shut those thoughts down. But they were always hidden down there in some crevasse, lurking like a... like Drake in a dark hedge. What did her failure to completely banish the *what ifs* mean?

Did part of her wish fate had directed her down an alternative fork in life that long-ago night, even if it meant no Joe and no Marcie?

HER DARK PAST

CHAPTER ELEVEN

Two weeks after admittance, I am released from the hospital. Mum and Dad don't visit or call me for the final two days, at my insistence. The day before that, the police finally admitted to the country that my attack was part of the Slasher series.

I knew it was coming and asked Jenny to tell my parents first, then bring them to the hospital. The ride over gave them time to absorb the news. Our chat that afternoon was awkward for me.

Mum was terribly upset that I was going to be connected to a serial killer, and a source of interest to the morbid, perhaps for a long time. She was also worried that a killer that smart might go undetected for years, and I would never see my attacker brought to justice. Dad was a little more blunt and even cracked a joke about it. It was something to boast about down the pub: my daughter kicked the Slasher's ass. And he wants to nickname me Doll.

It was very weird to hear Dad act as if attempted murder was no big deal, but Mum later told me his flippant attitude was a conscious effort to lighten the gravity of my attack. He hoped I would follow suit. I love him for the attempt. I felt real bad for both of them. It hurt them a lot.

When they left, I told them I didn't want to talk about it ever again. I gave them two days alone after that so they could deal with friends and neighbours who would flock to our door once the news came out. Hopefully, everyone would have lost interest by the time I came home. My parents were happy to do this, although I felt guilty that I was abandoning them to field all the hassle while I stayed in bed and watched TV.

That evening, Jenny broke the news at a press conference. Reporters found my location within an hour, but the hospital staff kept them away from me. Except one. I allowed one to visit my room. If I didn't talk to any of them, they'd keep hounding me. I figured the best tactic was to give one the scoop and hope it convinced others I'd been milked for all I was worth.

I didn't watch the press conference or any other news. If the hospital staff see it, they do a good job of keeping it to themselves. Those two days feel a little strange because I'm in a blank room, insulated against an outside world that boils in reaction to this shocking Slasher update.

On the morning of my release, Jenny turned up with my parents, to escort me out. But not home. Mum and Dad have arranged for us to stay at a hotel in Woodseats, about eight miles west of our house. My plan to have all our friends and neighbours bored of the story by the time I came home? A miserable failure.

Despite the scoop by the reporter I spoke to, the city is still eager to get hold of the only Doll to face the Slasher and live. Reporters are camped outside the house and my phone, which my mum took away, has been blowing up with messages and calls. My parents want to give it another couple of days, so off we go to the hotel.

We have to leave by a secluded delivery door because people are waiting out front to get at me. Jenny has arranged for a police officer to sit outside the hotel and fend off those who manage to find it.

Later that evening, one person who wants me is allowed to get a message through. Jenny phones and tells me that Joe Yorston, my saviour, wants permission to call me. On any day before my attack, this would have been glorious news. But now I worry that he wants to interview me. Has he been contacted by reporters who want him to get close to me? It's a worry and I ask Jenny about it.

She doubts he has an ulterior motive because as far as she can tell, the news hasn't reported on his role as the man who saved a Slasher victim. He was cleared of any involvement in the murders long before the story of my attack broke and it seems he's not told anyone.

Basically, no one knows. He could have bragged about being a hero, could have made money selling his story, and hadn't. How can I not love this? I say yes, give him my new number – my old number was compromised and Mum cancelled the contract.

Jenny gives Joe the number the next morning and he texts. I text back, too nervous to have a live voice chat. Within a couple of hours, I have my confidence back and ask if he wants to join me for a meal. My hotel has a restaurant downstairs and we agree to meet that evening.

My parents are a bit dubious about my meeting a new boy and try to convince me to wait until the frenzy around me cools. It's nothing to do with Joe himself, who has effectively passed the vetting process by saving me from a psychopathic butcher. But I insist, so before my date they head down to the nearby shops for gifts. A hat from my mum. Dad buys me a panic alarm and I don't know whether to laugh or cry.

I dress my best, put on make-up to cover the cuts and bruises on my face, and leave Mum's hat behind. The bandages are off my head and I wear only gauze over the wound and the shaved spot around it. I don't want to hide how I look, even if it betrays my anonymity.

The hotel is one of Sheffield's most popular and as I head down alone to the lobby, people do look. It's hard to know if they're just staring at my head or if they know who I am. Or maybe it's because I'm as pretty as a Doll, ha ha. Nobody says anything. There's other news in the world.

I see Joe standing by the restaurant entrance, a trellis archway wrapped in plastic palm leaves. No one with him: so, he hasn't brought a media crew, unless they're disguised as hotel guests. But I doubt it.

He looks good in a suit jacket over black jeans, his hair slicked back and face freshly shaved. Not just good, magnificent. Back at school I had considered Joe to be far too good for me and the feeling returns now. My cuts and bruises seem to glow, adding to my worry. He doesn't see me and I turn and flee back up the stairs. When I return shortly afterwards, it's beneath my new hat.

I take a breath and stride over. We shake hands and he comments on my face – I'll get him beaten up, apparently. It's just a joke and reminds me of my dad's tactic to try to relax me. When we head into the restaurant, he catches a palm leaf in the eye and I nervously laugh.

'Don't go blind on me,' I say.

Once we're seated, scanning the menu, I try to ignore the looks people give me. Joe seems to get glares from all the males, as if they think he's my abusive partner. We chat, but there is no mention of my attack. That feels a little wrong. It's a bond we can't break, even if this evening somehow makes us sworn enemies. Needing to bring it up, I say the first thing that comes to me.

'So the police let you go.'

God, that was silly. But he cracks a joke: 'I escaped.'

We pause as the waiter arrives to take our orders. When he's gone, I feel bold enough to go further. I ask his version of what happened on that fateful night. It's pretty much the same as the tale he gave to Jenny and which she relayed to me. But he didn't tell the police this next little gem.

'I recognised you while I was holding your hand. I had this mad thought that you'd probably be thankful that I saved your life. I figured I'd say you owe me a date.'

He's grinning, of course, because of where we are. 'Yeah, you got no chance,' I say, going along with it.

'Well, I was going to the same party, remember.' This surprises me: I had asked Petra to ask him to her party that night, but she hadn't mentioned me. 'Don't look so surprised. I saw you talk to your friend and then she came running over. I knew you'd sent her.'

'Oh, and why were you watching us talk?' I say, embarrassed.

'Not both of you. Just you.'

I know my cheeks go as colourful as the bruises on the rest of my face. Our food comes and this seems to signal the end of talk about that night. As if by silent agreement, we don't mention it again. We chat on all sorts of subjects. He makes me laugh like I haven't in months and the time flies, but sadness prevails as we prepare to part company later that evening. He wants another date, but I am in a quandary.

Joe is funny and sweet and normally I would have snapped at the chance to see him again. But we are bonded by my near-death experience and I am scared that he'll be a hindrance to healing. Everything seems fine now, but I have no clue how my mental resolve will shift and act as the days then months pass.

What if I think about the Slasher every time I'm with Joe? What if, in a Pavlovian sense, I can't help but relive my ordeal when we're together? What if I can't ever allow him, or any other man, to touch me, ever again?

Joe's awaiting an answer. The one I offer doesn't erase his smile, but it wipes the legitimacy behind it. 'We'll see. I can't answer that right now. I'm sorry. I just need some time to heal first.'

He understands, he says, and he kisses my cheek, reminds me I have his phone number, and leaves. I wonder if it's the last time I'll ever see him.

23

Joe's events venue, The Old Tiara, had been his baby for years and he didn't trust it in the hands of others. While he was wrapped up with a check-up phone call to the assistant manager, Sara took the opportunity to go next door and see Jenny.

The former detective answered Sara's knock red-faced and breathing heavy. She'd opened the sliding door to access the balcony, but had been unable to manoeuvre her wheelchair over the high sill. She'd been at it for a couple of minutes before giving up. Sara helped.

Out on the dark balcony, the two women spent a few silent seconds enjoying the view. The balcony was on the third floor, facing north, and Jenny didn't miss the intensity in Sara's roving eyes. 'See the church? Look a little left, just beyond the warehouse with the blue roof.'

Sara did, and there it was. Poking out from behind the warehouse was the top portion of a red-brick, squared building and the tips of three long annexes in white. Orrell Prison was composed of a central hub with six radial wings. Built in 1981, one of only a handful of Category A prisons in the UK, it was home to 551 convicts, none of whom was serving a sentence of less than four years.

A secure place to keep the undesirables of society away from law-abiding folk, yet in just a few hours she would be walking into that place. To sit and talk with the worst of the worst.

There wasn't much to see from a mile away, but she couldn't drag her gaze off it. Was Drake at a window in one of the three wing portions she could see? Did he somehow know she was staying at the Seven Apples Hotel and was even now looking this way? Did he have binoculars and could fathom every detail on her face? Again she wondered why she was doing this.

'A lot of effort has gone into this,' she said to Jenny. She finally ripped her eyes away from the prison to stare further afield, at nothing in particular. 'They're letting us in outside of visiting hours, and they're bringing in guards from another prison.'

'I don't understand. What do you mean?'

'Pressure. The prison officials, they haven't allowed this meeting for Drake's sake, or mine. They want information, don't they? The idea was that I talk to Drake and maybe he'll admit something. But it's not just an idea anymore, not in the eyes of the prison people. It's the plan. It's expected. That's why they've gone to all this trouble. They *expect* me to interrogate Drake. To them, I will have failed if I don't get him to admit to some old crime.'

'Maybe they do,' Jenny said, 'but you're under no pressure. Everybody else has failed to get him to open up, so you can hardly be blamed if he refuses to talk about his crimes.'

Sara looked down at the older woman. 'But you also hope I can get something from him.'

'I don't know why Drake wants this meeting, Sara. You're in charge here, not Drake and not the prison service or anyone else. If tomorrow can help a grieving family, good. If he says nothing about past crimes, that's on him, not you. I'm here to help you and you're here to face the man who tried to murder you and hopefully put him behind you. If you want to do that by sitting in silence and not even looking at him, so be it. You do that. And if at any time you want to leave, just stand up and walk out. If someone tries to coach you on what to say or gives you any kind of pressure, I'll put a stop to it. In fact, if you want it to all stop right now, say the word.'

'No, I want to do this. I need to. I want to sit in front of that frail little bastard and know I'm the better person. I want to know I could jump over that table and strangle him. I want to see him weak and useless and for him to see that I have no fear anymore.' Sara looked at Jenny and didn't like the expression on her face. 'What is it?'

'Nothing,' Jenny said. 'I was just thinking how much stronger you sound already. That's a good start.'

Soothing words, but Sara read a hollowness in them. She knew the former detective didn't buy into Sara's claims that the meeting with Drake would result in good news for her mental state.

And she doubted it herself.

HER DARK PAST

CHAPTER THIRTEEN

Like a fool, I am again in the middle of nowhere, alone in the dark.

I had taken a few driving lessons before my attack, but my parents made me ramp that up afterwards. Mum said she would never again allow me out on a bicycle late at night. I said, well, I'd need a car. Mum bought me a Skoda Fabia. I said, well, I'd need a kicking new stereo to scare off carjackers. Mum laughed in my face.

My dad taught me for at least two hours a day, and just ten days after I got out of hospital, I took my test and passed. That first day driving on my own was nerve-wracking, but soon I got over it. The car doors could be locked, and I've got Dad's hammer under the seat.

I had some time off work after leaving the hospital, but on my first day back I couldn't hack it. Too many bad memories of that night. It would be impossible to forget that I once walked out of that building and five minutes later was in the process of being murdered.

Determined to keep in touch with my friends there, I quit The Ball Centre and acquired a cashier job at the UGC cinema at Valley Centertainment, built on old steel-mill land. The throngs of people and bright lights make the late nights bearable.

Within a few days of my discharge from the hospital, journalists eager for new angles on the Slasher murders had got hold of me. I was his latest victim and someone who could talk, so they would not stop until I'd been milked for all I was worth. There seemed to always be at least one reporter hanging around the house, no matter the hour, so one afternoon I opened the door to a young man with a camera and a microphone.

The police had released some details of the attack, primarily the location, in their hunt for witnesses, so this man knew pretty much everything except if the killer 'said something to me. That's what he wanted to know: if there was a conversation between us. The police had made the same query and knew I could recall very little of the whole event, but this guy seemed to think the same question asked a different way would produce results.

Somehow, perhaps by leak from the police, the media had also learned of Joe's contribution to my survival. He was also bombarded by requests for his story, and he didn't back down. He told everyone who knocked on his door exactly what happened: saw a man about to kill a woman, yelled at him, went to her and called the emergency services.

Once that official account hit the papers, meaning a journalist had already got a 'first', the frenzy died down a little. After that, all who came at Joe got the exact same story. Soon they knew there was nothing new and they started to leave him alone.

And it worked for me. Finally, I had spoken to a paper about my attack. Someone had had the exclusive. Others came, but left unhappy. A fortnight after the attack, the public had new things to obsess over, all my friends and neighbours had come to terms with events, and the raging river of gossip became a trickle. I started to get on with my life.

Joe called me around this time, seeking my company again. My mum and dad had been eager to meet him because he saved my life, and were surprised when I hadn't introduced him to them after our restaurant date. But they understood my worries. I explained to Joe that I wasn't sure if it was a good idea to see him. But he'd be the first to know if I came to a firm conclusion.

When he called me a second time a few days later, there was no mention of meeting up. He wanted to know how I'd coped with all the media attention and was eager to learn what developments the police had made in the case. But I felt this was all a cover just to talk to me and I felt sorry for him. But again I had to stand fast on my decision: I can't see you because I'll associate you with my terrible ordeal.

He said he understood and I bid him goodbye, and that was that. I thought. How could either of us know I'd be hugging him the very next night?

It is 30 May, twenty-five days since the attack, and it is my second night at work at the cinema. After my shift, around half ten at night, I set off on what should have been a routine drive home. It is only seven miles, which should take me about fifteen minutes at night with little traffic. But it all goes wrong tonight.

As I cross the bridge over the M1, my car starts to lose power. As I pass the now-closed and run-down garden centre called Gulthwaite Nurseries, the engine starts to make a grinding noise. I will later learn I'd run dry of oil.

Seconds later, as hedges and fields appear either side, no houses around, the car makes a noise like a dropped bag of spanners and grinds to a halt. I manage to roll onto the grass verge so I don't block the road. That's the end of my car.

And I wonder if it's the end of me. It's very dark out here. I promised myself and my parents that I wouldn't be out alone again at night, but now look. I put the interior light on as my fear rises, but this only makes me worry that I'm advertising a lone young female in the middle of nowhere, like an item in a shop.

I call my mum, but there's no answer. Same with my dad's mobile. I call a few friends I know have phones, but only one answers and she's in Lincoln, unable to help.

An approaching car pulls up on the other side of the road and a young man steps out. I can see another man in the passenger seat. As the driver is about to cross the road, I shut off the interior light and wind my window down a jot. Not enough for a hand to get through, but adequate for my voice.

'Stop,' I yell at him. 'My dad and his brother are coming, so I'm okay.'

The man doesn't stop coming across the road. 'I can start it for you.'

Since my discharge I haven't been outdoors much, but when I do it is sans make-up and in dull clothing. I don't want men looking at me. Before my attack, such interest from men was always cause for a little glow, because what woman doesn't want to feel attractive? Now I read such scrutiny as sinister. Every time a pair of male eyes seeks me out in a shop aisle or from a passing car, I don't see a man flirting with a pretty girl. I see a monster selecting a victim.

It's a fear I have a balanced relationship with. I don't control it, but it does not control me. But right here, now, alone in the dark, the fear suddenly transforms into something far more horrendous. Now the man crossing the road isn't just another monster, but my monster. He is the invisible Slasher. I am his only failure and he's been seeking a moment like this to finish his work.

'No, don't come near me,' I bellow. 'Get the hell lost, you bastard.'

Beautifully, this works. The man flips me the bird and turns back. He gets in his car, and screeches out of there.

But my relief lasts moments. Maybe he wasn't the Slasher, and maybe the next man along won't be, either, but I'm still out here alone in a dead car. I need help. My rear-view mirror shows me the roof of a building poking above the top of the hill behind me, perhaps two hundred metres away: a collection of stone cottages I passed. I could run there in half a minute. But I dare not leave the car. I don't even want to unlock the doors.

I see Dad's hammer in my hand, but don't remember grabbing it from under the seat. My heart thumps as another car passes and I sink low in the seat, hoping not to be seen. Again I pick up my phone and I call people, but get no answer. Fear starts to turn into anger and I unfairly curse everyone for abandoning me. Should I call the police?

Then I see Joe's name in my phone book and jab the call button without thinking.

He's there within half an hour and I don't unlock the door until he's right outside. I leap into his arms, a gnat's hair short of bursting into tears.

'Thank you, thank you, I say.' He calms me down, still hugging me. 'I'm so stupid. I kept thinking the next man along was going to be the Slasher.'

'You're not stupid,' he says, and I kiss his lips.

The night Joe rescued me for a second time, when my car broke down, I knew I had to repay him. After he'd waited with me for the tow truck, I felt so indebted that I posted the question: 'Do you want to see me again?'

Our second date was in Barnsley, and the new surroundings helped me to concentrate on Joe, not on myself. For a portion of that evening, I even forgot about the Slasher. I knew Joe would be good for me, so I agreed to another date, and another, and each night out was a painkiller. He also finally met my parents, but they were professional enough not to even mention what he'd done for me. There was just a silent understanding, a silent thanks for saving their daughter's life.

By the middle of June, it was no longer a case of using Joe to calm my nerves. I think I needed him. I was effectively addicted to this painkiller. The next logical step was to introduce him to my parents. I had never considered him my boyfriend, but this was a term used by my dad one evening. He said, 'Is your boyfriend any good with car engines?'

'Yes, he is,' I replied. Dad then asked me to get Joe round to look at his car. But I hadn't been answering Dad's question about Joe's mechanical savvy. I had been talking to myself: wow, yes, I guess he is my boyfriend now.

There was only so much headache and worry that Joe could soothe though. The Slasher was still relevant, and so was I, as his last-known victim. I don't think I went a day without reading my name somewhere, or hearing it discussed behind my back.

Officially he hadn't targeted a victim since May – me – but other women were getting attacked out on the dark streets. Could a number of these have been his work? Some of these assaults deserved a closer look, but others seemed so outside his modus operandi I was surprised they'd even been considered. I guess people just wanted to blame the Slasher because that was juicier gossip.

Added to the influx of new attacks were the historical ones. Long-forgotten unsolved murders and disappearances across the country were in the papers and talked about around water coolers again, this time with the Slasher front and centre. The most high-profile of these crimes was a pretty recent one, the disappearance of Isla Greaves, ten years old, and the police did give a Slasher connection some thought. But more on that in another chapter.

History wasn't all about the dead and missing though. Women who'd been assaulted months, sometimes years ago were coming out of the woodwork to say, 'You know, I think it was the Slasher who jumped me.'

Some of these possible Slasher attacks were in Scotland, Wales, all across England, sometimes on the same night yet a hundred miles apart. At one point it seemed to me that the public was dispelling the notion that other bad people could be out there. But they all had to be investigated and none has been attributed to the Slasher, at least officially.

South Yorkshire Police seemed to take the opposite stance and were loath to add any attacks to the Slasher's catalogue, new, or old, no matter how similar. A month after my attack, there was an attempted murder that had all the hallmarks of this psycho's work: cracked over the head, stabbed, left naked in a remote area. It again got tongues wagging, sales of personal alarms, Mace sprays and karate lessons going through the roof, and sexist men offering to escort ladies home.

But the lack of a swimming cap made the police say no, not our boy's doing. That one is still unsolved.

I remember a psychologist on the radio talking about 'escalation'. He said that a killer like the Slasher never leaps directly into the deep end of depravity. He works his way there slowly, beginning his offending career with crimes like burglary, voyeurism, even animal torture. This is a sort of 'training exercise' where a sexually deviant and violence-thirsty individual builds his resilience, overcomes his nerves. For some, the thrill of such low-level offending satisfies and they never progress.

For a select few, though, stagnation occurs and that itch can only be scratched at the next level, and the next. This killer, he says, is experimenting with his sexual sadism. Various acts became ritual, like the swimming caps, but others were discarded and new ones appeared.

Victim one had her hands tied, but the next two didn't, suggesting this was an action that didn't excite the killer and was discarded. With victim two, the desire for greater violence resulted in a slashed throat, and it appeared the next time. Victim three suffered the additional carnage of a head crushed by a boot.

We have yet to see if this becomes part of his signature and what new brutality the killer will visit upon whoever becomes victim four. But the mind doctors are agreed on one thing. Victim one: fifteen stabs wounds. Victim two: thirty-seven. Victim three: fifty-nine. This madman is increasing the level of violence to continue to gratify his bloodlust.

Jenny's team of detectives were getting accused of laziness, naivety, and even a lack of care, but they hadn't been twiddling their thumbs. Aware of the 'escalation' process most killers go through, and with no new evidence to pore over, the task force hunting the Slasher had been delving into old files. They were seeking clues in minor crimes that could indicate a monster in the making.

All of the above activity kept the Slasher in the news and kept me from putting my attack behind me. Every mention of his nickname or one of his victims was like ripping open a scabbing wound. A friend said that I should write a book about my experience, and I nearly smacked her. Submerge myself in a world I wanted to leave far behind? Stamp myself as a Slasher victim for all time? Preposterous.

I knew that the only chance I had to really start moving on was for the Slasher to be caught. When he was, public interest would go neon for a while, but once he was convicted and sentenced and a cage door locked behind him, the world would move on.

But I feared the Slasher would not be caught for a long time, if at all. And he wouldn't stop killing. He'd lay low for a while, until it seemed people had turned their attention elsewhere, then he'd destroy another family and hit the headlines again.

So it was quite a shock when, on Tuesday 10 July, close to the anniversary of his first murder, DCI Jenny Pitchford called me out of the blue. She'd been keeping me abreast of the Slasher enquiry here and there, primarily because my parents often hounded the police for updates, but I hadn't heard from her in weeks. I knew the call had to be something real good or real bad.

I expected the latter: perhaps her team had found evidence that the Slasher didn't like unfinished business and was again targeting me.

But it was the former: real good news. She told me to sit down, then: 'I thought you should hear it from us before the news gets out. We've got him.'

24

A prison officer in a yellow high-vis jacket was waiting before the rear gate, a sturdy steel slab topped with razor wire, like the rest of the wall around Orrell Prison. Oliver Elliot's car was waiting here. As Jenny's Outlander pulled up, the gate officer checked a clipboard and scrutinised her registration plate. The quartet had to sign a visitors' book: name, company, time in, then both vehicles were allowed in.

Once inside, they drove a hundred metres down a blank road, past the end wall of one of the radial wings on their right. Sara was struck by just how much she remembered about this place, even though she'd never seen it live.

After Drake's incarceration, she'd read all about his new home. Some of it had been in the news as journalists sought to keep the story alive without rehashing the murders or Drake's past. Some of it she'd researched on her own. Strangely, she remembered a useless fact: it would cost the taxpayer £39,038.75 every year to keep Drake locked up. Over half a million would have been spent on that monster already.

At the next gate, a second officer searched their vehicles, including running a mirror on a stick beneath the chassis. He led them to a small parking area, walking ahead of the vehicles like a funeral conductor. After they'd disembarked, the visitors were escorted along a path between two wings, towards the central building.

Each long wing, just fifty metres from the path, was two storeys with rows of small windows. The entire length was covered with netting, presumably to prevent prisoners from launching items between the bars of their windows at people down below. Sara kept her eyes on the path, aware that she could be under scrutiny from dozens of convicted killers and rapists. Strangely, all was quiet.

Once through a heavy iron door and inside the central building, their ID was read again and they waited in a hallway. The solicitor made small talk with Jenny. Sara tried to talk to Joe, to get her mind off what lay ahead, but he seemed dulled by the whole experience. He was nervously squeezing a pen. She took his free hand.

'It'll be okay.'

He nodded. 'I'm sorry. I just hope this day doesn't mess with our heads too much. You can still back out of this.'

'No. We've come all this way. I'm fine. But you can wait with the solicitor if you don't want to come in.'

He kissed her cheek. 'I told you. I'm not letting the man who tried to kill my wife have alone time with her. Now don't worry about me.'

The escorting officer was soon relieved by the governor himself, a middle-aged man with thin limbs, a thin neck, but a large belly straining against his tucked-in shirt. He smiled a lot and had kind eyes, but behind was a stern voice.

He introduced himself and checked everyone's ID, which made it the third time, and said to Sara, 'Mr Mills is already in the visiting room. He'll stay there when the meeting is done and we'll take him back to his cell when you've all left the building. We don't want to move him while you're here.'

Why was he telling her such pointless information? To convince her she'd be safe? Was Drake a serious escape risk while being moved about the prison? If the governor was trying to make her calm, he'd just failed miserably.

'He's expecting only you and your husband. Ms Pitchford and Mr Elliot will have to wait outside. We have a staff kitchen nearby.'

'I understand,' Jenny said. 'You have wheelchair access to there?'

'We can get there without using stairs, yes. Now, I should point out a few things about the meeting–'

Jenny jumped in here. 'Where are the detectives?'

'Detectives?' The governor tried to sound puzzled, but he was a bad actor.

'Yes. Two of them from South Yorkshire Police. They signed the visitors' book about thirty minutes before we did. Look, Mr Jones, have detectives listen in to the conversation, video-record it, whatever. Sara does not want to meet with these detectives. She won't be taking any coaching on how to sit and listen to Drake. Because that's all she plans to do. Sit, listen. I completely understand that we have here a serial killer suspected of other crimes and who has refused to talk for twenty years. But if he's going to admit anything today, it's off his own back. She will not be pressured to ask Drake any questions or put any accusations to him. Now, it's your prison, your prisoner, and we'll abide by any rules you have regarding this meeting. I'm a former detective and I worked the Drake investigation, so I'll meet with the detectives. Lead on.'

The journey to the visitors' room involved three corridors, seven gates, and a lift on the western side of the central hub that took them to the top floor. The route was grey and bland and they passed various vital organs of the prison.

There was a door marked WOODWORKING. Sara recalled reading that prisoners got the unemployment rate of £2.50 an hour. It made her wonder: how much money had Drake earned over the last two decades? Had he invested or saved it? Was he quite rich today, hoping for freedom and a chance to buy a house and a car?

The kitchen was next. Its large double doors were open, exposing men at work. Sara knew they were prisoners, but their chef whites almost betrayed this. Only the presence of prison officers amongst them marred what appeared to be a scene she might have witnessed at the back of her favourite restaurant.

Another useless fact surfaced in her mind. Some prisoners engaged in pooling the food – called 'food boats' – they bought from the prison shop or got sent in from outside, then cooking meals for each other. Was Drake part of this social activity? Did he sit and chow down with others, laughing, having a great old time?

Eyes turned her way and she scuttled quickly past the kitchen. Next on the sightseeing tour was the library, where two prisoners in their own clothing were opening boxes of books under the watchful eye of a single guard.

Seeing prisoners in their natural habitat gave Sara a strange feeling; it was as if she was the convict and Drake, already awaiting her, the visitor. 'Do all guests have to come this way?' she asked. 'It doesn't seem right.'

'Oh, no, no,' the governor said. He then explained that standard visitors would enter through a reception area on the eastern side of the complex, pass a metal detector, and use a visitors-only lift.

'Why have we come this way then?'

'Outside of visiting hours,' was the answer; to her mind, no answer at all.

Joe put an arm around Sara's shoulders. To the governor, he said, 'We want to leave by the visitors' exit. I don't want my wife to have to come back through this way. I don't care if we have to walk right around the outside to get back to the car.'

'I'll see what I can do,' the governor said, but Sara noted that his smile had gone. Maybe Joe's request somehow was logistically awkward. She didn't care.

They rode the lift and stepped out into a corridor on the top level. Rooms lined each side, but the door at the end got Sara's attention. A sign on it declared it to be her destination and an officer stood outside.

This was it. She had cut down the miles, and passed beyond various walls, and now only a few metres and a little slab of wood stood between her and Drake. Was he really in there, just sitting and waiting for her? It suddenly felt as if the air was thick, weighted, making forward movement tough. She wanted to turn and run.

But she didn't run. Holding Joe's hand, she followed the governor. The rooms they passed had closed doors, but little windows in them showed her various staff-oriented spaces. Only one door was open, the last on the left before the visiting room. A staff kitchenette.

The governor directed Jenny and Elliot inside this tiny room, but the former detective ignored him and wheeled up to the window in the visiting room. Buoyed by Jenny's lack of fear, Sara copied. This was it. She leaned over Jenny and put her face to the window.

And gasped at the man she saw inside.

HER DARK PAST

CHAPTER FIFTEEN

Surprisingly, he's a weedy, rat-faced man. Barely over five feet, thin as a rake, the skin on his upper face pockmarked and greasy, the lower half covered in wiry stubble. He's certainly not the demonic monster I imagined. More like one of the homeless drug addicts I sometimes see under dingy bridges in the city centre.

For sure he looks like the type of man who couldn't ever woo a woman and would need to turn to taking sex by force. But he's probably a hundred pounds soaking wet and I'm surprised he's got the power to overwhelm anyone, even teenaged girls. Of course, he had the benefit of ambush on his side.

But which one is he?

'Are you sure?' DCI Jenny Pitchford asks me.

'I'm sure,' I say. 'I'm sorry.'

'Perhaps seeing him like this is clouding your mind. Perhaps you're nervous. We could go to the video.'

West Yorkshire Police have started using a technology called VIPER in place of their live line-ups. It was pioneered by a unit called the Viper's Nest and uses a database of images and videos of innocent people used as fillers. This virtual line-up saves time and money and the technology will be soon rolled out across the country, but it isn't used yet by South Yorkshire Police.

However, Jenny was worried that, because my attacker was violent towards me, I'd find it difficult to come face to face with him, especially in the oppressive atmosphere of a police station. As well as putting together this identity parade in record time, she had also pulled strings and got the software, and it awaits me in a colourful family room upstairs.

But I insisted I wanted to see the man live, close. I knew there would be a one-way window between us and he'd be unable to see me. I knew that I could be traumatised no further than I had been already. So I insisted: I will face him and point him out.

But I can't. The men in the line-up all look similar. Do they know which criminal stands with them? Once the Slasher is shown to the world, they will try to change their appearance? Maybe all get fat and shave daily? But I am digressing from the matter at hand. 'I don't remember enough. I can't identify him. I'm sorry.'

Immediately after the call from Jenny announcing the capture of the Slasher, I had run downstairs to tell my mum. She was already on her way up to see me, and there, on the stairs, we both blurted at each other in unison:

'They've caught him.'

Jenny had called me out of courtesy, as a surviving victim still worried that my faceless attacker would come after me – but how had my mum known?

The police were quickly forced into a late-night press

conference to admit that, yes, a man had been apprehended. Yes, evidence found at his home connected him to the recent attack on Sara Tasker. No, they wouldn't confirm or deny the method of his capture, and stop asking for his name. They were eager to stress the old adage that a person is innocent until proven guilty. I think that fell on deaf ears. I certainly believed the vile killer had finally been snared.

But why had the police been forced into hosting a press conference so soon, and why were they confirming the capture instead of delivering an exclusive?

The morning after the Slasher's arrest, Jenny picked me up from home, and on the way to the station for the identity parade, she told me how the police got their man. But I already knew. How?

At a little past eight on Tuesday 10 July, a criminal gang kicked in one of two doors belonging to bedsits above a charity shop in Grenoside. They were there to tax a drug dealer – meaning they were going to raid his home, steal his cash and drugs, and leave knowing he couldn't call the police. But the trio kicked in the wrong door. Unaware of this, they set about searching the empty bedsit for drugs.

What they found instead, behind the bath panel, caused the gang shock. A drum of electrical cable and a plastic bag containing a bread knife, another kitchen tool, and a rubber swimming cap. They'd just unearthed the Slasher's kill kit.

Nominal procedure upon finding the home of a serial killer: get the hell out and call the police. But these were three hardened bad boys, weaned on street justice and psychologically averse to dialling 999. So they took a seat.

The Slasher was ambushed as he stepped through the door. He was tied to an armchair with his own electrical cable and the swimming cap was pulled over his head, but not to restrict the mouth. These boys were clued up on forensics, so didn't touch the knife or the other kitchen tool. Instead, they tortured their captive with sewing needles, all over his body.

The drug dealer next door – he was actually in – called the police upon hearing screams. He admitted he knew full well the perpetrators had got the wrong door and might be back unless they got nicked. Officers arrived and manhandled the drug dealers, before hearing the wild story told above. Sans drugs, that is – the trio at first claimed they'd barged into the bedsit because they'd heard the tenant had stolen their friend's cat.

During the Slasher's torture by a thousand pokes, one of the gang had sent texts to his friends, and they to theirs. Tongues had begun to wag even before the police were called. By the time Jenny's team got involved, word had spread far and wide that the Slasher had been caught.

My mum heard through the friend of a friend, who probably knew someone in the gang members' social circle. By the next morning, before Jenny collected me for the ID parade, the entire tale was out. Including the serial killer's name.

The outrage and shock were most vehement in my community when the Slasher was unveiled as Drake Mills. Before relocating to Grenoside, he had lived in Hillsborough, just a few miles from my home and actually on the same housing estate as Joe. Even more unnerving, Drake Mills had also attended the same school as us both. I didn't recall him, but Joe did.

Drake Mills was the freaky kid nicknamed Peanut. Small world.

I hate to say it, even about the man who tried to kill me, but Drake was just one of those people it seemed impossible to like. There was something about him, maybe a chemosignal or an aura, that put people off. He drew bullies to him like moths to a flame. Apparently, even the teachers disliked him and intervened against the bullies only when forced.

I say 'apparently' because there were so many rumours going around about Drake that nobody knew what to believe. When I started my first year at that school, when Drake and Joe were in the third year, I quickly heard all about the kid called Peanut. A fact that was undisputed was that he lived alone with his mother, who had moved from Scotland to Sheffield, to be near her father, when Drake was three. Drake's granddad was the only man he apparently liked or got on with.

Beyond that, it was hard to distinguish fact from fiction, so wild were some stories. Some said he'd been born in a travelling circus, his mother having been a lion tamer who quit when she got impregnated by an unknown man. Some said he was an aborted child who'd been rescued from a bin outside a hospital by a tramp lady who brought him up as her own.

There were rumours that his father was an imprisoned terrorist, killer, paedophile. He'd had three brothers, but all four had had to play a card game to decided which one would remain with their mother, the losing trio having been sold into gypsy slavery. Anything wacky and worth a giggle that kids could come up with got attributed to Drake at some point, until the lines were blurred.

His cause wasn't helped when one day teachers found him in the woods at the edge of the school sport field, throwing stones at a rabbit he'd tied to a tree. Or maybe that was just folklore, too.

Kids reckoned he would become a male prostitute when he left school. Or he'd go live in the woods like Tarzan. Strangely, nobody ever said he'd end up as a serial killer. Too glamorous for the imagination of kids, I guess.

After Jenny phones to tell me about the capture of Drake, I try to share the news with Joe, but his mobile is off. About six the next morning I am woken by small stones hitting my bedroom window. Joe is in the back garden, and he looks bedraggled. I don't want to wake my parents by bringing him inside, so I go down into the backyard and we sit on the bench behind my shed, talking quietly.

Joe has already heard the news about Drake on the grapevine. Shocked, he went for an aimless drive, pulled into the car park at Rotherham General Hospital, and dwelled on things. Unable to sleep, he sat up all night, thinking, worrying, then waited until a decent hour to come and wake me. He turned his mobile off so he could think in peace. His reason why upsets me.

Even people not known for picking on others turned against Drake, but not Joe, although he did keep his distance from the boy. And, he admitted, sometimes he would laugh when Drake was ridiculed or pranked. If I was shocked to learn that a former schoolmate was the Slasher, Joe was flabbergasted. But unlike most people who expressed outrage, Joe's initial reaction was guilt. 'I could have helped him. He just needed a friend.'

Joe was not a bully towards Drake, so why was he overcome with enough guilt to keep him up all night? It was because on that first day of school, Joe saw a weedy, disliked kid and decided to become his friend. That lunchtime, he walked home with Drake and they ate their food together on the street, kicking a ball. 'I knew Drake wasn't used to having friends. So I chose to be one to him.'

But that afternoon, back in school, Joe's friends warned him about becoming pally with Drake. Joe was one of the handsome, groovy, smart gang, but friendship with Drake would pull all the respect he had right out from under his feet. And Joe believed it. At the end of the school day, when Drake again wanted to walk home with his new friend, Joe refused.

'I cut him loose,' Joe says, and begins to cry. 'I didn't want him to drag me down. It was wrong. He just needed help.'

Joe's got a good heart and I understand how he feels guilt that he abandoned a lonely kid. And if it had been any other kid, I would have said this. Instead, Joe's sympathy angers me. 'Drake Mills is a vicious rapist and killer. And he didn't turn that way overnight. The kid you wanted to protect was a psycho monster in the making.'

'Kids are monsters,' Joe says, a calm having descended. The tears have stopped. 'Maybe all he needed was one good friend. Someone to–'

'To steer him clear?' I shout, no care for if I wake my parents. 'To stop him becoming a psychopath? If anyone, that's his mum's job. Or psychiatrists. Or whoever. But not you. You can't blame yourself. If it was your fault, the police would arrest you too. Everyone in the school. None of us helped him.'

Joe says nothing, and I can't read his face. I do not know it at first, having put his demeanour down to shock, but a softening of Joe's personality takes place that day. He will no longer display his feelings as he once did. It's as if all the emotional pain caused an overload that dialled everything back, forever.

But this safety feature does not pick and choose, and he will also lose some of his suave, his brashness. He won't laugh as heartily, and his cheeky grin won't be quite as cheeky.

To some this might sound like a negative, but I think that day he became the man I love.

I put my face close to the glass of the door and stare at the five men in the line-up. Drake Mills, a boy I went to school with and probably saw hundreds of times. But I do not remember his face. I recall of my attacker nothing, because I saw nothing. I know he's short, skinny and bearded only because the police have arranged five of the type before me. But it doesn't matter, Jenny has promised me: the evidence will condemn him.

I don't believe it though. If they have enough to charge him, they should go right ahead and do it. I worry that they need my identification to progress.

'You needed me to ID him, I just know it. That's why you're so eager. And I can't and he's going to be released, isn't he? You're just going to let him go.'

Jenny shakes her head. 'We have him for a few more hours before he has to be charged. I'll apply for an extension if we don't have enough evidence by then. I'll see to it that he's already had his last day of freedom, don't you worry. We're still collecting evidence, and the more the better. But if we have to do without a witness ID, it really shouldn't matter.'

Her tone is positive, but she used the word SHOULDN'T, and that's a worry. But the police have been keeping what they know of the Slasher close to their chests, and now they have him, who knows what glorious evidence they'll find? So I focus on something else. If they don't need my ID, then there's no reason for her to deny my request:

'Which one is he? Tell me. I need to know.'

Before arriving here, I was told by Jenny that I cannot be shown my attacker, because at some point his defence solicitor might wish to repeat this identification parade. But I can't point him out, so it doesn't matter. And she knows this is important to me.

'He's number four,' she whispers, and all men but him blur as my eyes zero in. I shiver. The beast who'd picked me for slaughter is just feet away. Seconds away. It's a mental trick, I know, but I'm sure he suddenly looks evil. Behind me, Jenny rubs my arm in a soothing motion.

'Thank you,' I say. 'Now I want to leave.'

I let Jenny lead me from the room. At the front entrance of the police station, Jenny again tells me not to worry: they will find all the evidence they need to sink Drake. And when she has it, her first call will be to me. When she sees my doubt, she pulls me close and makes sure no one is around.

'Tell no one I told you this. In a bag hidden behind Drake's bath, we found electrical cord, a knife and a rubber swimming cap. And an apple corer. Only a handful of senior officers know that the stab wounds on the three murder victims were caused by an apple corer.'

It takes me a moment to understand. The police often keep important murder details secret in order to verify a confession and thwart cranks. Only the actual killer would know about the apple corer. 'So that's proof it's him? It's definitely him? So that's all the evidence you need, right?'

'Drake isn't registered as the tenant of that flat, that's the problem we have at the minute. We're working on it. He's saying he broke in that evening. In other words, the evidence found in the flat isn't his. His prints aren't on the bag behind the bath, anything in the bag, or even on that bath panel, and that's what's slowing us down. But we'll get him, so please don't worry.'

I think I understand. Whoever uses that flat is definitely the Slasher. The police just need to find proof it's Drake. I am not sure I'm reassured, I can't shake the image of an apple corer being thrust in and out of soft flesh. That was nearly my fate. I just want to get home and curl up in front of the TV, and watch cartoons that seem to take place in a world where murder and evil and grief don't exist.

Jenny calls me with an update that afternoon, and before she can utter a word, I ask the important question:

'Has Drake been charged yet?'

The answer is no, but there's a mirth to her tone that keeps me silent, aware that she's not done yet. 'There's good news.'

And there is. Her team has found the landlord of the bedsit in Grenoside, and he's done what I couldn't do: ID'd Drake. Drake Mills is definitely the man renting the flat from him, cash in hand, and he's lived there for months. Her second piece of news is even better.

'We didn't announce this information at the time and I'd like you to keep it to yourself for a little longer. Marcie Whitecotton's bike was swabbed for forensic evidence, and we got some. Under the back of the seat, on a sharp protrusion at a weld, we found a fragment of a rubber glove. It suggests the killer was wearing gloves and used the seat and the handlebars to throw the bike. The interior lining of that piece of glove contains DNA. We got a profile from it. We took Drake's and the result came back just a few minutes ago. It's a match, Sara. It's him.'

Now, the Crown Prosecution Service feels it has enough to charge Drake. He's connected to the third Slasher killing, and that's connected to the other two. He has seven hours left on his custody clock and is itching to leave. So Jenny plans to do some paperwork, doddle about a bit, and leave Drake in his cell.

He knows the time, knows when his twenty-four hours are up, and when there's ten minutes left and Jenny opens his cell door, he's going to think he's getting out. That's when she'll hit him with the charges. She can't wait.

So, Drake will be going on trial for three murders. Drake is still denying everything, including having anything to do with the disappearance of the ten-year-old girl, Isla Greaves, in June of 2001. His bedsit in Grenoside is only a mile and a half from Parson Cross, where Isla lived and was last seen, so Jenny's team will do some delving into that old crime.

'What about further charges?' I ask, nervous. 'I think you know what I'm getting at.'

She does. Before I left her that morning, I told her to leave me out of the whole thing. Three killings will put this guy away for life, so there's no need to hit him with an attempted murder charge. I don't want to have to go to court to testify. I fear the publicity.

'Let's not discuss that for now,' is her response, which I take to mean she's not eager to hear me refuse again. Witness evidence, especially of a violent attack, is very powerful, so I understand her worry. I agree to change the subject. I'm sure I'll have another chance to hammer it home that I won't be telling a packed courtroom about the day a monster tried to kill me.

Drake is charged late the next day and taken to the magistrates' court the following morning. He's only there to confirm his name, hear the charges against him and possibly make a plea. He refuses to plea at this time and his case is sent to the crown court for trial at a later date.

He's there for a very little amount of time, but hundreds of people turn up at the court. Some to protest, some to get a glimpse of a real-life serial killer. I do not go, but my father does, and he's allowed to sit in the courtroom. When he returns later, he wants to tell me what happened. I don't want to know.

After the short hearing, Drake is taken away, remanded to Orrell Prison in Wigan, Greater Manchester, to await trial. Although he's only a remand prisoner, he's a serious criminal and warrants Category A status. Orrell has a wing for remand prisoners.

I spend that evening worried. Not about the trial and whether he'll be convicted. Instead, I fret that Drake won't suffer inside prison. Earlier, I looked into HMP Orrell and this research left me less than impressed. I am only young and had an image of prisons as dangerous cesspits, of chain gangs and cockroach-filled dungeons, but that's not the case.

Drake will have access to free healthcare and education, he'll have his own room and his own belongings; he can buy food from a prison shop, borrow books from the library, and even wear his own clothing. As a remand prisoner, he can still vote, retain private cash and actively work on business interests, or continue to claim benefits. Plus, he'll get more visiting time than convicted inmates. Is this a prison or a damn holiday camp?

However, about a week later I read a newspaper article that put a smile on my face.

A month earlier, the paper had run a story on the state of the British prison system and Orrell had been featured. The story talked about a lack of appropriate qualified mental health staff at the facility. Prisoners who exhibited disturbing behaviour as a result of mental health didn't get much in the way of direct help to address their problems.

The most volatile of these men were put in the segregation unit, but the more vulnerable inmates were housed in the same wing as remand prisoners. This is a problem because remand prisoners have not yet been assessed and can be a danger to vulnerable convicts.

Following Drake's remand, the newspaper has run a follow-up story. Given the Slasher's vile crimes, Drake's small stature and weak disposition, he is a constant target and has been repeatedly attacked by violent remand prisoners in the short time he's been there. Perhaps his attackers felt the country's injustice. Maybe they just wanted headlines.

The newspaper for sure does. A piece supposedly concentrating on the prison's mediocre anti-bullying methods has been sewn through with the Slasher. It details how Drake had been moved into the infirmary for treatment and then into segregation for his own safety.

There, he can't associate with other prisoners. Segregation exercise time is in the evening, so he can't get to turn his face into the sunshine. He's not allowed to make his own food. He doesn't have all his luxury items. No more library trips.

Weedy little rat-face is no longer in a holiday camp, and he is suffering. This is why I am smiling.

25

'Now I understand your worry back on the hotel balcony last night,' Sara said. 'You looked at me in... pity. You knew I expected Drake to be a shell of a man, just like he was all those years ago. But you knew he was far from it.'

'Yes. I'm sorry,' Jenny said.

They were in Orrell Prison's staff kitchen, Sara staring out the barred window at the city beyond. She had fled to the kitchen here to get away from that visiting-room door, from that man on the other side. She needed to see the outside world, if only to be reminded there was one. Jenny and Joe had followed her, although Jenny had told the solicitor, Elliot, to go find something else to do. Joe stood against a wall, looking shell-shocked, and watched the women talk.

'Drake has thrived, hasn't he?' Sara said. 'I bet he gets all sorts of privileges. What happened? You told me he wouldn't last long. You said prison would be hell on earth for him. You even said he might get murdered. The man I just saw looks like the king of this so-called hellhole.'

'All true back then, Sara. Drake was probably the most hated man on earth. But there comes a time when all the big news about the murders and the trial is done and forgotten, and you're left with some guy rotting in prison. But he's still alive. Still has a future to make.'

'And you seem to be saying he made one. What happened?'

'He got in a fight.'

Until they were shut down a couple of years after Drake's conviction, the prison had held illegal fight clubs. Men would find unobserved spots to duel it out with rivals, sometimes for seniority, sometimes to pay off debts, and, in Drake's case, to end a bully's torment. By unwritten rule, a bullied inmate could officially challenge his tormentor, and if successful the antagonism had to end.

Drake had been suffering abuse at the hands of a man since day one of his incarceration, enduring many beatings. But on the day it actually mattered who came out on top, Drake won. There was no chance of comeback, because any loser who exacted revenge faced the wrath of many. So, by choice or force, the bully had to end his beef with Drake, and the Slasher began a trouble-free life inside prison.

'Trouble-free,' Sara said to herself. She didn't like that.

When the fight clubs ended, so did the rules they'd enforced. Drake's old bully came at him again, and was again put down, this time badly. The prison officials brought a judge into the prison and Drake admitted attempted murder. He got additional years and two months in segregation for the attack, but emerged with a new-found respect throughout the prison.

There were bigger, stronger, well-connected boys around, but they didn't want the hassle. Any of them could have killed Drake, but that meant another sentence. And kill him you'd have to, because he'd already proved that a psycho with a whole life term had nothing to lose.

Sara turned from the window. 'So he's controlling people by fear again. Just like when he was free.'

The prison's hard cases left Drake alone and the vulnerable inmates, as he'd once been, turned to him for protection. Soon, he could call upon a growing number of acolytes to do his bidding. He suddenly had the clout to start running things inside and make big money, like a serious prison gangster.

'Are you telling me he's still breaking the law? And no one is doing anything about it?'

'He never took that route,' Jenny said. 'Drake didn't bully anyone. He didn't abuse anyone and he didn't turn to crime. He just wanted a comfortable life. In fact, I hear he was trying to prevent marijuana from being smuggled into the prison and he ended various rivalries between others that could have caused problems. Apparently he's done a lot of good for the prison. He's a model prisoner. All he wants is a comfortable life.'

'A comfortable life?' Sara spat. She felt... violated, somehow.

With no need to go short or watch his back, Drake's attention turned to his mind and body, to bettering himself. He got his teeth sorted, started eating better, and began a serious exercise regimen. In addition, he took every course he could get his hands on.

Computers were his thing, something he'd never touched before prison. He created an animated guide for the families of inmates, which taught them about the visiting process and negated various macabre prison myths. That video was now available on Orrell Prison's website and its YouTube channel.

Enrolled with the Prisoners Education Trust, he gained his NVQ Level 2 in information technology and now taught a prison computer class. He was head of the basketball team, which often played against the officers.

Last year, he'd been allowed to create an online newsletter showcasing his fitness regime, including a weekly video, to help prisoners stay healthy. Somehow, its reach had extended beyond just the incarcerated, to their family and friends, and beyond, and he had hundreds of female subscribers. Some wrote him letters and were clearly attracted to him. Others had promised money. One wanted his baby.

Sara put up a hand: enough. 'Prison is supposed to be a punishment, isn't it? But he's got a better life in here than he had outside, hasn't he?'

Jenny was careful with her answer. 'He's still going to die in prison. Isn't it better that his existence at least can help others?'

Sara shook her head. Oh, she understood about reform and rehabilitation and giving back and all that. But that was for politicians, or the clergy, and anyone else who hadn't almost been gutted by a lunatic. 'No, it's not better, not for me. I wanted that man to suffer, every day. I still do. I don't want him to have one single happy moment in this place, and I don't want anyone to like him.'

'Do you want to leave?' Joe asked.

'No, I want to go face that bastard, get him out of my system, and never think about him again.' She paused. 'But I won't do this unless we both want it, Joe. It affects our whole family.'

Joe gave one of his slow shrugs. 'I'm in this with you. Whatever you want to do.'

Sara abruptly strode from the room, forcing Joe and Jenny to catch her up. They caught her at the visiting-room door. The governor and a guard had waited patiently, and they said nothing as Sara stepped to the door, face inches from the glass, and peered inside the room.

Bare walls, tables and chairs bolted to the floor, a room at the back probably used as a guard station where they could monitor CCTV.

And at a table dead centre, like a prize exhibit, there he was. The beast who'd picked her for slaughter, just feet away. Seconds away. Jenny rubbed Sara's arm in a soothing motion.

Drake wasn't looking around, or fidgeting. He just seemed

like a man with all the time in the world. And no nerves about meeting a woman he'd tried to kill. He hadn't even glanced at the door he knew she'd come through.

It was still hard to reconcile the man sitting in there with the monster who'd been convicted of serial murder. The skinny, dirty, rat-faced man was no more. The man awaiting her was twenty years older but looked even younger than way back. He was buff. His hair was neat, his teeth straight and white. He was even handsome, although it hurt her gut to admit this.

She reminded herself that he could have all the women followers he wanted, but they were naïve. He could look like an Adonis, but it was a shell. His brain might be full of new knowledge, but it still contained a black core. Bottom line: this man had still committed murder, he was still evil, and he was still going to die in prison. She still had the upper hand here, she told herself. Or tried to.

She put her hand on the handle, ready to turn it, but Jenny grabbed her wrist, surprising her. 'Look, I know I promised I wasn't here on police business, but there's a missing girl. It's been twenty years and the only viable suspect was that man inside there.'

'You wanted me to do this all along. You waited until now to spring it. You knew it would be too late to back out.'

'This is the first time Drake has ever agreed to speak with someone since he was locked up. You are our best chance at getting information out of him. At getting answers for the family of little Isla Greaves.'

Sara realised her fingers had abandoned the door handle and crept upwards, to scratch her old head wound. 'Stop, okay. Don't beg. You want me to ask him, so I will. For the girl's family. I will.'

Jenny looked a little thrown, as if she'd expected this to be harder. 'Okay. Good. Be careful, though, in case he clams up. And if you get upset–'

'I'll be fine.' Sara pushed the door open and stepped inside, before she could have second thoughts. Joe followed. Drake's eyes came her way, and he smiled. Right then, everything changed.

He wanted this, had waited for this, would do anything for this. She could antagonise him, insult him, even spit on him, but he would not shut down the meeting. She knew it, and in the blink of an eye, control was ripped from him and thrust into her palms.

So she came right out with it: 'Did you kill Isla Greaves?'

HER DARK PAST

CHAPTER SEVENTEEN

Parson Cross, Tuesday, 5 June 2001. Isla Greaves, ten years old, is walking home with her brother, Pete, having just left their grandmother's house on Adlington Road, on the western edge of Parson Cross Park. The time is about five in the evening, so well before dark and the streets are busy.

The typical route home taken by the siblings is across the roundabout ahead and onto Holgate Avenue, which would lead to their estate in just a few minutes. But on this day they choose to turn right onto Deerlands Avenue, along the northern edge of the park, and take a path that cuts through a small wasteland.

However, the siblings start playfully throwing small stones at each other and Isla hits Pete in the eye, causing him to yell at her. She climbs a small wall, onto a grassy area, and flees through a hedge, into the park.

Pete searches for his sister, but later admits to police that he was also shouting that he would bash Isla when he got hold of her. So she remains hidden and, angry, her thirteen-year-old brother storms off home.

When he arrives, without his sister, he knows his parents

will be angry that he abandoned her. But he believes Isla will soon be back because they've had spats like this very one before. Usually Isla will hide until she thinks he's calmed down and then she'll approach with a smile and her arms out for a hug and say, 'Forgive me, superfly?'

So, foolishly, Pete pretends Isla is still with him. He tells their mother he is going to his room with Isla and they don't want to be disturbed. He even comes down to collect both their dinners, pretending they've chosen to eat in his room. He tells his mother he's playing a game with Isla: he is her toy robot and must fetch and carry for her.

Neither parent realises something is wrong until Isla's nine pm bedtime, when their mother insists on applying cream to Isla's rash. When Isla doesn't respond to the summons, their mother finally enters Pete's bedroom, and discovers her gone. Only then does Pete admit what happened and that he left his sister in Parson Cross Park. Over three hours ago.

The family put off calling the police immediately and converge on the park, but find no sign of Isla. When the police are called soon afterwards, they mobilise quickly. By ten pm, officers are scouring the park for clues, dogs are sniffing for Isla's scent, and a helicopter with infrared searchlights is seeking her heat signature.

Just a hundred metres south of the park is another, Longley Park, and this, too, is searched. The police are out in the parks and the surrounding streets until nearly two in the morning, at which point the search is postponed until first light. Friends and family remain active all night, though, without success.

The next day, the search area is widened; every home and garden in the immediate area of Parson Cross Park is checked. Every conceivable hole, alley, shed, hedgerow – anywhere big enough to contain Isla's mass – is poked and prodded. Every piece of CCTV footage within five miles is pulled in and scrutinised.

Members of the public come from far and wide to help find Isla. Every person she'd ever known is questioned. Rewards for information go out, including £20,000 offered by a local businessman. Known child sex offenders across the city get their doors rapped.

In the first couple of weeks, the inconsolable parents host five TV press conferences. At first they plead for information from the public and ask them to search. Later, when it becomes hard to deny that Isla has been snatched, they beg her captor to return her. The public rally to help, but achieve nothing.

The abductor, if there was one, ignores the pleas. And the biggest missing person investigation ever launched by South Yorkshire Police will never even definitively uncover if there even was an abductor.

As the weeks and months pass, there are reported sightings of Isla all over the country, and each has to be investigated. Police also waste time dealing with crackpots who boast that they have clues, and fools who claim to know where Isla's body is.

Now, as I write this, it has been over two years and no sign of Isla has ever been found. There aren't many people outside the family who think she's still alive, but officially she's still a missing person. I don't know what to believe.

Of course, the Slasher was a suspect, but Drake has always denied snatching Isla Greaves. In his first police interview, he denied ever attacking any women, and then he clammed up and would say no more. But with Isla Greaves it was different. Until his trial, he denied that kidnapping, every time it was put to him. It was the only question he'd answer and that answer was always a single word: no. And after his trial, he shut down completely.

As of this writing, he refuses to speak to any psychiatrists or police officers who seek interview. Even Isla's parents tried to engineer a meeting with him, hoping he would see their distress and come clean. But no.

And Isla remains a mystery.

26

'Take a seat. Both of you.'

There were two chairs, but it had already been decided that Joe wouldn't sit by Sara. He wanted to, but had agreed with Jenny that a bubble containing just Sara and Drake would accord the killer a little more comfort. Perhaps enough to push him into admitting something he'd kept secret for two decades.

Sara agreed this was best, but for a selfish reason. She had to experience this man up close and personal if she had any hope of exorcising his poison. So Joe took a table by the door, facing Drake, and Sara stepped forward.

Drake was big, muscular, handsome, and looked young and powerful, and even as a weakling she'd feared this man. She should have been terrified. But, she reasoned, that must have been the man as a figure, an enigma, because now she faced him, she wasn't scared at all. Unless that had something to with the taser-wielding guard standing by each door.

She continued walking towards him, until only the desk parted them. But she wasn't ready to sit just yet. To enter his bubble.

'I've answered the question of Isla Greaves' disappearance,' he said. In his fingers was a pencil, which he twiddled and waved and generally played with. Nervous? She wondered if she appeared scared to this man.

'I know,' she said. 'You told the police you killed young adult women, not little girls. You had never kidnapped a victim, but left them where they were slaughtered–'

'Where they died, that was the term I used.'

'–and you only operated at weekends, whereas Isla was killed on a Tuesday. And these facts, according to you, are proof that you had nothing to do with her disappearance. And that was all you said. One time, twenty years ago. And you've refused to speak about her since.'

Drake gave a slight pause, which bolstered her. She yanked out the chair from under the desk and sat. But she leaned back: small steps.

'Not true,' Drake said. 'I granted the police an interview nine years ago. Back they came with their questions, and I again told them I had nothing to do with Isla. There was no evidence. Those who assumed I attacked her did so based on simple probabilities. What were the odds that a serial killer and a child killer were operating on the same patch at the same time? The whole country couldn't see beyond the fact that I lived just two miles south-west of Parson Cross Park, where she was abducted. And the result of that?'

'You said a child killer. How do you know she's dead?'

'How do you? You implied the same thing ten seconds ago. And if she's not then, wow, she must be really terrified of her brother. To still be hiding from him twenty years on.' Continuing to twiddle and tap the pencil, he leaned back and smiled. 'Sara, we're starting off on the wrong foot. I didn't ask you here for an argument.'

'You're worried we'll fall out? I didn't come here for a friendly chat. I didn't even come here because I was curious about what you wanted to see me for. I came to face you because it will help me get over you.'

'Ah, so you still have the nightmare. I read your book.'

She had to hold herself together at that statement. Of course he would have read it, she would expect nothing less. But hearing it confirmed dragged up old worries she hadn't had since she made the mistake of publishing the book. He would know about her family. Her pregnancy. Her marriage to Joe. She had laid out her inner feelings in that book, and he would have experienced them all.

'I bet you made a pretty penny off that book, right?'

He was still leaning back, so she leaned forward, elbows planted on the table. This all felt so easy now. She wished she'd done this years ago. 'I didn't do it for that. I didn't want money. I was forced to write that book. I...'

She nearly told him: one day after the trial, a reporter had approached her with a deal, and then a threat. The deal: we author a book together, you talk, I write. The threat: do this or I'll write the book myself, and you'll have no say in what goes inside. Sara didn't want to join forces, and didn't want to have a third party tell her tale.

So, backed against a wall, she beat everyone to the punch by creating the definitive account of the crimes of the Slasher. And she'd regretted it ever since. Thankfully, the publisher had held the rights only for a year, and once returned to her she promised the book would never be republished. The number of copies still out there had probably dwindled to next to nothing. She had bought and burned every copy she got hold of – except one, of course. She wasn't even sure why she'd always kept that one.

But she caught herself. She did not need to explain anything to this man. She returned to an earlier issue. 'Yes, I still have the nightmare. You tried to kill me. That would wreck anyone's head forever.'

He tapped the table with the pencil and spun it in his fingers. 'Not forever. You certainly ooze confidence right now. Perhaps it's worked. Maybe the enemy is no longer the enemy – the inner me.' Drake leaned forward and planted his elbows on the table, just like Sara's. She willed herself to keep her own elbows planted, but her heart was thudding. Now they were close enough that he could have reached out and touched her. 'I guess that means you can leave now. Have a nice life.'

Did he really mean that? He didn't mind if she just upped and vanished? She'd been here almost no time, and couldn't see what he'd achieved from this meeting. But she wasn't ready to just yet. A few more seconds. She relaxed her shoulders. She stared into his eyes. She said nothing. It was like a systems check.

And then she stood up. It was done. System all clear. Now she could get the hell out of this hellhole.

But she didn't.

She looked round at Joe, sitting there with his pencil and little notepad. He seemed a little scared. She thought of Jenny outside the room, and the others waiting. She thought about Isla's family, who might even know about this meeting. All waiting for her to work some magic here today.

She sat down. 'Let's talk some more. I came a long way.'

Drake leaned back again, with a smile. 'Did you read my letter?' he asked. 'The one I sent you after my trial?'

'No.'

He gave her a long look, assessing if she was telling the truth. 'Sure?'

'I got no letter. Did you admit to killing Isla in it?'

He actually laughed. 'Well, if that was the case, I'd know if you read it or not.'

'So, what was it, an apology? Save it. Apologies do no good. Just like the one you gave after your trial.'

HER DARK PAST

CHAPTER NINETEEN

As we await the murder trial of Drake Mills, I try to get on with life. I'm eager for fresh changes and the biggest is Joe. We start to date more and more often. He is still a very popular lad, but he starts to see his friends less and less, in favour of me. He no longer goes to nightclubs or for wild car rides, although I insist he does not give up his indoor football.

Joe even plays snooker with my dad a couple of times, which is a little unnerving for me. I know they'll discuss me, and Drake. I did ask both men about this after their first night out, but they deny that I was a subject of conversation. Joe did admit that my dad wanted to grill him about Drake. Both my parents are very intrigued that Joe knew Drake at school. But Joe has no gossip for them.

Nobody back then, especially schoolkids, could have had any inkling of the monster Drake would become.

On one occasion, though, Joe drops me off after a date at the cinema and my dad, a bit drunk, says, 'Why didn't you kill this bastard at school?'

My mum tells him off for that and Joe never again faces

that question. Mum, though, poses one a little less blunt: why didn't Drake's teachers ever spot his mental sickness and get him professional help?

The media soon learns of a shuddering new twist to the Slasher tale. His only known surviving victim had known him at school, and the man who'd saved her had actually been in Drake's class, and victim and saviour are now dating! There is a whole new invasion of reporters at the front door once that breaks, and they're now targeting Joe's family too.

Even when the press finally get it into their skulls that we're not talking, they just go elsewhere. Former classmates, and even teachers, are happy to talk, and the story only loses steam in time for a new boost with the start of the murder trial.

Fobbing off the reporters is actually quite easy. Joe and I are to be witnesses for the prosecution, and we're forbidden from discussing the case. Even with each other. Yes, I eventually change my mind about having my attack included in the charges against Drake. Jenny convinced me that no evidence works up a jury more than the words of a real, live victim. So I will sit in that courtroom and tell these twelve strangers all about the night Drake tried to kill me.

Drake's lawyers are going to call some of his former classmates and teachers to the stand. It's purely character evidence, Jenny says: they want to paint a picture of their client as a kid hard done by in life. The evidence against Drake is piling up and the prosecutor reckons even the defence team doesn't doubt he'll be convicted, so they're probably aiming to create sympathy for their client.

Joe will testify to what he saw the night I was attacked; is there any better way to that desired compassion than to cross-examine such a powerful prosecution witness and get him to describe the incessant bullying Drake suffered? I suspect it could mean the difference between a minimum and a whole life term.

I ask Jenny if it's possible that Drake might one day walk free. Her response is: 'Three murders, one attempted, a city in terror for a year? Are you joking?' I take that as a no.

Because of the trial and our roles in it, it becomes hard to get Drake out of our lives. We've got plans to go away for a week, perhaps to the Derbyshire Dales, but that isn't possible until after the trial. It seems like every day there's some appointment or phone call with the police or lawyers from the Crown Prosecution Service. I can't wait for this episode in my life to be dust in my rear-view mirror.

'How do you feel knowing you wouldn't be with Joe if not for the Slasher attacking you?' is one question I get by journalists and strangers. I never respond, but I often contemplate the answer.

Without Drake, no Joe: would I change that fateful, murderous night if given the chance?

In January of 2002, I would finally move out of my parents' house and into a rented flat with Joe. Five months later, we'd start looking to buy our first house. With a nursery. It's a baby girl in my belly. We haven't picked a name yet.

Joe wants to leave Sheffield and he thinks a new city could help me get over my attack, but I'm not so sure. Sheffield is the city I know and love and far more good things have happened to me here than bad. I feel connected to it, as if by umbilical cord: it feeds and grows me. Drake is in prison in another city, no longer a threat to me, and I want to stay near my friends and family.

Although I have to admit that friends have fallen by the wayside. Partly down to how much I see Joe, and partly because I don't like to be outside much these days. Other than periodic texts, I haven't been in contact with any of the boys and girls from my old workplace, The Ball Centre. I hate to say it, but they're all a reminder of that night.

The Slasher's poison is still with me: I continue to nightly have the dark dream about being connected to him, forced to accompany him as he hunts and murders. I know his face, but the killer in the dream is still a featureless black humanoid. I will try various ways, perhaps even therapy, to banish the nightmare, and if nothing works, I will consider relocating far away from ground zero. It depends on what's best for the baby. I think she should be near her grandparents.

I'm thinking hard about my future, but such a thing was impossible just a few months earlier. I didn't count in years, but days, like a cancer victim. There seemed to be a dead zone in my mind that wouldn't allow me to imagine the road ahead beyond Monday, 3 December 2001. The day Drake Mills' murder trial started.

It is a media circus outside the court as I arrive with my parents and two friends. As well as the media, members of the public have turned up. A lot. You'll often see such crowds when an infamous killer is due in court. Most are probably just there to get a glimpse of a real-life serial killer, but the police are out in force because gawkers aren't the only ones in attendance.

Some want violent justice. Apparently, the van containing Drake arrived a little earlier and was almost besieged by wannabe vigilantes, including a man who lobbed potatoes. I wonder what it's like to see a crowd baying for your blood. Perhaps, if convicted, Drake should be hung by his feet from a rope and dangled into that crowd.

We are taken in the back way to avoid the crowds and led to an empty jury room upstairs, where we will await the start of the case. My family and friends will get to go into court when the trial starts, but I can't. I am a witness for the prosecution and am not allowed into the courtroom until after I've given my evidence, which I know won't be until tomorrow, once the opening statements are concluded.

Joe and his people arrive at court separate to us. It's well documented that he and I are an item, but why feed the media's hunger for sensationism?

It is out back where I meet the parents of Marcie Whitecotton, Drake's third victim. Despite knowing and working with Whitecotton for months and visiting her house, I never met her mum and dad. Here, in a private patio at the rear of the grand building, they are both smoking.

I get a hug from Whitecotton's mother, but also a look I don't really like. It seems accusing, as if she's wondering why God chose me to survive and not her daughter. I suppose I will meet the other parents over the course of the week. We have a bond none of us wishes for.

That turns my thoughts to Drake's family. I know he has a mother and a grandfather here in South Yorkshire, and cousins and uncles and aunties up in Scotland. Perhaps there are others, maybe many. None of them are here for him.

Because Joe and I are witnesses and unable to enter court until our testimony is given, we leave the building once the court session begins. Our parents are inside, watching the pantomime, but we spend the morning in a park close to the courthouse. There's a giant chessboard painted onto a patch of concrete and we watch, and sometimes play against two old men who admit they are there religiously, day in, day out. I watch them stare at the giant board, take their moves slowly, chat periodically, and I'm jealous of their carefree lives.

But I don't know their history. They might have lost wives, children, or years of their lives in prison for murder. I should really stop assuming the grass is always greener on the other side.

When court breaks for lunch, we are joined by our families, and we find a secluded part of the park to eat packed lunches. I really want to head over to a café across the street from the courthouse for a bacon roll, but there's no way we'd get peace. As per the rules, we don't talk about the trial. Sounds hard, but it's the last subject I want to discuss anyway.

In the afternoon, we return to the empty jury room to wait. I know Drake is in the building, perhaps only a stone's throw from me, and I lock the door. Even though big, strong Joe is by my side, I can't help but have this recurring fear, albeit silly: Drake escapes his guards, and searches the courthouse for me, to finish his business. Of course, it never happens and I don't see him.

But I will when I give evidence.

Despite being unable to discuss the case with me, my parents tell me all about the Drake they saw in the flesh. From photos and videos in the news, they already knew he wasn't a hulking, vampiric demon with horns. But they were unprepared for the weedy little man who walked into the courtroom overshadowed by big guards. But, of course, it is the inert human appearance of people like Drake that allows them to commit their crimes and go unnoticed.

In his opening statement on that first day, Drake's

barrister tries to paint a picture of his client as a hard-done-by man with a sorry past, as we expect. Abused by his father as a baby, until his mother fled south to England to raise him alone. He had glue ear as a toddler and could barely speak properly, leading to developing no friends.

Later, he was bullied, in and out of school, because his mother was Scottish and was often arrested for shoplifting and disturbing the peace – her nickname in the estate was Common Scold. She would make Drake shoplift his own meals and clothing. He had to clean the house for hours every day. Most evenings, he would have to apply make-up to his mother and comb her hair, again sometimes for hours.

There was no father figure. He was mostly invisible at school and missed a high percentage of days. Later, in secondary school, this all continued. His mother managed to convince the authorities on three occasions that she was not negligent and he avoided going into care. Bullying was a constant in his life.

The overall gist of the barrister's statement seems to be that society, life and luck didn't just ignore his client, but beat him down. We knew Drake's defence would angle for sympathy, but to me it almost sounds like the barrister is saying Drake is just the sort of guy who could be wrongly accused. Is the jury supposed to feel sorrow and be lenient? Or to believe Drake became a monster through no fault of his own and let him walk free?

Ultimately these words strike no chord with those in the audience and two people are removed for yelling out in defiance of the strategy. The jury is made up of such people.

At the end of the day, we all go home. Our families head off, but Joe and I hang around a bit and find a recessed shop doorway to watch from. I want to see Drake's prison van leave. Why? To make sure he's far, far away? Or because it feels nice to watch protestors hurl things at the van and know he is a hated man across the world?

The defence and prosecution teams leave together, as if they did no more today than compete in a game of chess like the two old men in the park. The crowd splits and people saunter off to the shops or home. The reporters flee to go write their copy. Soon, the street outside the court is back to business as usual and the building shuts for the evening. The frenzy will repeat tomorrow, and for many days to come. It feels very strange.

Joe points at a café down the street. 'We can go get you that bacon roll now.'

The news comes that evening. Jenny once promised me they'd find enough evidence to put Drake away forever, and in the months since his arrest the authorities have indeed strengthened their case against him. I haven't been party to the ins and outs of whatever fibres, fingerprints, DNA or whatever else they have against him, but Jenny had been growing in confidence as the trial approached. Drake, like any cornered wild animal, fought to the end, but eventually had to see the light.

Jenny calls me as I'm preparing for bed, and comes straight out with it. 'Drake is going to plead guilty.'

I almost drop the phone. I know this means I won't have to give evidence, Joe too. I have to ask this just to make sure.

'No, you don't,' Jenny says. I realise she sounds a little drunk and there's unmistakable party chatter behind her.

Later I'll find out she took her murder squad out to a pub to celebrate another case closed, the biggest of her career. 'The trial is over. Court will go ahead tomorrow, but the guilty plea will go down and Drake will make a statement.'

'What statement?'

'An apology, probably. You're no longer a witness, Sara, and that means you can come.' My head is so muddled by this sudden twist in the road that I have to ask her what she means. 'Come to court. Sit there and watch Drake try to pretend he's sorry. And watch the judge tell him he's evil and then sentence him. You want to watch that?'

I so do, but Drake doesn't give me that satisfaction.

The killer wasn't due to take the stand until much later in the trial, so the crowds we saw yesterday weren't even the half of it. Now that the news has travelled that the Slasher will stand up in court and talk, the interest in the case is mammoth. The next morning, the street outside the court is heaving, far more so than on day one of the trial. Inside, every seat in the gallery is taken, many by reporters. I've heard this statement is going out live on TV. Everyone wants to see Drake in action.

None of our families want to sit in a courtroom and hear that monster pretend to be sorry, but Joe and I will not miss it for the world. Yesterday evening, he gave me a sparkling new yin-and-yang necklace. I see the pendant for what it is: a symbol of bonding between us, of our opposites needing each other. But Joe says it's to celebrate the end of a dark night, and the start of a new dawn. I promise to wear it everywhere, always.

The police numbers are massive, but when his van arrives, hardly anyone accosts it. No one wants to see a disruption to today's climactic events. But it's his last day in court; when the van leaves again, it will be the last time

Drake is outside a prison cell. The last chance anyone will have for street justice. The police are ready for it.

Either Drake came to the building to get out of prison, or he got cold feet at the last moment. Regardless of the reason, he's down in the cells under the courtrooms and he'll stay there: his barrister will read out his statement. This last-minute news annoys me and I can see the same emotion on every face in the courtroom. Even the judge looks a bit annoyed that he can't stare Drake down when he passes sentence.

I am prepared for a lengthy statement from Drake, but what we get is weak, and an utter surprise. Or not, given his lack of a soul.

'I am bringing this trial to an end for the sake of the families of my victims. I do not want to put them through any more grief. I accept what I did and the punishment I will receive.'

Utter bullshit. Not a single word of remorse for his barbaric crimes. It is at this point I leave. The judge passes sentence, thanks police and prosecution for their hard work, and praises the dignity and bravery of the victims' families as they prepared for the trial. But as these words are spoken, I am with Joe in the park behind the courthouse. We do not talk about what we just witnessed and instead pretend to be like the two old men again playing chess: oblivious.

But the trial is over. Drake is in prison. Later, Mum tells me about the sentence imposed by the judge. Three life sentences and eighteen years for my attempted murder. These are concurrent sentences.

In cases like this, the judge always sends his recommendation to the Home Secretary, who is David Blunkett. My mum has actually met him. He's MP for Sheffield Brightside, so he will be acutely aware of the pain and horror this city endured while the Slasher was rampaging. Mum is not surprised at all when the Home Secretary subsequently imposes a whole life term. He agrees with the judge's words that, '...evil like this cannot be allowed to walk the streets, therefore it is my hope that you will die in prison.'

27

'Your apology to the families was bullshit. You wanted out of that courtroom. You didn't like being under the microscope. You didn't want your crimes and psychopathy broken down for the watching world. You hated being stared at like a caged animal. That first day in court broke you and you couldn't face another. If you'd really felt sorry, you would have read that statement out yourself. Hell, you wouldn't have even had a trial. You would have told the police everything, pled guilty immediately, and gone quietly off to rot in your cell. We're done here.'

Throughout Sara's scathing attack on him, Drake's eyes had spent an equal amount of time on her and staring over her shoulder, at Joe. When she looked round at her husband, he seemed terrified by what he had witnessed. She wanted out of here for his sake as much as hers. They both stood at the same time, but Drake snapped his pencil and yelled:

'*Sit down.*'

Joe almost fell into his chair. The shout was so loud it prompted one of the guards to step forward, hand on his taser. But Sara, still standing, held up a hand to stop him. Because there was no threat of action from Drake: he still leaned back, casual. Joe waited. The guard waited. Sara took her chair again.

'Why did you bring me here? Clearly, it's not a deathbed confession. You don't have bowel cancer, do you?'

Drake's first slice of irritation showed here. 'That your diagnosis, doctor? Don't you need to stare at me a little longer for a real deep analysis first?'

'No, I'm not here to do anything. You wanted to see me, not the other way round. It's clear you won't admit to killing Isla and I see no point in being here. So talk. Last chance.'

His eyes went from her to Joe, her to Joe, back and forth. 'I did talk. I've told you all you need to know. It's up to you what you do with my wisdom. Bear in mind a quote from the Chinese philosopher Confucius. *Ignorance is the night of the mind, but a night without moon or star*.'

Drake stood up. He pointed at her yin-and-yang necklace, and said, 'I used to have one of those, by the way,' and walked towards the guard-station door at the back of the room. It took Sara a few seconds to realise this wasn't a trick. He really was leaving. And she felt left hanging. She wanted more, but not to let Drake know that. So she waited, hoping he had something planned. And he did: to leave.

He entered the guard station and sat down. The guard shut the door. It was over.

28

Waiting outside the visiting room with Elliot and Jenny were two detectives, who wanted a little private chat with Sara and Joe.

'It's okay, Sara,' Jenny said. Peripherally, she noticed the look Joe was giving her and tried to ignore it. 'They stayed back so you didn't feel pushed into pressing Drake for information. It'll take five minutes, that's all.'

Five more minutes in this place would send her insane. 'I'm saying nothing until sunlight is on my face,' Sara said, and pushed past the detectives.

The sky was solid white, no sun visible, and the air was chilly. But it was fresh air. Sara took a deep breath. The female detective took her onto the grass on one side of the path and pulled out a notepad. Over the sergeant's shoulder, Sara saw her husband chatting with the male detective over on the other slab of green. Elliot, the solicitor, had remained inside. Jenny watched from the path.

On the way out through the prison, the detectives had explained that they'd heard the entire conversation, having recorded it using the facility's CCTV system, in case Drake incriminated himself. The female detective, Hanson, said, 'There was mention of a letter. Was there a letter?'

'No,' Sara said. She focused on the woman's face, to blur out the wing they were standing nervously close to. 'No letter came to my house. Unless my mum or dad got rid of it. But maybe it got lost in the post.'

'I imagine that it would have turned up somewhere, got opened at some point, and we would have heard about it. Did your parents not mention a letter?'

'You mean, did they say, "There was a letter from the man who tried to kill you, but we threw it away"? What do you think?' Before the detective could answer, Sara regretted her outburst. 'Sorry. I got no letter. Do you think he admitted something in it?'

'Doubtful. As you heard, he wasn't sure you'd received it. If he'd admitted additional crimes, he would have known because you would have told the police.'

'An apology, maybe?'

'Also doubtful, based on his conduct just now. Or maybe your lack of reply upset him. Would you meet with him again if we can arrange it?'

'No,' Sara snapped. Then, again, she regretted this burst of emotion. 'I mean, I'm the only person he's been willing to talk to for twenty years. If he just lied to me about abducting Isla Greaves, he's hardly going to admit something next time. I don't want to see him again. I want to move on and forget him. I won't go back in there. It won't do any good.'

'Okay, we'll leave that for now. We looked up that quote he gave you. *Ignorance is the night of the mind, but a night without moon or star.* What do you think he meant by that? We wondered if that was a code. Have you heard it before? Did it mean anything to you?'

'No.'

'And his claim that he'd given you his wisdom and now it was up to you what you did with it? What did that mean?'

'I don't know. Look, detective, I'm sorry to be brusque, but you heard what I heard. I thought he meant that he'd said he didn't abduct Isla. Do you think there's more to it? Was it a threat or something?'

'We don't know. We'll look into it. Perhaps it was just some nonsense. Now, you said there was no letter. And you can confirm there's been no other contact between you and Drake since he was locked up?'

'Of course there hasn't. Look, I have no idea what he meant by that quote, and there was no letter. I've had nothing to do with the man for two decades until he called this meeting. I don't know why he did it and I don't know what he wants and if there was a secret message in that quote, it's gone over my head. Maybe he was just trying to sound clever. If you work it out, let me know. Is there anything else?'

'No, Mrs Yorston, not for the moment. Perhaps we'll be in touch.'

That sounded a little like a threat. Maybe the detectives were just angry that their big chance to solve a cold case had turned to dust. But that wasn't her fault.

Sara saw that Joe had finished with the male policeman and they were now free to get the hell away from this place. Sara thanked Detective Hanson and walked past her.

29

Sara's eyes were locked on the prison until Jenny's car took a corner and it was lost from sight. Only then did she face front. Joe, in the back seat, was still staring, lost in thought. Ever since she'd woken that morning, she had wanted to ask a question, but didn't dare. Now she needed the answer.

'Is someone going to tell Isla Greaves' parents about this meeting?'

Jenny, driving, said, 'They were live on one of the detectives' phones while you were inside. They didn't hear your conversation with him, but they were told that Drake is still denying it.'

'I bet they're distraught. Are they okay?'

'I don't know. There's no real proof that Drake's responsible, remember. He might be telling the truth. The parents have gone twenty years without answers. I wouldn't worry that today is going to break their hearts.'

'But I do worry. They only waited twenty years because that bastard Drake wouldn't say a word. Now he has, and it was my chance to help them.'

'Chance, yes. Obligation, no. Don't let it worry you, Sara. The police will help the parents if they aren't satisfied by what happened today. You should concentrate on nothing but you. Today was about helping you get over your attack. How do you feel now you've been before the man?'

'We'll see tonight if it's worked.'

'Yes. If he's still in your thoughts now, it's only because we only just left. You need to get home, get back to your life, and then see.'

No, Drake was still in her head because this business wasn't yet finished. The original plan had been to face him and eject her own demons. But it had changed, hadn't it? She'd agreed to interrogate the serial killer about little Isla Greaves, and that part had been a big failure. 'I want to meet her. I want to tell her myself.'

'Who? Isla's mum?'

'Obligation or not, I agreed to get information from Drake, and Isla's mother was waiting for it, and I didn't deliver. Please don't tell me it won't do any good to see her. I want to. Call some old detective friend and get her address, and take me there. Please.'

30

And so it was that that afternoon Jenny's car pulled up outside Isla's mother's home. It was the same semi-detached house Isla had lived in. Sara remembered it from the news all those years ago, the only difference was a tarmacked front yard where there had once been scraggy grass.

Actually, the toys, too. There had been toys. There had been an Isla. She recalled an interview given by the mother, Wendy, when Isla was three days missing. A reporter had asked if she'd move house, given the bad memories it contained. A strange question, but Wendy Greaves had offered the perfect answer.

'This house has no bad memories. It was the streets out there she went missing from.'

Sara hadn't wanted to turn up completely unannounced, so Jenny had called one of the detectives working with Wendy and got permission for this visit. Both women had stressed that it should happen in solitude. There were no police around.

The front door had a small sign saying PLEASE USE BACK DOOR. Sara found the rear via decking down the side. The backyard was just a plain lawn, but it stopped her in her tracks.

There were toys here. A swing, a large trampoline, and

others. During the first televised public appeal Isla's parents had given, Wendy had spoken directly to her daughter: 'You're not in trouble, sweetie. Your brother isn't angry with you. We want you back and we'll be waiting in, no matter how long it takes.' Had she literally done so: remained in this house, and kept all the toys, even if it took Isla fifty years to return?

The door opened before she could knock. Wendy Greaves was tall, slim, pale, and she wore a bandanna over her head. She had no hair. Was it cancer? Sara wondered. She would not ask.

She would not get time. Wendy wore shoes and a short rain mac, and she stepped outside. A girl of about twelve, in school uniform, was by her side. She could see the resemblance.

Wendy immediately grabbed Sara in a quick hug. 'Good of you to come. I have to take Miriam here back to school. She's been to speech therapy. But I just had to wait in for you. Thank you for what you did.'

It all happened so fast that Sara was stunned for a moment. She'd expected to be blamed in some way, or at least told she could have done a better job getting Drake to admit further crimes. 'I didn't do anything. Drake said he didn't kill your Isla. It means nothing one way or the other. I'm sorry.'

Wendy turned to lock the back door. 'I think I'll take it as a final answer. Maybe he did it, maybe he didn't. Today I found out we'll never know. So, as of today, I'll know in my heart that Isla wasn't killed by that man. Not while he hasn't said he did it. That makes me feel a little better.'

Sara had to stop herself. She wanted to say no, that's not right, Drake could still have killed Isla. But Sara had taken a bizarre step today to try to come to terms with events at the turn of the century; this was Wendy's way. No one had the right to say it was wrong, however strange it seemed.

'I'm sorry about what happened to you and your family,' Wendy said. 'But don't pity me. I can't and won't forget Isla, but

I've moved on.' She indicated the little girl. 'Some say I tried to replace Isla. But you can't choose if you have a girl or a boy. And we're allowed more than one child, aren't we?'

'Yes, of course.'

'So I'm okay and I hope you believe that. It's Peter, her brother, who needs help though. He's living in South Africa. Went when he was twenty, so thirteen years ago now. I think he had to get away. But he's doing well for himself, at least on the outside. I don't hear from him much. He blames himself, I'm sure of it. But anyway, we have to go.'

Both women and the girl walked around to the front of the house. In her Outlander, Jenny watched as the trio approached a car parked in front of hers. The little girl climbed in the passenger seat and Wendy shut the door before turning back to Sara. 'It would have been nice for Miriam to have met her older sister. And to see her big brother more often. It's been years.'

Sara had a sudden, irrational thought: the big brother, Peter, throwing stones with Miriam down at Parson Cross Park. She hits him with one and runs away to hide...

'Anyway, I need to get going, but thank you,' Wendy said, cutting into Sara's daft image with another hug. 'I know you went to see that man today because of your own problems. I hope you got what you needed.'

I'll find out tonight, Sara thought.

31

When Joe and Sara got back home in the middle of the afternoon, the house was empty. The roofers were absent and Sara remembered they'd booked the day off. Joe wanted to clear his mind by escaping into old snooker footage on YouTube, so she headed out to the barn to try to work. But her head wasn't in it. She sat at her table until she heard a car pull up outside and Marcie bid goodbye to someone.

She got to the living room as Marcie entered. Joe wasn't here. Immediately, the teenager said, 'How did the meeting go?'

'Okay. I sat right in front of him and... yeah, it was fine.'

'Were you scared? Did he say anything bad to you? Tell me everything.'

'I don't want to get into it. I wasn't scared. Like you said, he's a weedy man who looks like a castaway and he means nothing to me. And now it's done. So let's move on. I'd like to never bring it up again. You okay with that?'

'If that's what you want, and if that's the best way for you to move past this, then hell yes. Starting now, we don't bring his name up again.'

She sounded sincere, but Sara knew Marcie was itching for

details. That would fade. An awkward silence was broken by Joe's return to the living room.

'I just got a call from work,' he said. 'A wedding party, some drunks and damage and... I need to pop in.'

'Okay. How long will you be? I thought we could all go out for a meal tonight.'

'Sounds good,' Joe said, heading for the door. 'If I'm not back in time, you two go without me.'

He was gone just seconds later. If Marcie noticed her dad seemed a little off, she didn't mention it. She went upstairs to bathe, dress and put on make-up. Sara put the TV on, just to kill the silence, and pottered about.

An hour later, Marcie was ready, but Sara had bad news. 'Your dad's not back yet. And I don't really feel like going out now. I know you just got ready, so why don't you go out with friends? My treat.'

'Are you okay? I can stay.'

'I'm fine, just fine. I think I want some peace and quiet after the long day, that's all. So you go and have a free meal.'

Marcie gave her mother another chance, but eventually accepted that Sara didn't feel sociable this evening. She took a proffered twenty-pound note, called friends to arrange a meet, and skipped out of the house.

The TV could no longer entertain Sara, or ward off unwelcome thoughts, so she set about doing some odd jobs that nobody had got round to. Fixing a loose plug socket. Varnishing the dining-room tabletop. Putting a new frame on a family photo.

Two hours later, Joe still hadn't returned. She called, but his mobile was off. Now, she found it impossible to ignore a growing urge. Once again she attempted to switch channels by fiddling and fixing, but it was no good. The fight was lost.

Sixty seconds later, the house was empty.

32

Arkwood Academy had endured, but St Mary's Catholic Primary School had shut seven years earlier. Its land was now a supermarket. She parked here, unwilling to stop outside the house.

As she left the car park, she stopped to stare. A man was plugging his electric car into a charging point and he gave a puzzled glance at her scrutiny. But she wasn't watching the man or admiring his car. That charging point now sat where once there had been a toolshed. Roughly in the spot where the man now stood had once laid the mutilated body of nineteen-year-old Kymm Dymock.

Staring too long superimposed an image of that corpse over the modern scene, so Sara shuddered and moved on.

The school-bus park behind the row of houses was now a standard bus stop. Nobody there. The back fence of the houses had been replaced with a similar one, but there were no gates now. Sara circled homes and approached number six from the front. The street had had potholes retarmacked and all six homes had solar panels clogging the roofs, but otherwise everything was how she remembered it.

In the driveway of number six was a tradesman's van. The front curtains were shut. The old ornamental stone was still in place under the front window, although the paving slabs on that section of garden had been swapped for smooth concrete.

She hadn't seen her old house since her parents sold it and moved out, some twelve years ago now. But there was no time to hang around. She considered knocking, but if someone answered and refused her request, she didn't know what she'd do. Better to seek forgiveness than permission on this occasion.

She followed the path that led down the side of the house. A high gate had once blocked access to the rear, but today there was no obstacle. The backyard was much the same although the old brick shed her father had built was gone, replaced by a cheap, flat-pack wooden one. But, best of all, the concrete patch behind it was still there and she could see the old bench poking out from behind. She made sure no one was in the kitchen to see her and crossed the garden.

Even twenty years ago the bench, set into the concrete, hadn't looked new, but today it did. The wooden seating slats had been replaced and the hollow metal tube sections repainted. Best of all, the plastic end caps on the backrest were originals, still scuffed and battered, so it appeared they hadn't been removed.

She took a spoon out of her pocket and started to pry one of the caps free. Her heart was thumping, and not because of the fear of being discovered trespassing.

When the end cap was free, Sara dug a finger into the hollow abyss. And touched something. If someone had removed this end cap at some point, they hadn't discovered the piece of paper she'd slotted inside the tube all those years ago.

HER DARK PAST

CHAPTER TWENTY-ONE

It is January 2002 and in just days I will be moving into my new flat with Joe. The trial has been over for a couple of weeks now. The media have finally realised that it's pointless to hound Drake's surviving victim. The funerals of his three kills are done and dusted. The magical aura of the Slasher is, thankfully, draining away.

Interest is lowered enough that I no longer get stopped in the street, but the die-hard serial-killer fans from all over the world have begun contacting me via email.

Some of the authors are sweet, sympathetic individuals, sorry for what I've been through. They pray for me. They send me little gifts and flowers. They want to meet and talk. One even said I could come and live on her farm in Texas, USA.

Some are desperate for all the little details of how each murder occurred. We know some of this already because of the police investigation, but that's not enough for the inquisitive. They want to know what Drake said to his victims, what they said back; what tortures there might have been that didn't leave physical evidence; what wounds weren't released to the public from the pathology report. Everything.

The worst of the emails are the angry ones. It's surprising how many people ask why I was so special to survive. I made the mistake of responding to the first few with anger of my own – special? For nearly getting killed? – but it only made things worse. Then I started to ignore them, even the nice ones. Now I no longer use that email address. No one has my home address or mobile number at least.

But the main question people want answered is: why? The human psyche has been studied for hundreds of years and many a serial killer has opened up his or her mind. There are a lot of answers out there as to why humans embark on killing sprees. But the broad causes don't quite define every single case. The masses want to know exactly why Drake Mills chose to stalk the streets and kill young women. That can only be achieved by professionals asking the right questions, but Drake is saying nothing to anyone.

Apparently the authors of the emails I receive think I can explain everything.

But I must now admit, for the first time ever, that there might have been an opportunity for the world to know the why, and, equally important to some, the how. Because Drake sent me a letter in which he might have bared his soul.

But why did I say might have?

Because I did not read that letter, and I told no one of its existence.

When the envelope comes through the letter box and I realise it's from Orrell Prison, I run into the backyard with it before my parents get wind. Something prevents me from tearing it into pieces, but I also dare not open it. In my parents' backyard is a metal-and-wood bench set in concrete, and I roll it up and slide it into a hollow part of the back.

I will take some time to think about whether I want to read it. But as I write this, it's been over a year and a half, and I still do not want to touch that letter. I can't bring myself to destroy it either.

Some might say that letter could have contained vital information, perhaps in regard to other crimes – maybe even poor Isla Greaves – but I doubt it. Letters sent from prison are scanned so they don't contain dangerous information or threats or contraband, so if Drake did send me something improper, it would have been seen and acted upon.

Or maybe it wasn't from Drake at all, since I only have the prison postmark to go by. Maybe another inmate contacted me. Just because a man is locked up for a crime, it doesn't mean all crime sits well with him. A fraudster or bank robber will be as appalled by Drake's actions as the next man.

But I'll never know, will I?

I plan to cut reference to the letter from the finished book, so why write this section at all? I just wanted to create a true account for myself, to see and feel the words, in the hope that it helps my healing process. If, in the future, someone finds that letter still rolled up and hidden in that bench, and it does indeed contain vital information about Drake's unknown crimes, I apologise. Of course, no one will see this apology, so why write that too?

Again, the healing process.

33

Sara sat in her car, in the supermarket car park behind her old house, and clutched her phone, waiting. It rang just two minutes after she'd sent the picture message.

'Did you have the letter all this time?' Jenny said. Sara had taken a photo of the letter and sent it to her. No text in the message. She knew Jenny would need no explanation, except for where Sara had hidden the letter for almost two decades. She now gave a quick overview, including that she'd never read it until today.

'But there's nothing in there about Isla, is there? It sounds a bit cryptic, but she's not mentioned, is she?'

'You sound worried. I think I now understand why you wanted to see Isla's mother. You were scared that Drake might have admitted things in that letter, but you hadn't read it or passed it on to the police.'

'Yes. And there's nothing, is there?'

'Calm down, Sara. No, there's nothing in it about Isla Greaves or any other possible victims. Yes, it's a little cryptic, in fact downright strange, but he was exactly the same in person. That Confucius quote he came out with at the meeting today?

But from reading it and seeing him in action today, my sense is that Drake feels a connection to you. We already discussed this possibility. He feels a bond to all his victims, only three quarters of them aren't able to respond to him. That, to him, makes you special.'

Sara took deep breaths to allow her heart to stop thumping. 'So I ignore the letter? It means nothing? Or do we give it to the police?'

'The police probably won't do anything with it. It doesn't talk about victims, and Drake is already convicted and rotting. I would just destroy and forget.'

'The destroy part will be easy.'

After the call, Sara headed home. She was shocked to realise it was early evening; she'd been out for three hours, most of that spent in her car, debating whether or not to inform Jenny of the letter. She drove fast to get home, sure that Joe would be worried.

But Joe wasn't home yet. As she pulled up, she saw his car was missing. Sara parked and called his mobile. It rang off. Inside the house, she tried again, and this time heard Joe's mobile ringing somewhere upstairs. She hadn't realised he'd forgotten it when he went to work.

Around midnight, she heard a car pull up and went to the living-room window. But it belonged to one of Marcie's friends. When her daughter entered the house, Sara said, 'Have you been back since? Did your dad come home?'

Marcie shook her head. 'Something wrong? He went into work, didn't he?'

Yes, about seven hours ago. Sara told her daughter there was nothing wrong, but wasn't sure she believed it herself. When Marcie went upstairs to get ready for bed, Sara pulled her mobile out again. This time she called his workplace, The Old Tiara. She got the overnight security guard.

'Jimmy, hi, it's Sara Yorston. Joe around?'

No, he wasn't. Everybody had gone home following the closure of the bar at eleven thirty. Jimmy had been on-site since eight and hadn't seen Joe.

'Might he have been in and you didn't see him? Maybe the back way?'

No. Jimmy had done his rounds when the bar shut and hadn't seen a soul. Joe's office was locked. Plus, Jimmy's car was the only one left in the car park. Sara thanked him and hung up.

'Something up with Dad?'

Sara spun to see Marcie in the living-room doorway. 'No, not at all. He's probably just left work and is on his way home.'

Marcie vanished without a word. Sara knew she didn't believe it, but–

Headlights cut through the chink in the curtains. Sara rushed over. Joe's car was pulling up. She sat on the sofa, with the TV on low, and tried to act like nothing was wrong. When Joe came in, he said, 'Did you call me? I left my phone here.'

Sara shook her head. 'Work problem fixed? Did you only just leave?'

'Yeah. Problem sorted. But I'm tired now so I'll go to bed.'

He did look tired, dejected even. The lie about work suddenly seemed so bad. He had probably been bombing in his car, his head a mess. It had been a tough day. The meeting with Drake had affected him more than she probably understood. She'd been too concerned with her own feelings to consider his, but would change that tomorrow.

She bid him goodnight and he went upstairs. Sara was tired, too, but, she had to admit, also a little nervous about going to bed. Because tonight would give her answers, wouldn't it? If she didn't have the dream, then her plan had worked. She would have banished Drake's poison.

But if it didn't, then she was cursed forever.

34

'Another woman?'

Marcie was sitting on the scaffolding outside her bedroom window, phone to her ear, watching the dark clouds slip across the moon. It was past midnight, peaceful and eerie at the same time. 'I don't know,' she told Louise, the girl on the other end of the phone. 'I bloody hope not. I'll kill him and leave the body for Mum to crap on.'

'Nice image,' Louise said. 'Maybe he was at work like he said and nobody saw him.'

'No, Mum asked that question on the phone. If Dad was called into work, someone would have talked to him. And he went straight in the shower when he got home.'

'Sounds like another woman then. What you going to do?'

Below, she saw the lawn blacken as the living-room light went off. Dad would be coming up to bed shortly. 'I don't know. It better not be another woman, that's all I'm saying. I hate all this secrecy.'

Louise laughed. 'You've got your own secrets, sweets. We've been together five months and–'

'That's different,' Marcie cut in. 'We're doing nothing wrong.

I'm just waiting for the right time. Anyway, we're not talking about that right now, are we?'

'Okay. Try this. Listen out for your mum and dad having sex.'

'Oh, bog off. Why?'

'My mum's brother. He cheated on his missus. He said the best thrill was sleeping with his bit on the side and then his wife right afterwards. So if your dad–'

'I get it, Louise. Proves nothing. I wish I could just find out where he was tonight, if he didn't go to work.'

'Easily done, sweets.'

Louise outlined what she had to do. It was easy, simple, and she was dismayed she hadn't thought of it herself.

They chatted for another twenty minutes, with Louise yet again asking her to promise that she wouldn't run off with a pretty African girl when she was away. After the call, Marcie went out onto the landing, to listen at her parents' door. Not for disgusting middle-aged sex sounds, but for voices, or snoring. All was silent. They were asleep, or settled with their books and unlikely to come out and catch her in the act.

She gave it ten more minutes to be sure, then sneaked downstairs, for her father's car keys. Louise's trick worked a treat and soon she had her answer. Her father's workplace was in Gawber, Barnsley, about eleven miles north of home. But according to his onboard satnav, which stored all routes taken, he had driven to a postcode to the north-east, in Doncaster. She googled the postcode. It belonged to a small village on the A18 called Dunsville.

So Dad hadn't been at work at all today. He had lied, but why? Did he have a bit on the side who lived in Dunsville? Marcie threw the car keys at the kitchen wall, angry. After the day her mother had had, this was so unfair on her. But Marcie didn't know what to do. It could wreck the marriage if she told her mother.

35

'Sweets dreams this time, I hope?'

Sara rubbed her eyes at morning sunlight streaming through a crack in the curtains. She saw Marcie standing nearby, and that Joe's side of the bed was empty. 'What time is it? Where's your dad?'

'Nearly ten.' Marcie put a cup of tea on her mum's bedside table. 'Dad's gone to work. I went out for breakfast with friends. I'm off in a minute. I just wanted to know if you had sweet dreams.'

It was a strange thing to ask – until it wasn't. Ten in the morning: Sara couldn't remember ever sleeping in so late. Slowly, it dawned on her and the cup of tea shook in her hand. 'My God, I didn't have the nightmare.'

Marcie gleefully clapped, like someone half her age. 'You're cured.'

Sara blew out her cheeks. 'Wow. I can't believe it.'

'How cool. Bet you wish you'd faced Drake earlier, eh?'

'Let's not get too happy just yet. It was one night.'

'Don't be so pessimistic. So Dad doesn't know yet?'

That made Sara pause. Yes, she'd slept in, but it was still a bit puzzling that Joe hadn't woken her. She checked her phone.

'No hope-you-had-a-good-night message from him?' Marcie asked.

'He was probably in a rush. Anyway, young miss, skedaddle so I can get dressed.'

As Sara was pulling on jeans, her phone rang. She grinned at the name in the screen, knowing exactly why Jenny was calling.

'No nightmare,' Sara answered.

Jenny made a noise of glee. 'You're cured.'

'You're the second person to say that.'

The women chatted for a few more minutes and agreed to meet at the weekend to catch up. After the call, Sara stood at the window, staring at her garden. She hoped Marcie and Jenny were right about her being cured, but she was fearful it was too early to start celebrating.

Still, it was a good sign and she could already feel the benefits of an unbroken sleep. The morning seemed brighter, and not just because of the rare winter sunshine. She felt more awake, and it wasn't all down to a lie-in. The day had the vibe of something... different, like the first of a holiday. She hoped this perky mood wasn't just a one-off. Time would tell.

Meantime, a new bounce in her step had to be taken advantage of. Something productive was called for. She would load up a box with pottery and tour the shops, make some sales. Clean her car. Throw out old clothing. And the dripping bathroom tap, that needed attention.

She pictured Drake, back in that visiting room. She wouldn't ever forget the man, but hopefully imagining him in the future would give his form a little less substance, like a line drawing. Seeing him now didn't raise her heartbeat. She even felt a little embarrassed that she'd felt so much worry about sitting across from him. It had been easy.

And necessary. Without his invite, she wouldn't now be, as Jenny and Marcie had put it, 'cured'.

'Thanks, Drake,' she said aloud, and she was smiling.

36

'Your father won't be back until late,' Sara said.

Marcie dumped her handbag on the kitchen table and snatched a piece of one of the carrots her mother was chopping.

'Where is he?'

'A problem at work, so he's had to stay. He just called me.'

Marcie stopped chewing her carrot. It was just after five in the evening and Dad had been at work all day. The number of times he'd stayed late at work could be counted on no fingers. She'd never known it. Plus, he had a deputy to take care of problems. Plus, plus, the fact that he'd lied about going into work yesterday, and he'd skipped out today without asking Mum about her nightmare. She had never known him to do that.

Was dad falling out of love with Mum? She hoped not, dearly. Things were looking up for her mother, and the higher she sailed, the bigger the drop. She would not let that happen.

Marcie got changed into comfortable house clothes and went downstairs for dinner. There was a spare plate on the table for Dad, and Marcie kept looking at it. It was hard not to imagine that seating place empty every day. What if her dad was having an affair but refused to end it, even if Marcie confronted him? What if he moved in with this woman?

'You okay?' Sara said. 'You were telling me about your day and just stopped.'

Marcie got her father out of her mind, as best she could, and they ate.

Joe came in the door at almost eight pm. He bid everyone a weak hello, but it was clear something was on his mind. While Mum plated up his dinner, he went out to water the backyard plants. That was a first for him, too. He wanted time to think.

When his food was ready, he sat at the table, still a little moody, although Mum seemed to have missed it. While Mum asked about his day, Marcie grabbed his coat. 'I'll hang this up for you.'

In the hallway, she fished in his coat pocket and found his phone. No calls or messages received or sent all day.

She quietly opened the front door and jogged to her dad's car. She loaded up his satnav and was appalled to learn he'd been back to the same postcode as yesterday evening. The housing estate in Dunsville, Doncaster, nowhere near his place of work.

However, when she clicked on the postcode to load the route on a map, the destination pin was located a little way south of the residential area. She zoomed in, puzzled. According to the pin, her dad had stopped on a portion of the A18 that cut through woods. No houses nearby; the only building was something called Windermere Hall Care Home.

She used her phone to access the internet and realised she'd made a mistake last night. The housing estate and the care home shared the same postcode – DN7 6TZ – but a google search of that postcode had yielded only the former. It was why she'd assumed he'd been visiting another woman's home. She now knew he'd been to this remote care home on both occasions.

The website for the care home showed pictures of a massive edifice more befitting the home of a vampire than old grannies. It was an ancient Victorian building with grotesque gargoyles and lit up by ground spotlights. Woods surrounded it on all sides. On a sub-menu she found information about an intended construction project that would erase some of the roadside woods and install paths and benches and ponds.

Why had her dad been to this place? Visiting a resident? None of her family were homed there. The old relative of a work colleague? But he hadn't entered the grounds, according to the pin: he'd parked on the main road. Perhaps his mistress worked there. That was it: he'd gone to pick her up, and waited outside so her friends wouldn't know about him. He probably had a secret phone.

After making sure her parents weren't watching at the living-room window, Marcie started with the driver's door pocket, then tried the passenger one. Nothing. The boot. Nothing. Next, she lay across the back seats and felt under the front ones.

No secret phone. No secret love notes.

Something else puzzled her. According to the satnav her dad had driven straight home from that spot on the A18, and he'd been there for hours. Sure, it was a pretty desolate road overshadowed by trees, but would he really have sat in the car with a woman for all that time? Right there near the entrance to the care home, where staff might see them?

None of this made much sense. But Marcie was determined to get to the bottom of it.

37

'Okay, what's wrong?'

Joe stopped. Sara was in bed, playing a game on her phone, and Joe had just entered the room. He'd been downstairs, watching TV alone. It was past midnight. He shut the door. 'What with?'

'With you, Joe. You've been out of sorts all day. And yesterday. Ever since we came back from the prison. I'm surprised Marcie hasn't noticed it as well.'

'Well, it's that bastard Drake, isn't it? He made my skin crawl in there.'

'Is that all? You've been distant with me. You left without saying bye this morning.'

Joe started to unbutton his shirt. 'You were asleep.'

'And you aren't wondering why? I didn't get woken up in the middle of the night by a certain nightmare.'

Joe leaned over and kissed her forehead. 'That's great. I didn't realise. I'm sorry. So you're cured?'

'Well, I wasn't diseased or anything. But, yes, I might just have made the step over the line. Fingers crossed.'

From blank to joyful to angry, in five seconds. Joe tossed his shirt hard into the laundry basket and headed for the bathroom. 'Trust me, that bastard is very much a disease.'

When he'd finished in the bathroom and climbed into bed, Sara asked, 'Is there something else?'

'Work, Drake, bellyache, Marcie going off to another country soon, all sorts. Just give me a day or two. I'm sorry if I upset you. I love you.'

'And you,' Sara said. 'And you'd tell me if there were any other problems I need to know about, right?'

He grunted a yes and shut off the bedside cabinet lamp.

An hour later, Joe stepped quietly out of the dark bedroom and moved down the stairs. He got his shoes and car keys and slipped out of the house. When he drove away, he covered the first thirty metres without his headlights on, just to make sure he caught no gossip's attention.

But he'd been watched by Marcie, staring through a crack in her bedroom curtains.

38

'Where did you go, Dad?'

Marcie flicked on the landing light. She was standing in her bedroom doorway. Joe was at the top of the stairs, about to sneak back into his own room.

'Couldn't sleep. I went for a bomb,' he said. The light made him squint.

'No, you went to a place called Windermere Hall Care Home. And Mum doesn't know anything about what you've been doing there.'

Joe moved towards her. Marcie stepped back so he could enter. He shut the bedroom door behind him.

'Were you watching me, Marcie? How did you know where I went?'

Marcie ignored the question. 'Are you seeing another woman? Does she work at this care home?'

'Does your mum know I went out?'

'No, not yet. And she knows nothing about another woman. That's what's going on, isn't it?'

He shrugged, which she knew meant he wasn't denying the accusation. 'Don't tell her. I'll talk to her.'

'Don't wake her now. But tomorrow. When you're alone with her. And I think you should take the day off work. You can't just break her world in two and go out.'

'Okay. I will. So leave this all up to me, okay? Don't tell her that I went out.'

'I won't, as long as you come clean about it all. And leave me out of it. Now I need sleep, Dad.'

He took the hint and left her room. Her mother had warned her never to leave her bedroom window open while the scaffolding was up, but she broke that rule now. She needed it open so she could hear the outside world. Just in case her father decided to sneak out again.

39

In the morning, Sara woke to find Joe sitting on the bed, watching her. She took a moment to gather herself, and smiled at him. 'Day two. No nightmare.'

He gave a little nod. Something was wrong, she realised. He said, 'I wanted to wait until you woke up naturally. I have something to say. You won't like it.'

She sat straight up. 'Don't tell me you've met another woman.'

'How did you know? Did Marcie mention it?'

It had been a joke, but the seriousness in his eyes said he wasn't playing along. 'Wait a minute. So it's true? And Marcie knows?'

'I haven't met her. I haven't slept with her. We've just been messaging.'

'And Marcie knows? My God.' He started to speak, but she told him to wait. She rushed to the bathroom, sat on the toilet, and waited for her head to clear. Joe was standing by the door when she returned. She sat at her dressing table, fiddling with a hairbrush, watching him in the mirror.

'Start talking,' she said. 'Who is this woman?'

'She came into my work. We got chatting and swapped numbers. I arranged to meet her last night, but backed out at the last moment. I won't do it again. I promised Marcie that I'd tell you.'

'And how did Marcie know about it and I didn't?'

'She caught me going out last night,' Joe said after a pause.

'So, you told me only because you got caught?'

'Well, I–'

'You're going to be late for work.'

Joe started to fidget. 'Perhaps I shouldn't go today. Don't we need to work this out?'

'Are you going to see this woman again?'

'No, no, I–'

'Then there's nothing to work out. I'll get over it. But I don't want to see you for a few hours, so you should go to work. We'll talk later.'

Joe headed downstairs. Sara remained at her dressing table, waiting until he'd gone. Once he had, she dressed and aimed for the kitchen. Marcie was eating breakfast at the table, and she could tell the teenager had either heard her parents' discussion or Joe had spoken to her before leaving. Sara didn't want any tension between them and needed to air this dirty laundry.

'So, you know about your dad's affair. He said you did.'

Marcie nodded. 'Are you okay? I caught him going out last night. I said he should tell you.'

Sara sat at the table and picked up Marcie's mobile, just to give her hands something to do. 'And he did.'

'I know we shouldn't talk about it. But I know that sometimes men can't control themselves around women. Are you going to leave him?'

Sara shook her head. 'We'll get through this. He said he didn't go with this woman and I believe him. He reckons he won't see her again. I didn't ask about future women though. He's got a loophole there.'

It was meant as a joke, to relieve tension, but Marcie looked so sorry for her mother that Sara had to hold back tears. 'Don't worry about me, Marcie.'

'But I do. I'm away for six months in a few weeks, and I don't want to be all the way over in Africa when I find out my dad's had to move into a new flat.'

'That won't happen. He can have the barn.'

This time Marcie understood her mother was diffusing the heavy air and smiled. 'In time, we can all forget this, I hope. So, starting now, how about we don't mention this again?'

'Yes. We won't. But I need to know one thing. After that, we forget it. How did you find out? Did you see his phone or something.'

Marcie took a big bite of her breakfast. Playing for time, Sara realised. 'What did he tell you?'

'Are you scared of telling me something I don't already know, Marcie? I spoke to your dad upstairs. He told me everything except how you knew.'

Sara's trick worked. Marcie said, 'I suspected for a few days that he was up to something. So I did some online noseying and found out he'd been to the care home twice.'

Sara nodded. 'He mentioned the care home. I can't remember the name. What was it again?'

Marcie bought more time with a mouthful of food, but this time Sara's trickery failed. 'I don't know the name. Why is that important? You're not going to go there, are you? I don't want you going round and fighting with this woman.'

Sara put her hands below the table. 'I guess I don't need to know. Let's forget about it.'

Marcie's breakfast was finished. She got up, kissed her mum's head, and headed for the door, calling back that she hoped her mum would be okay today.

'I will,' Sara said as Marcie thumped upstairs to use the shower. Sara waited a few moments and removed her hands from under the table. She still had Marcie's mobile. She got up and moved into the living room, where she opened the mobile and found the internet search history.

And there it was. Windermere Hall Care Home, Dunsville, Doncaster.

It took a few moments for her brain to make the connection; when it did, all of Sara's muscles tightened – except those in her fingers, which let the mobile thud to the carpet.

40

The Old Tiara, next to Barnsley Hospice, had once been a large Victorian library, now fully reconstructed with new annexes and a car park. Joe had been the general manager of the weddings and corporate events venue for over ten years, and as his wife, Sara, knew many of the staff. So she knew they would alert him to her arrival.

There were businesslike men and women gathered out front, smoking. A banner above the door said THE INJURY CLAIMS LAWYERS MERGER PARTY. Sara hadn't expected a function other than a wedding party to be on in the afternoon, but the commotion helped her to slip through the main doors and past the receptionist unnoticed.

Strangely for a subdued and quiet man, Joe didn't like a muted atmosphere at work and his office was a back room behind the drinks bar in the pub. The lounge was bustling, but Sara didn't escape the beady eyes of the barman as she lifted the counter flap and stepped through. Too late to alert the boss by phone anyway.

She pushed through into his office, but it was empty. There

was a pager on the desk, which she activated to summon him. It was for emergencies, and this was one.

But not according to Joe's face when he turned up a minute later, a little out of breath because he'd obviously jogged back from wherever. He was clearly shocked to see his wife sitting in his chair.

'Windermere Hall Care Home,' she said. She saw from his expression that he knew exactly what she meant. 'That's where you went to meet this so-called other woman. You didn't mention that.'

Joe shut the door behind him. He stood before the desk, but wouldn't look at his wife. His eyes roamed the walls of his office, where there were photos of the staff, various events the venue had hosted, and images of the venue before, during and after construction.

'I was going to tell you. Honest. Tonight, when I got home.'

Sara stood up so fast his desk chair rolled into a cabinet behind her, rattling it so violently that a standing calendar toppled off. 'I remember that name, Joe. How could I not? Why, Joe? On the same day we met with Drake Mills, why the hell are you suddenly sneaking around a place that played a big part in his life?'

HER DARK PAST

CHAPTER TWENTY-THREE

Five weeks after his trial, Drake is back in the headlines again. Hopefully for the final time. Again, it involves a death, but, thankfully, this time not a victim.

Drake's mother moved from Scotland to Sheffield to be close to her father, and it's reported that he's the only human Drake had a good relationship with. The only person on the planet who didn't have a bad word to say about the future serial killer.

In fact, rumour has it that his grandfather, Albert, refused to believe the stories about Drake, even after conviction. After all, this was the young man who used to visit two or three evenings a week, and bring him satsumas, and play chutes and ladders. The two men got on like a house on fire.

And now Drake's grandfather is dead. Albert was found in his bed early in the morning at Windermere Hall Care Home, where he'd been a resident for three years. When Drake received the news, it is alleged, he cried for hours.

Drake refused to comment on his loss, but there's rumour that a prison guard read a letter Drake composed to his mother, in which the killer blamed himself for his grandfather's death. He wrote of his belief that the old man finally accepted his grandson was a monster and the shock to his system simply shut him down. Apparently, the letter contained the line, 'Forgive me. My murder count is now four.'

In response to this story, a female care worker at Windermere gave an interview about the moment Drake's grandfather switched sides. She said she had wheeled him out of the lounge, back to his room, where he would soon be taking a prison call from Drake. Albert sat at his desk and the cordless phone was brought in. The care worker would wait until the conversation between killer and grandfather was active, then retire to the hallway to give them peace.

She said Albert was in joyful spirits. His own daughter's visits had ceased when she fled back to Scotland after Drake's arrest for murder, but his grandson was ever loyal. He often liked to talk about his Drake, although 'this was awkward for us, the staff, you know? Because he was that Barbie Doll Slasher lunatic. But Albert loved him, refused to believe he'd done those things. I'd just nod and stuff and then try to change the subject.'

On that afternoon that everything changed, the phone rang and Albert put his finger over the answer button. And paused. On it rang. The care worker asked him if he remembered how to answer. He turned to her and asked if she'd heard 'them things they're saying about him, them murders?'

Of course she did. Everyone did. Half the old folks living in the building refused to talk to Albert, 'as if he was somehow responsible for his grandson's soupy brain. The other half, I think they're a wee bit too out of it to know, you know?' I just nodded.

'The phone kept ringing. And he said to me, do I believe

it? I told him, well, he was convicted in court. And Albert, he just thought for a wee moment and he ended that call. He gave me the phone and said I had to block his grandson from ever calling again, and never mention him again.

'The rest of that day, he was withdrawn. I mean, he ate his dinner and he answered when spoken to and stuff, but he wasn't his normal self. Not as bubbly. Albert was always bubbly. Because I think he never believed what the papers were saying. And then he went to bed, and the next morning Shana was on, and Shana said she went in his room and he was just lying there, like he was asleep. But he was dead. I think the boss, she called the prison a bit later to tell his grandson.'

Natural causes is the official line, but given the short time frame between the trial and the death, perhaps a broken heart can truly be fatal.

But it is not the death as such that returns Drake to public attention; the story gets minimal coverage outside of Sheffield. It is the furore surrounding the funeral a week later. A Home Office spokesperson refuses to state whether or not Drake Mills will attend, leading some to assume the government is trying to hide the fact that he's been granted compassionate leave.

Six reporters lurk outside Rose Hill Crematorium, hoping for a snap of the serial killer. That takes the total number of attendees to nine – the other three are one staff and two residents from Windermere Hall Care Home. But Drake does not show. Some say this is probably because his conviction is fresh, the terror he unleashed upon South Yorkshire not yet cooled, and the government feels it wouldn't be right to open the prison gates for him.

Others say it's because the gates couldn't open.

The uncle of Drake's second victim, Sheila McGirr,

decided he wouldn't wait to find out if the Home Office had granted Drake leave. He would make sure Drake couldn't take it. On the morning of the funeral, he left his coach-driving job and travelled to HMP Orrell.

While pensioners wait around for another ride to Blackpool, McGirr's uncle is sitting in the King Long luxury coach he'd absconded with, engine off and ignition key snapped, doors locked, blinds drawn. The thirteen-metre length of the coach is enough to block the rear exit road and grass verges of the prison, much to the delight of a gaggle of objectionable-placard-wielding protestors across the road.

By the time the authorities shift the coach, the funeral of Drake's grandfather is over. If there had been plans to sneak Drake out, they'd been foiled.

This story amuses me. I know that sounds horrendous, but I can't help it. I don't know Drake's grandfather, have no opinion of him, and I don't doubt he was a worthwhile member of society. But he's someone who meant a lot to Drake and losing him will hurt that bastard for a long time.

I doubt I'm alone in this sentiment. Drake left countless parents, aunties and uncles, brothers and sisters with broken hearts, and he deserves to feel the same kind of pain. But he gets off lightly.

At least his grandfather died asleep, without pain, as God intended. He wasn't butchered to satisfy a demon's sexual desires.

41

'Tell me. Now, Joe. There's no other woman, is there?'

Joe leaned against his office door. Still his eyes roamed the walls, alighting here, there, anywhere but his wife. 'No. I lied because... it was Drake. Drake passed me a note along the floor.'

Sara was shocked. 'Drake? In the prison? What note? For me? Where is it?'

'The note was for me, not you. I think he realised you wouldn't help. Maybe he knew I'd come along to the meeting, even if told not to.'

'Help? With what? Where is this note? I want to see it.'

'I'm sorry. I was shocked and angry. I tossed it out the window on the way home.'

'And you never mentioned it to me?'

'I didn't want to upset you.'

Well, upset she was. 'That was foolish. That would have been proof for the police. What did it say?'

A smashing sound and then raucous laughter from the lounge made Joe glance that way. 'He wanted photographs of the care home staff.'

'Photographs? Why ask you? Why do it by secret note? And what does he want photographs for?'

Joe started to pace. 'I think he's suing someone there. Something to do with his grandfather's death. The note doesn't exactly say that, but it's the gist I got.'

Sara dropped into the chair behind Joe's desk, her head spinning. 'This whole thing makes no sense. Why would Drake want to sue someone nearly twenty years after his grandfather died? Why use you with a stupid secret note instead of a solicitor? He contacted Elliot and Harmon in order to get to me. Hell, this place is full of claims solicitors at the moment.'

'I don't know,' was Joe's weak reply.

'But the biggest question is: why did you agree, Joe?'

'He said we owed him.'

42

'So there was no other woman,' Sara said. It wasn't a question.

'No.'

'Drake didn't want to meet one of his victims for some kind of sexual thrill, he just wanted to get a note to you.'

'Yes.'

'And he set all of this up, all those people involved, so he could get some photographs of a care home.'

Joe shrugged. He had excused himself from work and they'd exited into an empty rear beer garden. Here, they'd taken a bench at the far end, near a stream. Joe stared into the water. Sara's eyes were glued to her husband.

'And Drake wants us to do his bidding because he thinks we're in his debt. And for some reason you agreed. Do you think we owe Drake? Why, because he's in jail? Because I didn't die that night?'

'No, I don't agree. I don't know why he thinks we owe him. Maybe exactly what you said. But I know he thinks it. And I guess I figured doing this job for him could get him off our backs.'

'Well, we're not doing it. I need to make a phone call.'

'Why? To who?'

'Why? Because Drake is an evil monster, and I don't see him as the sort to sue people.'

After hearing her plan, Joe didn't argue. Sara let him go back to work. When he was gone, she made the call.

'Can you find out something about Drake for me?' she said as soon as Jenny Pitchford answered.

There was worry in Jenny's tone. 'Why, what's happened? Is it the nightmare? It came back?'

'No, I slept fine. I just need some information. Drake's grandfather died in Windermere Hall Care Home, didn't he? I want to know if he holds a grudge against anyone there, or the care home itself. Any legal action pending? Anything like that.'

'That's a strange request, Sara. Anything I should know about?'

'No. I was just thinking back to when I wrote about it in my book.'

'And you wrote that Drake blamed himself. You don't sound like you believe that now.'

'I don't know. It was just something bugging me. It's probably nothing.'

'Well, I'll look into it and get back to you.'

After the call, Sara knew Jenny suspected something. How could she not, if the shiver in Sara's tone had been anything to go by? Her worry, which she'd been loath to inform Jenny of, was that Drake did indeed blame the care home staff for his loss and did want pictures of these people. Not for legal justice though.

He was a bringer of death, and it was all he knew. She suspected he might be planning bloody revenge and wanted to draw her and Joe into his evil plans.

43

Back home, Sara spent the whole afternoon worrying about Drake, until she literally knocked some sense into herself. Frustration and fret weighed so much that she put her head against the tall freezer in the kitchen, pulled back, and headbutted it.

'Stop this shit, Sara.'

And it worked, just like that. Suddenly, the whole notion of a revenge mission by a twenty-year convict seemed ludicrous. What if the note Drake had passed to Joe had been handed to the police? The care home staff, identified as targets, would have been guaranteed safety, foiling his plan. Of all the people to try to recruit, Drake had chosen the husband of an attempted murder victim – someone he had to know would be highly unlikely to help. Passing that note and expecting aid made no sense.

So, what did that leave? A game. Drake's lone intention had been to mess with Sara's head. He wanted her and Joe to discuss the note, worry over his intentions with the care home staff. And worry about the price of refusal. He knew – or suspected – she had long ago got over him, and he hated that. He'd stewed over this for years, possibly, until he was unable to fight the urge to act. So this was all just a game designed to make sure he never left her thoughts, to torment her, and it was best ignored, or ridiculed.

Joe didn't seem to be on that page though. She was cooking dinner when he called to say he wouldn't be back until later: 'Johnny sent me a text. He wants to run over a new song.'

Johnny was one of the members of Joe's band. In their twenties, they'd played pub gigs every weekend, but as time passed and the members acquired families, meet-ups had become less frequent. Over the last couple of years, the band had got together perhaps five times to rehearse, and their last gig had been back in June of last year. On any other day, Sara wouldn't have questioned Joe's claim.

'Forward it to me,' she said.

'Forward what?'

'I want to see the text message Johnny sent you about the song.'

'Why? I deleted it.'

'There was no text, Joe. You want to go back to the care home, don't you? After work. It's not happening. We agreed. Come straight home after work.'

Joe hung up without another word said, but he was at home when she expected him. He found her in the barn. She almost called The Old Tiara to make sure he hadn't left early and sneaked in a little detour to Windermere Hall Care Home. But that would have displayed a lack of trust.

He wasn't in a good mood. He went straight into the garden to water the plants. When his dinner was ready, he took it into the living room to eat. Marcie was in her room, no witness to her parents' tiff. Sara chose to give Joe some space. She called Jenny for an update; the former detective had tasked an old friend and active police officer with contacting Orrell Prison, but no word had yet come back. Sara had hoped she could cheer Joe up with good news, but that wasn't on the cards for this evening.

Around seven, Sara sat alone in the living room while Joe cleaned the kitchen, just for a reason to stay away from her. Marcie came downstairs, ready to go out and meet friends. Once she was gone, Sara saw an opportunity to clear the air with Joe, even if it involved an argument. But before she could get off the sofa, Joe appeared.

'Going for a bomb. Don't wait up.'

He entered the hallway for his coat and car keys. 'How do I know you're not going to Windermere?'

Childlike, he tossed his car keys by her feet and thumped upstairs. She followed and found him with the frame of their ottoman bed raised. He pulled a sleeping bag out of the storage area.

'Really? How old are we?'

The remark was a little unfair, but Joe ignored it. He took his sleeping bag and laptop into the spare room and shut the door. He was still in there when Sara went to bed a few hours later. Marcie had returned and gone straight upstairs half an hour before. So, for the first time since he was away at a conference two years before, Sara would sleep alone. So be it. Maybe they both needed space to think about things. She put the TV on low, unwilling to lie in a silent room.

Jenny called her soon afterwards, with news that bolstered her theory that Drake was playing mind games. One of Jenny's old team members, now a superintendent down in Kent, had fostered a good relationship with a prison officer at Orrell when Drake was remanded there after his arrest. The officer still worked there and had been happy to help his old friend. As far as the officer knew, Drake had never shown any anger over his grandfather's death. Not once in twenty years. In his opinion,

Drake did and always had accepted old age, not negligent staff, as the cause.

This was good news, but it did little to soothe Sara. Drake was still in her thoughts – as per the game. As soon as the light was off, the old wound in her head, painless for years, started to itch. She locked her hands together and refused to touch it. But she did switch the light back on.

44

Early the next morning, one of Marcie's friends knocked on the door. Sara answered with a smile. She recognised the tall, boyish redhead as Louise, a girl she was pretty sure had more than a friend's interest in Marcie.

'Hi, Mrs Yorston. I'm here to take Marcie for a café breakfast before college. I just saw your husband's car. Have you seen it? Looks like someone vandalised it.'

Sara followed the young woman out onto the street, where Louise pointed out twin scratches, like train tracks, along the entire side of Joe's car. Deep. Intentional. Sara was disgusted. And then a little scared.

Upstairs, Sara slammed a fist on Marcie's door to wake her for Louise, who'd followed her upstairs. She entered the spare room. Still fully dressed, Joe was dead to the world in his sleeping bag. It didn't last long. Sixty seconds later, they were standing in the street, eyeing the damage to Joe's car. He lost the last of his sleepiness in an instant.

'This is Drake's doing.'

She'd had the same thought, but refused to entertain it. 'But he's in prison.'

'Then he's got people on the outside, Sara. I don't think this is coincidence. We meet him, and soon after this happens? No way. This is a warning because we haven't done what he wants.'

'Calm down. How would Drake already know that? How long did he give you?'

'The note just said to be quick. And we wasted too much time.'

'It might just be thugs, Joe. I should be the paranoid one, but even I know what you're saying is a little far-fetched.'

He waved his hands at the street. 'No other cars have been done. This is probably a warning. Now you have to take this seriously, okay? I need to take those photographs for him. It's nothing. Just pictures?'

'I don't like it. I don't like all of this. It doesn't make sense. I...'

Here she had to pause as Marcie and Louise exited the house. Marcie didn't seem half as concerned by the damage. 'Idiot joyriders, probably. Check out Anita's CCTV. You might need it to stop the insurance company stalling. Anyway, see you later.'

'That's a good idea,' Sara said to Joe when Marcie and her friend had gone. She pointed at a house across the road. 'Anita has CCTV that will show the car. I'll go watch it and if it shows someone damaging the car, we'll show it to the police.'

'Police? We're not involving the police. Why?'

'Because Drake telling us we owe him is one thing. Threatening us is another.'

Joe held his hands out in surrender. 'Okay, look. You're right. If it's serious, we'll go to the police. But let's find out for sure. I'll go see Anita.'

Sara went inside while Joe went across the road. She watched out the window, hoping to read good news in his demeanour before he could tell her. Anita opened the door to him, they spoke for a moment, and in he went. He was out within ten minutes, and was that a calmer demeanour she sensed?

It was. 'I watched the CCTV and all it shows is a bike rushing past, close to that side of my car. I think he scraped alongside. It looks like just an accident. I guess you were right about Drake.'

'He's rotting in prison, Joe. This is all just a mind game to him. Messing with our heads. So, can we give up this photographing care homes silliness?'

Joe nodded. 'Maybe he gave the note to me because you looked confident in that visiting room. You were a match for him. He probably knew I'd freak out and... do exactly what I've been doing. Fretting.'

'So can we just forget about Drake and get on with our lives?'

'Yes.'

'And can I put the sleeping bag away?'

He laughed. 'Yes.'

Joe said he needed to shower for work and headed upstairs. Sara took a moment to compose herself and called Jenny. She knew this conversation would make the former detective suspicious, but she didn't care. She had played down the seriousness of the car vandalism in front of Joe, but inwardly it had her spooked.

'I need another favour. Ask your friend to contact the prison officer again. I want to know about Drake's friends. He's popular now, isn't he? People write to him and people in prison look up to him. I need to know about anyone he could have contact with. On the outside.'

Sure enough, Jenny seemed a little alarmed. 'Sara, what's happened? Has someone Drake knows been in contact?'

Jenny would connect the dots if given any more information. Sara's best bet now was not to lie, but to beg.

'Please don't ask. Not now. I'll explain later. I just need this favour. Can you get on to the prison and find out about people he knows? People he could get to do things for him outside prison. Please.'

Jenny gave a long pause. 'I can probably find out about any visitors Drake might have had, his phone calls and letters. And I won't ask what this is about. You can tell me when you're ready. But if you're worried about someone becoming a threat, the police need to know. I would also add that it's unlikely Drake could arrange a threat against you. Given his status, even twenty years later, he's monitored very carefully.'

After the call, Sara went up to her bedroom. She retrieved the sleeping bag and slotted it back where it belonged, in the ottoman bed. She then picked up Joe's discarded clothing from the floor.

The trousers were heavy and she found four AA batteries in one pocket. Joe walked out of the en suite dripping wet, a towel around his waist. Seeing the batteries, he said, 'From work. For the clocks. I'll swap them out. But later. Ask me why I can't do it right now.'

She could work out *why* from the sly eyes and the way he loosely held his towel in place. But she asked anyway, playing along. He let the towel drop, exposing his nakedness.

'Bit presumptuous, don't you think?' she said, but she was already closing the bedroom door.

She needed to hide her concern from Joe, to ease his soul. He didn't show emotion much, but that didn't mean he didn't feel it raging inside. So she submitted to his wants, if only to give him half an hour's reprieve. She got no such peace from a maelstrom of terrible thoughts, though, even as she lay beneath her husband.

Jenny had been convinced that Drake couldn't get word to

the outside without the prison knowing – but his letter to her all those years ago had slipped through unnoticed. Jenny had also doubted there was someone in the free world with a bond to the serial killer – but Sara felt there could be one man. It was a very loose 'could', but still a severe cause for worry.

45

'Drake hasn't made a phone call or written or received a letter in months,' Jenny said. 'That's straight from the governor at Orrell Prison. Because of his infamy and category A status, the governor personally checks all his mail, including email. Nothing. As for visitors, the last apart from us were a pair of cold-case detectives about five years ago.'

Sara was in the kitchen. Joe had just left for work, albeit late. In the hour since she'd been tasked with finding information, Jenny had worked fast.

'What about phone calls?' Sara said.

'Well, that's the tricky bit. Drake hasn't made any. All outgoing calls are recorded, but only a small percentage are listened to by the prison staff. If Drake got someone to make a call, it could have slipped through. That's what we're talking about here, isn't it? Could Drake have got word outside the prison through one of his connections inside?'

Sara ignored the question. 'But you said phone calls are recorded. The meeting with Drake was only days ago. There can't be that many calls to sift through.'

'That was mentioned, Sara, but they won't do it. If Drake got word to someone outside, he could have done it months ago. If he wanted something done it could have been set in motion with a code word in the last few days. The prison won't analyse months of phone calls from hundreds of prisoners without proof that Drake did indeed set something up. The plan could even have been arranged at visiting times, so there's an extra workload. They just won't do it.'

Sara was unimpressed and didn't know what to do next.

'Sara, talk to me. Has there been a threat? Did Drake threaten you somehow that the rest of us missed? You're obviously worried that he might send someone after you. Tell me.'

Sara unloaded it all. The secret note passed along the floor. The task to photograph staff from Windermere Hall Care Home.

Jenny listened carefully, and afterwards said, 'That's a strange story. If Drake has someone on the outside, why not use that man to take these photographs? Instead of this, which could draw attention since there's no guarantee Joe wouldn't have just immediately handed that note over to the prison staff.'

'I know, I know. I'm worried it was just a silly ploy to scare us. To keep me always looking over my shoulder.' Sara then detailed a new worry she'd been having. It had sparked in a moment of paranoia and hadn't released its grip since. What if Drake had long-term plans? What if he was playing an extended game? If Sara and Joe delivered photographs to him, he could call another meeting and deliver another ultimatum. Task after task, underlined by the threat of harm.

Today, silly photographs, just to test the waters. Tomorrow, something heavier. Meeting after meeting, he could watch Sara crumble, as he propelled her towards his ultimate goal. A task unholy, immoral, criminal. Perhaps violence against someone at the care home, if that place wasn't just a red herring.

Jenny said, 'Did Drake want addresses of the care home staff too?'

'Joe didn't say that. Just photographs. So you think Drake might want addresses as well? Might he ask for those next? To hurt these people?'

'I don't know anything yet, Sara. But I plan to. This whole thing needs investigating–'

'But no police, Jenny. Please. Not yet.'

'It's okay, Sara. If Drake has said he only plans to sue, there's no crime yet and the police wouldn't do much. So I'll sort this out. I'll dig deeper into the care home staff and see if there's a connection to Drake beyond just his grandfather. I'll also get back on to the prison about this note Drake passed. But until I have some answers, don't do anything. Stay away from the care staff. If you think you see anyone strange hanging around, call the police. But until then, please don't panic.'

'No photos and don't panic. One of those will be quite easy.'

46

Forty minutes after Joe had left for work, Sara got another call. It was from The Old Tiara. One of his staff, distressed.

'There's been an incident,' the woman said. 'Joe's car was attacked as he drove here. He's okay, he's having a sit down to relax.'

Thirty minutes later, Sara burst into the security office. Joe was sitting on a sofa, with two female staff members by his side.

'I'm okay, you didn't have to come,' he said. He looked a little shaken, and a bit embarrassed that his wife had driven down to comfort him.

'What happened?'

'I was driving here, and there was a car...'

After leaving the M1 at junction 37, a white Ford with no registration plates cut in front of him. Joe was forced to spin the wheel and hit the brakes to avoid slamming into the back of it. Stalled in a lay-by, he watched in shock as a man got out of the white car. He was dressed in black. He wore a balaclava.

The man was at the driver's window before Joe could react. Just in time, he averted his face as the man swung a hammer and sent glass spraying all over the interior of the car.

Seeing a break in the traffic cruising the motorway exit, Joe rammed his gearstick into reverse and pulled back. The man just watched as Joe cut a turn and blew past him, past the Ford, away. He watched his rear-view mirror for a pursuit, but he never saw the white car again.

'That's terrible,' Sara said. 'Are you sure you're okay?'

'Carjacking, like I said,' one of the female staff announced. 'My brother got done once, but that was late at night in Sheffield centre.'

'Leave us alone a minute,' Joe told his employees. Once they'd shut the door behind them, he grabbed Sara's hand. 'I didn't drive away, Sara. I just said that for their benefit. The truth is I froze like a deer in headlights when he broke the window. He could have done anything. He could have stolen the car. But he wasn't after the car. Drake sent him. I knew this would be bad.'

She'd been thinking the same thing, but she said, 'There's no proof of that.' She prayed he wouldn't have any.

But he did: 'Drake threatened us in the note, Sara. I didn't tell you that because I didn't want to worry you. But things have upped to a whole new level now. That man, he said something to me and then he left. That's how I know Drake sent that man and that his threat is for real. The man said, "You know what you have to do."'

47

Joe claimed he was good to finish his working day, but Sara wouldn't hear of it. She also wouldn't let him drive, so they would take her car home. But first she called Jenny and found a quiet spot to do so. She didn't even want Joe to hear the content of this conversation.

'Joe was attacked,' she said the moment Jenny answered. And she told the story as related by Joe. Including his revelation that the missing note actually contained a direct threat to harm them if they didn't obey his commands. Like Joe, she finished with the masked man's threat: *You know what you have to do*.

Jenny's reaction was immediate. 'This escalates things dramatically, Sara. Now it's time to call the police.'

'Joe said not to. I agreed, but only because I wanted to get away and tell you. And ask you something. I didn't want to bring this up in front of him. You were the lead detective on the Slasher case, Jenny. You know it better than anyone. You will know details that weren't in the trial. Things the newspapers didn't know. Things you didn't even tell me. I'm talking about someone Drake could know on the outside. And I think you know what I'm getting at.'

Jenny paused. 'It's been twenty years, Sara. That would be twenty years of silence. How would Drake have contacted this man? If there is one. Nobody was certain.'

'But it was possible. I know that from back then. I know your team looked into it. I know there was something that made you wonder if Drake didn't attack women alone. I need to know.'

'Yes,' Jenny said after another pause. 'There was no proof to say a definitive yes, but some of my team were convinced that Drake had an accomplice when he murdered those three women.'

HER DARK PAST

THE FINAL CHAPTER

Now that my story is told, I need to touch upon one more aspect, just to give a sense of totality. And, I must admit, if I do not cover this detail, it opens the door for others to do so. I want this book to be the first and last anatomy of the Slasher case so I never see my name in another.

The aspect I speak of is the theory that the Slasher had an accomplice.

That two men performed the murders is not absolute fact. The police always treated it as a possibility and the theory had its most momentum in the media, which requires new and exciting twists to keep people entertained.

I was asked by the DCI leading the investigation, Jenny Pitchford, if I had been attacked by two men, but as you know from these pages I do not recall the event that well. My partner and saviour, Joe, saw only one man by my side under the bridge that night. And if I had to swing one way or the other, I would say that it didn't feel like two sets of hands that threw me off the bridge on Black Lane. As lead investigator, Jenny's opinion carries more weight than any other and she feels it's 'probably' one man.

For help writing this story I managed to interview Jenny on one occasion, and I asked her to play devil's advocate. Convince me there are two Slashers. All of the below information is in the public domain, but scattered, and this is the first time it has all been assembled. I'll repeat that I am not asserting that there are two men killing as the Slasher, but this list does raise my eyebrows.

Kymm Dymock, Arkwood Academy, Aughton, Sheffield.

Three hundred metres south of Arkwood Academy, at the junction of Main Street and Aston Lane, is an inn called the Friar Tuck. Around seven pm, between three and four hours before Kymm was attacked, two men were sitting at one of the outdoor tables, a sports bag between them. They wore baseball caps. When the landlord approached and asked if they were going to buy drinks, the two men left without a word.

At around the time it was believed Kymm was attacked, a taxi driver was parked in the entrance of Ulley Country Park, just five hundred metres north of the crime scene. He said he saw a green car buzz rapidly past along the A618, going north, with two men in the front. Drake Mills owned a dark-blue vehicle, which could be mistaken for green at night.

Sheila McGirr, Church Lane, Dinnington, Sheffield.

The chain-link fence inside the wood, just beyond which Sheila's naked body was found, was six feet high. Sheila could have scaled the fence under duress, or even before she was confronted. There was a scrape along the back of her calf that police attempted to prove could have happened by climbing over the fence. They sent officers over, but none could replicate the wound. It was more consistent with a body being passed face-up across the fence, but one man alone couldn't achieve this.

Two hours before Sheila was murdered, two men discussing the murder of Kymm Dymock were seen at a cashpoint outside a supermarket on Undergate Road, half a mile east of the crime scene. CCTV from the area shows them leave by van. The picture quality was not adequate to rule out Drake as one of the two men, but it should be noted that he's not known to have had access to a van.

Marcie Whitecotton, Lady Field Road, Thorpe Salvin, Rotherham.

Early in the afternoon on the day of the murder, a car was seen parked right around the spot where Whitecotton's body was found. The witness could not recall the make or even the colour of the car because he was on his phone as he walked past. But he did say he clearly heard two men's voices from the vehicle.

Around midday the day after the murder, around four miles east of the crime scene, two men were spotted by a stream running through Holbrook Industrial Estate, washing themselves. The witness, walking his dog, said both men were in their twenties, but he did not see their faces or any other details because he caught only a glance between two buildings.

Other individuals spotted by witnesses close to the crime scenes at relevant times were found and eliminated, but the people mentioned above were never traced.

48

When they pulled up at home, Joe got out of the car and headed into the house. Sara sat behind the wheel, needing a moment's silence to think about her conversation with Jenny. The woman who'd led the Slasher investigation was best poised to offer a professional opinion, and she had doubts.

She found it unlikely that Drake would or could have remained in touch with a man who'd helped him murder three women. If there was an accomplice, it was a man who'd been careful and clever enough to hide his inner monster for two decades. A man that skilful just didn't strike her as the sort who'd expose himself now, for the sake of a convicted man's cruel game.

If Drake had a helper, Jenny said, then it was someone connected to someone he knew in prison. And the police needed to be involved.

Sara knew she should accept Jenny's opinion. South Yorkshire Police had invested hundreds of thousands of pounds and thousands of working hours into the Slasher enquiry. But it was hard to raise logic above a growing gut feeling. As for involving the police, Sara had had to promise she would. And she would. Soon. But she was worried about the story getting out and–

A rapping on the car window startled her. Anita stood in the road, grinning. Sara wound the window down. 'I hope you got your clocks working again.'

Puzzled, Sara said, 'What do you mean?'

'The batteries I gave Joe. Were they not for clocks? I thought he said clocks.'

'Oh. Yes. Thank you.' She made an excuse to end the conversation and quickly went inside the house to get away from the nosey neighbour.

Inside the house, Joe was making tea. Sara sat at the table and let out a big sigh. She looked up at the wall clock. She could hardly believe it was still morning, so much had happened today already.

The clock made her think of something. 'Anita just told me she gave you the batteries for the clocks. You said they were from work.'

Joe passed her a tea and sat across from her. 'Oh. Did I? Okay. Yeah, they were from Anita. What's your plan for the day? I need to go get my car fixed. We should have stayed there and called a garage.'

'Too late now. Get a taxi if you want, or call someone to fetch you. But not right now. Let's just stay here a bit.'

When Marcie returned just after five pm, Joe figured he should go fetch his car and called a taxi. Sara went upstairs to run a bath. While stripping, she spotted the batteries Joe had got from Anita on the bedside table. Something puzzled her.

She'd found the batteries in his pocket that morning. Unless they'd been in his pocket while the garment hung in the wardrobe, he must have got them that morning. When he'd gone across the road to view Anita's CCTV. Why had Anita only mentioned the batteries and not their damaged vehicle?

Sara dressed again and headed to Anita's house. The middle-aged woman answered with a mixing bowl in her hands. Sara gave her a beaming grin. 'I wonder if I could just view your CCTV for last night. Our car got damaged.'

Anita's reply: 'Oh, those scratches. Yes, I saw those. I suppose my camera would see that. I guess it would help with the insurance. Sure thing.'

Not: 'But your husband has already viewed the footage.'

Upstairs, Anita left Sara alone after showing her how to work the playback. The monitor showed Anita's garden and the street and, in the top left corner, the portion of the road where Joe always parked his car. So, she would see exactly how Joe's car got damaged.

Sara selected to start the video from the point when Joe got home from work yesterday. It was getting dark, but the picture quality was excellent and a street lamp on this side of the road handily illuminated the side of his car. Scratch-free, so the damage hadn't happened at his workplace. She played the recording in time-lapse, five minutes between frames, watching carefully for the moment when something happened.

She didn't catch the act of vandalism using this method, but she saw the scratches appear out of the blue on the side of Joe's car. That meant the event had occurred in the previous five minutes. She clicked to jump back to the previous, scratch-free frame, and selected to play the tape in real time. The time code said it was just before four in the morning.

Shivering, she watched a man move alongside the car, hunched over. He was trying to be sneaky, but she clearly saw his hand run down the length of the car, leaving twin lines behind. Then he circled around the vehicle, stood up and walked away casually. In the direction of Sara's house. She hadn't seen his face, but there was no doubt about the identity of the vandal.

Joe. Her own husband.

49

As she was heading back to her house, Jenny called. It was starting to get dark. Sara got into her car to take the call. And she locked the doors.

'I got back on to the prison and they sent me a video,' Jenny said. 'The CCTV in the visitors' room. I just watched it, Sara. It clearly shows the whole room, an angle from behind and above Drake, and you can see the floor between the table and where Joe sat. It's good quality because the prison staff have to be able to detect if contraband is passed to or from inmates–'

'What did you see?' Sara interrupted.

'There was nothing, Sara. Joe made no move to bend down as if to pick something up. Drake dropped nothing. Sara, there was no note.'

'What does that mean? He got a message to Joe another way?'

'If at all.'

'You mean there was no message? But that would mean Joe lied.'

'I know. I don't know what's going on.'

'He's been acting strange. Hiding things, hiding where he's

been. Lying. Something is going on, but if it doesn't involve Drake, then what could it be? Why would he blame Drake? Why would Joe be going to the care home at night?'

'Joe's been going there?' Jenny said. 'I figured you meant he was following some of the staff.'

'Yes, my daughter caught him going out late one night. He gave her a story about having an affair with one of the staff. Perhaps that was actually the truth and this whole Drake thing... just a lie he told me to deflect me from the other woman. But he should have realised how bringing Drake into it would mess my head up, so that doesn't really make sense, either. I just...' Sara felt a headache coming on. This whole thing was becoming too convoluted.

'Sara, I'm going to look into something. Make sure I can reach you on the phone, maybe tonight, probably tomorrow. And report that attack against Joe.'

'Don't call tonight,' Sara said. 'I'm going to be busy having a raging argument with my husband.'

50

Sara was at Marcie's bedroom window, watching as Joe's car pulled up outside. Instead of a replacement driver's side window, Joe had simply attached a clear plastic sheet. The timing was perfect because Marcie had run to the corner shop.

She went into her bedroom to wait for him. After calling her name and receiving no answer, up he came. Aware from her red eyes and folded arms that something was wrong, he shut the door behind him.

She got right to it. 'There was no message from Drake. Jenny watched the video. You vandalised your own car. I suspect you broke your own window. All bullshit. Just cut past the denial and tell me why.'

Joe paused, as if indeed he was considering a denial. He sat on the floor, right there in the doorway. 'I lied about it all, yes.'

'That's not a why. That's just you admitting what it would now be foolish to deny. Let me help you. Marcie caught you at the care home and you told her you were having an affair with someone who works there.'

Joe nodded. If he'd done that annoying shrug of his, she might have flown at him.

'Marcie told you to tell me. But an affair has long-lasting consequences. Could have ruined your marriage. So you came up with another story. Drake. He had a connection to Windermere Hall Care Home, so that story would work. The bullshit about photographs was so you could continue to visit the care home.'

Joe nodded again.

'But I told you to stay away. To have nothing to do with what Drake wanted. So you scratched up your car. When that didn't work because I wanted to see the CCTV, you discarded that idea and tried again with the imaginary masked man on the motorway slip road. All to promote the idea of a made-up threat by Drake, to convince me to let you keep going to that care home. That was your mission here. To keep visiting that care home.'

Another nod.

'And the reason? Is it another woman after all? Just like you told Marcie?'

Joe had hung his head, but now it jerked up. He stood and took a step towards her. 'Yes, but I haven't slept with her. And I don't plan to. In fact, I ended it today. I texted her.'

'Show me.'

'I deleted it.'

'Oh, like the bullshit text from Johnny about a new song?'

Joe sat on the bed and hung his head again. 'I know it was dodgy, involving Drake, but I panicked.'

'Dodgy?' Sara shouted. 'That man tried to murder me, and in twenty years I never got over it. You lied about his threatening us and you call that dodgy? What do you think that did to my head, thinking he'd sent someone to attack you? That he had an accomplice out there who might hurt me, or hurt Marcie?'

'I didn't think. I panicked, like I said. I'm sorry.' Joe softly kicked at a small branch by his feet, like a kid plucking up courage. 'So what happens now?'

Sara didn't answer for what seemed like a long time. Joe waited, head hung. She felt her anger subsiding, but for the wrong reason. Still, it was departing, and that allowed rational thought to seep in. She sat by him on the bed.

'The first thing I'll say is I'm glad to find out this doesn't involve Drake. But I can't forget the fear you put me through. It's the lies more than the affair that bothers me. But I'll get over it. There's still the affair to deal with.'

'Marcie is away soon for six months. I could move out. Maybe a trial separation.'

'Never understood such a thing. You have a trial to see if you like something. Sounds to me like people who get back together after trial separations do it because it's worse to live apart. You want that?'

'No.'

The front door slammed. Sara said, 'Marcie's back. We need to put this behind us for now, and we'll deal with it later. Maybe tomorrow.'

'Sorry for the door slamming,' Marcie said when Joe and Sara entered the living room. 'Wind got it. How's things?'

Things were fine, apparently, although Marcie very much doubted it. She could see straight through their expressions – her mother's, at least. When Marcie went up to her room shortly afterwards, it was to give her parents peace. And time to continue the argument she'd interrupted when she got home.

Upon opening the front door, she'd heard her mother's voice from upstairs:

'...more than the affair that bothers me. But I'll get over it. There's still the affair to deal with.'

'Marcie is away soon for six months. I could move out. Maybe a trial separation...'

She'd waited in the garden for a few minutes, to see if they'd finished bickering. When entering the house the second time, she'd slammed the door to make sure they knew she was back.

Now, in her room, she left the door ajar, eager to hear what came next. But all she got was silence. Maybe the argument was over. Maybe it was on pause because Marcie was present. At least they were together downstairs, not stewing in separate rooms. But maybe that, too, was for Marcie's benefit.

Hopefully they would work out their problems before Marcie left for South Africa. How could she relax over there, never knowing if she'd get a call to say Dad had moved into a crappy bedsit?

Around eleven that evening, Marcie heard the landline ring. Her parents were downstairs still.

'It's work,' she heard her father say. Then the call went onto speaker. She figured it was so her mum would know it wasn't Dad's bit on the side.

The call was from a security guard at work, who'd found the security office locked. Her dad said he had the key, must have pocketed it when he left the office earlier. He'd bring it down. The call ended.

'You can run it down there if you want. Or come with me. Or I can take Marcie.'

'No,' was her mum's reply. 'I trust you. But don't be too long.'

Marcie loved and pitied her mother at the same time. It was good that she trusted Dad despite an admitted affair. And it was naïve. Marcie certainly wasn't ready to give him the benefit of the doubt just yet.

51

Sara was drifting off when she saw faint light splash across the wall above the fireplace. She jerked awake. She got off the sofa, crossed the dark living room, and looked through the chink in the curtains. Joe had returned. It was half-past four in the morning. She waited until he got out of his car, then she considered going upstairs.

But she stopped. She would not pretend she hadn't sat up, waiting for him. He was the one who'd had an affair and nothing she did could be called unjust. So she sat and waited.

When Joe came into the living room, he turned the light on, but then straight back off when it stung her eyes. He remained in the open doorway.

'Are you okay?' he asked.

'Yes. Waited up for you. You've been gone over five hours.'

He pulled his phone and tossed it onto the sofa. 'I got talking to security, that's why it took so long. Guy's all alone all night. Call him and ask him if you like.'

Sara stood up. 'No, I believe you. Are we going to bed now?'

His answer was to head up the stairs. A minute later, she

followed with an urge to berate him. Why was he giving her the cold shoulder when all the blame was in his court?

Joe was already in bed, the room dark. They hadn't discussed the sleeping arrangement and she was annoyed that he'd assumed everything would be as normal. But she hadn't told him otherwise, had she? She slipped in beside him, but she did so dressed, and kept her distance. His back was to her and he said nothing.

She shifted as an excuse to touch him with one hand, to see if he'd undressed. A bare back confirmed that he had. Again his audacity stung. He'd ignored her and scuttled off to bed as if nothing had happened.

She clutched the quilt tightly, as if to anchor herself to the bed. She was fighting a desire to go downstairs and check Joe's phone, see if he really had been at work for so many hours. Joe was the one in the wrong and no one would blame her for losing trust in him. She also didn't dare sleep, certain that the nightmare would make a return simply because she had spent so much of today with Drake in her thoughts.

When Joe started to snore, she could fight the urge no longer.

52

On her husband's phone there were no messages to or from any numbers she couldn't explain. All were to named people she knew except two, but one was a freephone 0808 and the other, which she determined through googling, was a garage. Nothing untoward in his call history, either. As Sara was cycling through Joe's internet history, Marcie entered the dark living room.

'What are you doing?'

'Nothing,' Sara said. She tossed Joe's phone back onto the sofa. Both women stood in the dark, barely able to see each other's face. 'Why have you come down?'

'Why are you looking at Dad's phone?'

'No reason. Why are you up so late?'

'The same reason as you. Because Dad was a regular early to bed, sleep-through man until the last few days, and now he's going out late at night. You were checking Dad's phone for that other woman, weren't you? I already did that.'

'Marcie, go back to bed. Or to bed.'

Marcie flicked the light on, making them both squint. 'Mum,

I heard your argument tonight. I know Dad's still seeing that woman. And we both think that's where he's gone.'

Sara made no reply.

'You wouldn't have checked his phone if you believed him. But I know how to find out. Ask me.'

'What is this, a game, Marcie? I won't ask you a thing like that. I want you to go to bed.'

Marcie immediately left the room. And the house. Sara followed when she heard the jangle of keys and then the front door open. She watched Marcie enter Joe's car. Sara couldn't fight her curiosity and climbed into the passenger seat.

'Here,' the teenager said, tapping the satnav. She turned on the ignition, but not the engine. The satnav lit up. 'This is how I found out where Dad had been. If you trust him, let's just leave now.'

Sara didn't move. Marcie waited.

Sara leaned over and tapped the satnav. She found the recent journeys. And there it was: DN7 6TZ – Windermere Hall Care Home, Dunsville. Marcie cursed.

But there was another entry, sandwiched between the trip to the care home and Joe's journey back here. One hour and fifty-one minutes after he'd arrived at Windermere, Joe had driven further east for another mile and a half. He hadn't left this new location for two hours and eight minutes. The pin in the map was located in woodland and was marked SMALLWAYS.

Marcie loaded the postcode into her phone and got:

'Some kind of little shop. Farm and garden supplies, it says. But it's closed. Closed at five in the evening. Why would Dad go there? Looks like a place where the owner could live.'

'Get out,' Sara said. Marcie obeyed, but Sara didn't follow suit. She slid across into the driver's seat and shut the door. Through the temporary plastic window, she ordered Marcie back into the house. 'Stay there and keep your phone on you.'

'You're not going there, are you? You can't just confront some woman at this time of night.'

Sara started the engine and drove away. She wished Joe's secret trips to the care home were about another woman, but she had started feeling the reason was something far more sinister.

53

The satnav directed her past Windermere Hall Care Home, which she slowed down to take a look at. The entrance was a driveway through trees, dark and eerie. The sign out front was a smooth-faced boulder with coloured lettering carved into it. Further along the road she was on, where the trees ended, was a fenced area for what appeared to be the embryo of a building site.

She passed it as she continued in a north-easterly direction along the A18, then took a fork east, away from the built-up areas of Dunsville and into fields. Soon she passed Carrside Business Park, and reached a bridge over the M18.

Here she parked and took comfort from the lesser darkness and the sounds and sight of vehicles whizzing by below. The sense of relaxation told her just how tense she'd been during the drive. When had she last been out alone this late?

Stopping killed her momentum. Her destination was less than two minutes away, but she suddenly didn't want to continue. It would be the easiest thing in the world to turn around, drive back, climb into bed. Let Joe have his secrets. She would have her peace.

But no, she wouldn't. She needed to know.

Just past the bridge, as the road curved to the left, trees rose up on both sides. She wanted to speed quickly through them, but the satnav ordered her to turn right in just a hundred yards. She slowed, but there was nothing to see ahead except tarmac and trees.

And then it appeared: a break in the trees, just like back at Windermere. And another sign, this one a more standard slab of thin wood on posts. SMALLWAYS GARDEN AND FARM SHOP – A FRIENDLY FAMILY-RUN BUSINESS.

She willed herself to drive past, but her mutinous hands spun the steering wheel. The path through the trees was thin, and she would not be able to turn around. She had to go on. Fifty metres down, a wooden gate blocked passage. A large padlock secured it and a sign confirmed what Marcie had told her: the farm shop was closed. Apparently the family included a dog, whose barking picture and I LIVE HERE caption was also on the gate.

Beyond the gate she could make out a cluster of small buildings, barely visible in the dark. None had any lights burning. Only one looked big enough to house a family, but it was a flat-roofed, single-storey building, so probably the main shop. If there was a house, it was off to one side and not visible from her position because of the trees.

She stopped the car and put on the interior light. It would give her away to anyone watching from the house, but she couldn't sit in the darkness. She put the radio on just low enough to hear. She needed noise, but didn't want to block any that might come from outside. Her ancient head wound started to itch again.

Was this where Joe had come? To visit a mistress? Or for another reason? To find answers, she would have to get out of the car, here in the dark woods, and climb that gate. She would have to walk amongst those dark buildings. Even if there was a house on the land, she had no idea who lived there, apart from the snarling dog.

Whatever Joe had been up to out here, she could wait until morning to find out.

Suddenly, Sara screamed as a hand knifed through the plastic side window, just five inches from her head, and ripped it away.

54

The same hand snatched the keys from the ignition. Frozen, Sara watched the man walk around the front of the car, cutting through the headlights, and pull open the passenger door. Once seated, he shut off the interior light.

As the darkness closed around her, her phone rang, which made her yell out once more. The device was in her hands, although she didn't recall taking it from her pocket. She got time only to register the name on the screen – Jenny – before the man took the phone from her.

In the meek green light from the radio, she saw worry on his face in the second before he gave her a smile that now, more than ever, seemed alien to him.

Joe said, 'One of the care home staff owns this place. Drake... he...' Joe stopped. 'I reckon there's no point in that story any longer, is there?'

Sara shook her head. 'The one about a lawsuit you made up while your workplace was hosting an injury lawyers' party.'

'You ambushed me. I needed to think quick.' He paused. 'Good job my place wasn't hosting a product launch for a new sex toy. That would have been a strange story.'

Sara didn't laugh.

'How did you know I was here?' he asked. He seemed to notice the faint radio noise, but didn't turn it off.

'Where's Marcie?'

'Back home. I said I was going to go look for you. So, what brought you to me?'

'Your satnav. Marcie's idea.'

'Ah. Stored journeys. Everyone's spying on me, it seems.'

'What's going on, Joe? I don't think this is about you having an affair. This is about Drake. But not about silly photographs.'

A long pause as he considered his options. And a sigh as he determined such options were limited, and unfavourable. 'No choice now, have I? Come, I'll show you.'

He got out, came around to her door, and waited. She shook her head. 'I need to get back to Marcie. Give me the keys.'

He opened her door, and took her by the hand. His was cold, clammy, and she felt disgusted by it. But she was too scared to break his grip. He led her off the path, deep into the woods.

She thought she'd known darkness before, but this was another world. She could barely see his shape only two feet in front of her. Her legs were weak with fear, but she followed obediently, saying nothing.

When he stopped and let go of her hand, nothing seemed different. All around her were trees, just like before. But she knew she was supposed to see something, so her eyes, which had slightly adjusted to the deeper gloom, ran across the ground. And saw it.

A fresh patch of earth, clear of forest debris and slightly raised because what had been excavated couldn't all fit neatly back inside the hole. Because something else had been put in the cavity first.

'Isla Greaves.' It was her voice, but it seemed out of her control. But little Isla couldn't be in that hole... that... grave.

'Yes, but not by my hand. I mean, you know that, right?'

Now the terrible notion was real. It hit her like a truck and she felt her entire body go weak. But she kept her balance, barely. She needed the truth, and that drive was all that held her together.

'Drake killed her. How could I? I was with you.'

There seemed to be more energy now. She felt the slight breeze. Feeling was returning. And pain in her palms: she had clenched her fists, driving fingernails into her palms. What she had just discovered was the worst shock possible, and she had survived it.

'But here you are.'

'Because of Drake. That message he got to me. He admitted he killed her. He said where she was buried. He told me to get rid of the body. He said he'd have us killed if I didn't do it.'

Her mind flashed into the future, seeing a whole new media frenzy and tidal wave of hate and grief. A twenty-year secret would expose itself with the impact of a megaton bomb. She had to drag herself back from that world. 'How did Drake get a message to you? We all know it wasn't by some note slid along the floor.'

Joe paused. Half his face was obscured by total blackness, but she saw the visible portion creased in thought. Then it relaxed, and she knew he'd opted for the truth. 'Code. Like semaphore. You don't need to know the details. Drake and I developed a code when we were friends. Before I turned on him. I didn't realise I still remembered it until he started using it in that prison visiting room.'

'You knew him one day before you turned on him. In one day you developed a code for the entire English language and remembered it two decades later?'

'It's true.'

'And Drake would trust you? You stopped him killing me.

You married one of his victims. You were going to give evidence at his trial. He would trust telling you about Isla? And why would he think you'd do it? What could he have on you? What could he threaten you with?'

'Murder. He would send me to hell.'

'Hell is certainly where you're going. For the rape and murder of three innocent women. Women you killed together.'

The man before her wasn't the one she'd always known, but here he showed a flash of that vanished identity: a shrug. *It is what it is.*

55

Even killers, it seemed, had standards.

Joe shook his head and wagged a finger, like a disapproving headmistress. 'No, no, no, I raped no one. Dirty business, and it was all Drake. I had looks and charm. I was the popular boy, not like that scummy bastard. Which one of us do you think had to resort to rape?'

'But you don't deny murder. The slaughter of innocent young women. The attempt to kill me.'

'No one tried to kill you, Sara. I wouldn't have it. I'll explain, I will. But there's no time right now. As for the others, I can't help how I was born, Sara. My sin was the desire to stab and kill. There. I said it. God cursed me. He could have given me a disease. He chose this instead.'

'You sound happy about being born an evil monster.'

Joe took a step back and put his hands up, as if to promote that he was no danger to her. 'I'm not a monster. Not all the time. You know me. Back then, I only got those urges at certain times. You think I'd be sitting on a sunny beach and start imagining mutilating girls? You think I did that while I was wheeling a trolley around the shops? It doesn't work like that. You don't understand.'

He seemed angry at her gall to assume he was bad because of his actions. If she'd been surrounded by bodyguards, or twenty feet tall, or armed, she would have laughed. But she was a female alone in the dark with a man pleased by butchering such creatures, and she remained silent.

'But that's not me anymore, Sara. Not since you came into my life. Drake and me, I think we fed off each other. We were a team. Two halves of the same.' He pointed at her. 'He was the yin to my yang. He gave me that, you know.'

Sara grabbed the yin-and-yang necklace and yanked it from her neck. The old string snapped easily, but not without causing pain. She threw it into the woods. Her hand seemed to burn where she'd clutched it. She didn't want to believe his words, but she remembered her time back at Orrell Prison. How Drake had stared at the necklace. *I used to have one of those, by the way.* She felt sick.

'Without him by my side,' Joe continued, 'I never again felt those desires to hurt women. I needed him. No, what I mean by that is the monster inside me needed him. To survive. To come out. But that monster inside me died when we parted. When you came along. That man I used to be is gone. You got rid of him. I was trapped with that other person inside me. You released and saved the real Joe.'

She gave a look at the grave between them. The itch in her head had become a throb, but she ignored it.

Joe also looked at the grave. 'You think I enjoy this? You think I can dig up the bones of a murdered little girl without feeling anything? This appals me. That's why I kept going back to the care home. I just couldn't bring myself to start digging up some poor girl's grave. This is different. I haven't hurt anyone.'

He sounded panicked, desperate to convince her he wasn't a

threat to her. But why? He hinted at a forthcoming answer to this with, 'Sara, there's a reason I'm telling you all this.'

'Because I won't be a living witness,' she said, before she could stop herself.

He was horrified. 'No. Because there's still a chance for us.'

56

Despite her terror, she managed a laugh.

'No, hear me out, Sara,' Joe pleaded. 'This can work. We can come out the other side of this if we work together. Nobody is looking for Isla, not after twenty years. She can stay right here and nobody needs to know. No one's life will change.'

'You're mad,' she spat.

'No, think about it. All we have to do is make sure Marcie suspects nothing. We tell her the affair is over. We tell her never to mention the care home to anyone, especially the police if somehow they ask. If she's already told friends, we get her to tell them she was wrong. We get rid of my phone and the satnav. This can work. And Drake won't ruin us. You just need to think straight to realise this can turn out good for us.'

'You need to think straight. You're mad for believing I'd agree to this. You're evil. You're a killer.'

'Not anymore. I promise you, ever since I parted from Drake, since I met you, I haven't had the urge to kill. I haven't attacked a woman or even thought about it. I'm still the Joe you always knew. That old me is gone, like I said. I was a mirror. I mirrored Drake's evil, but that wasn't the true me. When I knew people who were the life and soul of the party, the fun people, I mirrored those. You remember the old me, don't you? Charming, humorous, kind. I can be that man again.'

He had become panicked and irrational and unlikely to understand her position. She no longer wanted to press her point, fearful that he'd lose control in the worst possible way.

But he suddenly seemed to grasp what she'd been trying to say. 'Look, Sara, I know. Despite being normal now, I still did those things, and how could you possibly stay with a killer? You don't, that's my point. We don't have to be together. I can move away, only see Marcie at weekends. Or never, if that's what she wants. I just want to live a normal life. I'm reformed and it would be such a waste for me to go to prison. That old me... what I did... that was all so many years ago.'

Sara said nothing, but her core was virtuous, always had been, would never falter, and certainly not under an onslaught of dross from the mouth of a beast. He managed to get his rotten mind straight for long enough to realise this, and it caused him to change track. He laughed at her.

'So, you're willing to ruin your own life. Do you want to be infamous, is that it? Because you will be. When the world finds out that the Slasher was actually two men and you married one of them, what do you think will happen? You're going to need aliens to land at Buckingham Palace to get your name out of the news. The world won't talk about anything else. You think it was bad for you way back? You have no idea what's coming. You'll never get peace. You'll have nightmares for the next twenty years, guaranteed. And will everyone assume you're totally innocent, that you spent all this time married to me and didn't know what I'd done? Good luck with that.'

Sara said nothing. There was no point. He could not be reasoned with.

'Okay, so you don't care about yourself, fine,' he snapped. He was angrier, his breathing more of a snort. 'What about Isla Greaves? Right now her family still have hope she's out there. Maybe she's a prostitute run by a drugs cartel in Mexico. Maybe she's a slave working fields in Africa. Beats knowing she's dust and bones. But you'll change that if we don't do this. They'll know she was killed by Drake all those years ago. All those thousands of days they spent in hope. All for nothing. It will destroy them, and you'll have done that. And Marcie, think about her. Daughter of a serial killer? Bang go any hopes she'll have of a quiet future. No more dreams of charity work abroad. She'll be an outcast, and she'll die lonely, sleeping rough under a bridge. You'll do that to her?'

She no longer could see a way out of these woods. She knew she was going to die here if she didn't submit to his way. But she couldn't, and silence seemed the best answer, even if it provoked him.

He took a step forward, and there on the fresh grave of a child murdered years ago, he got down on one knee, extending a hand towards her. Despite the terror, the cold, the utter sense of hopelessness, the sight of him in that position dredged up a memory.

HER DARK PAST

EPILOGUE

As I write this it is July 2002, and this epilogue is actually the first part of the book committed to paper. I have chosen to start with the end because telling this tale will be hard. It will drag me down into the dark depths of my mind, it will assault me with memories that, before now, I hoped to never recall. It will be a journey into mental hell and there's a chance I will exit the other end a wreck. So, I want to begin with something sweet.

Perhaps it would be better to save the happy moments until the end, because that may help me emerge in good spirits, but I have made my choice. Today was a fabulous slice of my life and it's the freshest memory I have, and so I will embark upon this journey from that high point. Maybe, like a cyclist launching from a hilltop, I will race quickly through.

Joe and I visit Newstead Abbey in Nottingham, a large country house and former home of the poet Lord Byron. It is a hot Saturday and there are hundreds of smiles around me. Kids are playing, old folks are strolling, and at the house a young couple is getting married.

It's an almost dreamlike world and I have to remind myself that pleasant places and scenes like this surely outweigh the bad ones. Right now, across the world, more people are marrying than divorcing. More are laughing than crying. There's more sun than rain. For every death, there are two births. These are facts that might not be such at all, but it helps me to believe in them.

Joe and I make a whole day of it. We explore the abbey first, then move into the park to hunt out some of the hidden oases and visit the Venetian, Japanese and French gardens. We watch the children playing in the play park, which makes me rub my belly. Inside is a little one I hope to see running and dancing and giggling one day; in fact, she's kicking inside me, as if she can hear the kids playing and yearns to join them.

After eating sandwiches at a café, we head off for a woodland walk, and it is here, with the warm sun piercing down through the treetops, that Joe tells me to stop. He walks a few feet ahead, turns, and gets down on one knee.

I almost faint in shock as he holds out a ring. His words are not traditionally romantic, but they capture my heart. I did not expect this today, but I already knew my response should it happen. To the little girl in my belly, I apologise for what is probably going to feel like an earthquake.

'So, babe, how about you and me forever?' Joe says.

'If you can catch me, I'll be yours.'

I turn, and run.

57

'So, babe, how about you and me forever?' Joe said.

Sara turned, and ran.

She knew the route back to the track, but it was a bad idea. Even if she'd had the key, Joe would catch her before she could start the car – and there was no driver's window, so locking him out wouldn't work. And when they hit flat ground, his longer legs would close the distance between them in seconds, until there was no distance, and that would be game over.

But the alternative was to thrash through the woods, not knowing if she was approaching a fence or travelling deeper in, away from the hopeful safety of other people. Her only chance was to try for the main road and hope that an early, early morning jogger, milkman or whoever was in the vicinity.

If not, she would pound for the bridge over the M1, run down the embankment and onto the motorway, and stop a car.

She risked a glance back. He sounded so close she expected to see him right there, a snarl on his face, one hand reaching for her collar. But he was a black shape about at least five metres behind. It boosted her confidence. She might just escape him.

She stopped dead suddenly, fiery pain in her chest, and for a moment thought he'd somehow circled around and she'd run right into his arms. But it was the car. Because her head had been turned, she'd blasted out onto the track without realising it. Had she not hit the vehicle, she might have pushed onward, back into the woods, totally unaware that she'd missed her exit.

Joe burst out of the trees as she pushed away from the car. Her chest thundered and sucking in lungfuls of freezing air was killing her throat, but she increased speed, now able to make bigger strides. The hole at the end of the track was close, tantalisingly so, and it would hurt more than she could imagine if he snatched her backwards just feet from the safety of the road.

But it didn't happen. Another glance back showed him hot on her tail, but he was rising to his feet. He must have tripped. She faced forward and gave it her all.

She exited out of the dark tunnel, onto the road at full pelt, and screamed as a car blew past just inches from her. The shock made her stumble forward, sprawling onto the road, scraping her hands and knees, banging her head. The world started to swim.

As the car screeched to a halt, her muddled brain made two realisations. It wasn't just one car, but many – three, was it, or seven, or more? And second: they pulsed with flashing lights. Blue, flaring up the road, the trees, the smooth, dark sky.

Police.

She sat up, facing the dark hole in the woods, and there was Joe. He was in the mouth, awash with blue light. She heard shouting, but not from him. He made no noise at all. He looked straight at her, and then turned as if to flee, and she understood why when other men flowed into her line of sight, converging on him.

58

The police didn't immediately question Sara. A paramedic gave her a once-over, declared everything fine, and she was put in the back of a car to wait. She saw Joe being dragged out of the woods and at that point put her head down and fingers in her ears. When she next looked up, he was nowhere around, probably already being driven to a cell. She watched uniformed officers block off the road and secure the scene.

Detectives arrived soon after, as well as a forensics team. Except for a female uniformed officer who poked her head in every five minutes to see if she was okay, everyone seemed to ignore her.

The reason for this treatment became clear when Jenny's Outlander arrived at the scene soon after. Sara transferred to the former detective's car and used her phone to call Marcie. Her daughter was fine, also in the company of the police, but very worried. Marcie was the reason anybody knew of that night's events and exactly where Sara and Joe had gone.

Sara calmed her daughter and said she'd be back soon. She couldn't lie, so she told Marcie nothing except to wait until she was back home. Then everything would be explained.

'How do I start such a story?' she said to Jenny. 'Marcie, by the way, your dad is a serial killer?'

Sara didn't *know* everything though. Jenny detailed how the police had managed to turn up here at the most outlandish moment.

Once she knew that Joe had been visiting Windermere Hall Care Home, Jenny had called upon a colleague to access the old Slasher files, to refresh her memory. Drake had been questioned about the evening of Tuesday, 5 June 2001, the day Isla Greaves vanished, and his alibi had been a visit to Windermere Hall Care Home. The file entry was simply a notation that a care assistant had confirmed Drake had been there to see his grandfather 'not long after teatime', which was around the time Isla disappeared.

Isla was younger than the other victims, abducted in the middle of a weekday instead of late on a weekend, and the body wasn't dumped for all to see. These details didn't fit the Slasher's signature or MO and he was never considered a viable suspect. So his alibi wasn't thoroughly investigated. Even Jenny had believed Drake was innocent of this crime.

Until she learned that Joe was doing Drake's bidding and had been visiting the care home. Too much there to be a coincidence. Google and a map had provided the answers, and a worried Jenny had sent the police to Sara's home before getting in her car for a fast drive from Birmingham.

'The snatching of Isla must have been simply an opportunistic attack,' Jenny said. 'To reach the care home, Drake would have travelled east to the M1 and then the M18 north to Doncaster. This route would have taken him by Isla's home area at the right time. If only my team had looked into this route and the timing in detail. Best guess, until we know differently, is that he saw her somewhere near the park she was hiding in, snatched her, and continued his journey.'

'He killed Isla and then still went to see his grandfather as normal?' Sara said. She needed to hear it aloud to believe it, but even that didn't work. Could anyone really be so callous?

'I think Isla was probably dead by the time he got to the care home, yes. Once there, he either buried her first, or he left her in the boot of his car, visited his grandfather, and disposed of her afterwards. It could have been a handy spot because he didn't want to spend too long driving round with a body in the car. Or he specifically chose a place he knew he had an excuse to regularly visit.'

'The second one. That's what an insane demon would do. So he could be near her grave and relive it.' Sara rubbed her eyes. She'd expected to never sleep again, but she'd had an adrenaline dump and lethargy was taking hold. 'So Drake never wanted to see *me*. It was Joe all along. His accomplice. The whole point of the meeting was to get near Joe, to talk to him. I still can't believe this. And I can't believe Joe was never a suspect before this.'

'Well, there will be an enquiry into that and I'm sure we'll have answers soon.'

'I can give you one right now. Joe told me he and Drake had a code. Like semaphore, he said. That's how they spoke in the prison.'

'We'll get to the bottom of it all, Sara. I promise you.'

Sara turned her eyes away from the activity on the road. The noise and lights were making her headache worse. Noise and lights were going to be a big part of her life over the next few weeks, months, perhaps even years. 'But one thing I have no clue about is why? Why now? Why did Drake suddenly want Isla's body moved after twenty years?'

'Again, this early it's all guesswork. But that guess is construction at Windermere. When I looked into the care home, I saw that it's getting a new garden. A lot of the woods out front will be torn up for a series of pathways. That care home is a direct connection to Drake, so if the workmen found Isla's body, that's bad news for him. He's got a comfortable life in prison, and respect from his fellow inmates. But there's a lot of serious men in there, and–'

'And prison is no holiday camp for child killers. So he needed help, and there was only one man he could trust.'

'Or one man with enough to lose to help him. We don't know the full story yet, Sara. We don't know if there was a friendship pact, or if Joe was threatened. I guess we need to hope Joe tells us, because Drake won't.'

'Everyone thought I could get Drake to admit things, but I doubted it. But I can promise you I'll get my husband to talk.'

Sara lifted her fingers to her old head wound, to scratch. But the site had gone dormant.

HER DARK PAST

FINAL EPILOGUE

Your first question, upon reading this epilogue and noting the date of July 2021, will be: why did you add to, and rerelease, a book you claimed you wished you'd never written?

The reason is the same as before. The very reason I wrote the book in the first place, two decades ago. To give my version of the story. And in a year or twenty, I will probably again wish I'd never written this book. I only want to give the truth, not to defend myself. I don't care about money either. All profits will go to the families of the victims of the Slasher(s).

The surviving relatives of Kymm Dymock, Sheila McGirr and Marcie Whitecotton have denied my request to speak with them. There are those who think I could not possibly have been oblivious to my husband's dark secret all these years, and it has been hard for these grieving family members to not wonder. I was never a suspect in the eyes of the police, but those family members reckon it's probably safest just to ignore me. Just in case. I understand.

Isla Greaves' family do not feel the same way. Joe had said that it could only hurt Isla's family to know their daughter had been dead all along, raped and killed by Drake, but he is wrong. Her mother, as before, is grateful for my actions. She got the truth... even though it resulted in yet more grief for her.

Upon hearing the news that his sister was not only dead but had been for two decades, her son, Pete, leaped off the top of his penthouse apartment building in South Africa. A suicide note confirmed what his mother believed: he blamed himself for her death. As wild as it sounds, perhaps he had somehow convinced himself Isla was still out there, hiding, and any day now she'd waltz in the door with a grin and a 'Forgive me, superfly?'

Like Isla's mother, there are those who commend me for discovering my husband was a serial killer and not hiding this terrible truth. They overlook the fact that the police got involved before I could tell them anything. Isla's mother wrote me a letter, professing her sadness for me and eternal thanks for engineering the return of her daughter. Now she has answers. If she can't have her daughter back alive, answers will suffice.

Isla Greaves' body was little more than a collection of bones, no clothing, but these remains were returned to the family for burial. The post-mortem exposed no evidence of trauma, leading investigators to suspect she was strangled. The hyoid bone in children is not yet fully formed and thus flexible, and a lack of damage here is no indication strangulation didn't happen.

Perhaps the truth about Isla's final moments will never be known, but, tellingly, the pathologist found fragments of rubber lodged between her teeth. It's likely she was suffocated by a swim cap, which she tried to chew a breathing hole in. But she wasn't the last to suffer this fate. More on that soon.

Some of what has happened in the last year and a half since Joe's arrest you may be well aware of from the news. My husband never denied a thing and was co-operative. I got word to him through the police that I might be able to forgive him, if he confessed everything. Maybe that was the reason he talked. Maybe not, since he never once asked to see me.

Either way, he talked. He cleared up all the mysteries, except one. There was one subject he refused to talk about. Drake, however, has again remained silent about everything. He has not confirmed or denied. He said not a word.

Also except for one subject.

Joe talked about his friendship with Drake. It is true that Joe befriended Drake on their first day at secondary school, and on his second day unfriended him. But unknown was that this was a trick. After that first day at school, walking home, Joe and Drake took a detour to head alongside a stream in the woods. Here, they found a fox with a broken leg, and they tortured and killed it. Right there was the spark that began a long, volatile partnership.

The boys had been bonded in an instant. After that day, they would meet in secret to stalk animals to maim and kill; and as grown men to hunt women. There was a blood pact: if one needed help, the other would always be there; if one was caught, never would he give up the other; if one stalked, both stalked.

On what they termed a 'stalk', the duo would move through the land in Drake's car, cruising remote areas to find a suitable location to snatch a victim. At first it was the mere idea of attacking someone that fed their depraved desires. They would park, walk into a possible crime scene, and just sit and describe to each other exactly what they'd like to do to a captive young woman.

Soon they would begin to act out these violent scenes

with a victim made from women's clothing stuffed with pillows. These dummies were soon swapped for a whole mannequin that Drake found in the bin out the back of the charity shop below his bedsit. They had a lot of fun.

But soon that lump of plastic would not suffice to satiate their needs. There was clear 'escalation' at play, and there are no prizes for guessing what kind of object they required for the next stage.

The plan was hatched, edited, refined over a number of weeks. Drake would leave his Grenoside bedsit and drive south-west. Joe would leave his parents' house and drive north-west. Their two straight-line journeys converge at a busy pub in the village of Worral.

The pub held a karaoke session every Saturday that brought people from all over Sheffield, so strange cars in the car park went unnoticed. Here Joe would transfer to Drake's car, and the stalk would begin.

At a secluded spot somewhere, the two men would slip out of their clothing and into gear that Drake had bought from charity shops around South Yorkshire. Black bin liners would be used to cover the seats and carpets of the car.

After the kill, they would drive to another remote location, strip, bag the old clothing and the bloody bin liners. They would find a pond or stream or river and wash each other with a portable water pump that plugged into the car's cigarette lighter. After dressing in their original, clean clothing, they would drive back to the Worral pub so Joe could collect his car and head home.

Drake would burn the bloody clothing and bin liners at some point over the next week, and wash the inside of his car. If, somehow, the police took an interest in a village pub nowhere near the crime scene, hopefully no one questioned would recall a car whose occupants hadn't been present at the karaoke night.

Initially the plan had been that Drake would rape the victim while she struggled for breath under the rubber swimming cap. She would be on her back, hands secured underneath her, Drake between her legs. Facing him, Joe would kneel with her head locked between his thighs, watching the action. To prolong her life, Joe would lift the bottom of the swimming cap every thirty seconds or so to give her air.

When Drake was done, they would remain in place and watch her suffocate to death. This part of the attack was all for Drake. His dream: to rape a terrified woman and then watch her die.

Drake would move away and Joe would plunge his weapon into the dead body. He had chosen an apple corer simply in case the police pulled Drake's car over and searched it – best not to be discovered carrying a knife. This final segment of the attack was all for Joe. His dream: to stab and gouge at young female flesh.

First up was Kymm Dymock. Joe had heard that the grounds of Arkwood Academy were popular for teenagers on a Saturday night, sometimes bringing them from miles away to watch or ride quad bikes. They hoped to see a girl they could follow home and snatch at the right moment. Upon arrival, they found Kymm alone, riding around in the dark.

Joe, handsome, charming, had no problem getting her to stop and chat. Drake leaped out of the shadows and slammed a rubber swimming cap over her head. Joe cable-tied her hands behind her back.

This was where the plan changed. As he raped her, Drake

told Joe not to lift the swimming cap. He wanted to climax as Kymm died, not before. Joe obliged, liking this new twist to the plan. But as he watched her suffocate, Kymm's head between his knees, Drake thrusting away between her legs, Joe was overcome with his own urge to adapt the plan. Suddenly, the thought of stabbing at a dead body no longer appealed.

He did not wait for Drake to finish. As his partner raped Kymm, Joe started driving his weapon in and out of her flesh. Instead of shocking Drake, the blood excited him, and the rape acquired a new energy. Both men completed at the same time, with Drake ejaculating into a condom and Joe into his underwear. Both were surprised, and overjoyed that they'd found a new commonality between their paraphilia.

Afterwards, they stripped Kymm naked and moved her next to the toolshed. For Joe, the act had quelled his hunger for sadism, and he wouldn't feel the pangs again for months. It was different for Drake, who kept Kymm's clothing for two weeks, using this totem every night to gain a new high.

When they drove away after collecting Drake's car from its hiding spot, it was north along the A618. It indeed was Drake's car spotted by a taxi driver parked by Ulley Country Park, as mentioned in a previous chapter.

When the killer duo took their next victim, Sheila McGirr, in woodland off Church Lane in Dinnington, they discovered that the activities of last time were no longer satisfactory. Initially, stabbing a dead body had no longer excited Joe and he'd plunged his weapon in while she still breathed. Now, mutilating a defenceless victim fell short of pleasing him.

Police had theorised that the killer had been unable to secure Sheila's hands behind her back, leading to myriad defensive wounds on her arms and hands. Not the case. Joe had wanted her to struggle, to flail her arms uselessly as the sharpened apple corer bored into her flesh. Sheila's frantic attempt to survive increased the pleasure of both men. When Drake yelled that he was about to finish, Joe slit her throat so his friend could climax as her heart beat a final time.

They had not chosen Sheila as a victim – she chose herself, Joe claimed. They had parked by the eventual crime scene to scout it as a location. They left their car on the road and stepped into the woods, seeking a place to hide and a spot where a girl could lay down. But when they found the fence just a few metres into the trees, they decided the area was no good and turned to leave.

That was when a car pulled up next to Drake's. A young woman got out and yelled at them, somehow of the belief that they were fly-tipping.

So, in opposition to popular belief, Sheila had not entered the woods for a sexual encounter. Her killers had not been punters. She had not gone willingly, for Joe described how he and Drake had knocked her unconscious and passed her over the fence, one man each side. Once they got her awake again, the two men got to work.

By the night the killers ensnared their third victim, they were confident in their ability to thwart the police and careful stalking fell by the wayside. Driving along Lady Field Road, deep in farmland near Thorpe Salvin, they spotted young Marcie Whitecotton riding her bike towards them. They had been heading elsewhere, but a quick look between both men decided things.

Drake spun the wheel and his car cut in front of Whitecotton, who went sailing over the bonnet as her bike crashed to a halt. She leaped over a low stone wall and tried to flee across a field, but was quickly caught. It was so easy, Joe had said, that the pair decided it was going to be girls on bikes from then on.

And once more, there was an escalation in the violence involved. This time Joe did not blindly hack at his victim's body, but chose his sites carefully. After the first stab, Marcie Whitecotton tried to ward off the apple corer, flailing wildly because she was blinded by the swimming cap. Joe made a game of it, waiting patiently for a break in her defences to drive his weapon at her chest and belly.

Fifty-nine times he was successful, not a single blow having caught her arms or hands – and there we have an answer to a mystery I long ago said would never be solved.

This slower, more methodical approach increased the attack time, so to keep her from suffocating before her time, Joe allowed Whitecotton the odd gulp of air. Unfortunately for Drake, he couldn't pace himself like Joe and climaxed long before the victim perished. Frustrated, he stepped away, leaving Joe to his game.

Once Whitecotton's arms had fallen by her sides, and Joe had slit her throat, Drake vented his anger by stamping her skull into pieces. According to Joe, Drake was very upset he'd been denied his ultimate pleasure.

'On the next one, I want to do some stabbing,' Drake had yelled. 'I want to stab her eyes out. I want to cut her ears off. I want to slice her open from pussy to ass and fuck that hole until the pain kills her.'

I was the next one.

Joe said he needed Drake's personality to react with his own to create a monster, like a binary explosive, and this much seems true. But he also admitted that the passage of time had not fully expelled those deadly desires. That look Joe gave Jenny after the meeting at Orrell Prison? Nothing to do with blaming Jenny for my anguish, as she'd assumed.

She was old, infirm, helpless, and, in his own words, he 'wanted to smash a fist hard into her face, and I only just stopped myself. I guess those few minutes in the same room as Drake reanimated the dead beast inside me'.

Long before the duo turned to murder, Joe was adamant no one could know of his and Drake's depraved alliance. He was the handsome, smart, popular boy at school, and it would harm his reputation if he was friends with a sad, pathetic loner like Drake. Mostly they communicated on the sly using untraceable Pay as You Talk prepaid mobiles bought from Woolworths. But what about at school, where they were in close proximity and it would be awkward to ignore each other?

The answer, developed over months, was a code. Akin to semaphore, it involved creating letters and some whole words by waving pencils in the air. With it, they could talk across a classroom or from opposite sides of the playground without anyone knowing. Good for cheating at classwork, too.

Despite this, Joe didn't think of Drake as a close friend. He had casual girlfriends, a job and a busy social life, and it didn't leave much room for his partner in crime. Drake, on the other hand, had nothing else going for him, and their sick escapades were all he lived for. Night after night he would sit with his secret phone, waiting to see if Joe called to ask him to hang out at the cinema or the park. But Joe wasn't interested. Only when the desire to stab and mutilate became unstoppable would Joe seek out his friend.

A few months after they had become triple murderers, Drake got fed up with sitting alone with nothing but a TV that couldn't dampen his insatiable urges. He drove to Joe's house, hoping his friend would come out. Instead, Joe called from his secret phone.

'Get lost, Drake. Get away from my house. Don't ever come around here. You know how we do this.'

'I'm sick of waiting. I want one tonight.'

'You know I can't tonight. I'm going to a party. And I don't fancy one tonight. I'll tell you when it's time.'

'Why is it always on your clock? We never stalk when I want to. Why can't I do one on my own?'

'Because you'll balls it up and they'll catch you, and then me.'

'We have a pact never to tell on–'

'I'm talking about messing up the kill. Leaving evidence. We do it together so I know it's been done right. Now get lost. I've got to go out soon.'

Drake drove away. But Joe felt guilty and called him later. 'I'm bored.'

Drake gave an excited yelp. 'What about the party you're going to?'

'That's later tonight. I'm bored now.'

'So we can stalk?'

'Why not, eh? See you at the spot,' Joe said, referring to the Worral pub.

Remember I said there was a single subject that Drake spoke of and that Joe refused to comment on? My attack. It was the night described above.

After their first kill, a little too close to home, the killers had sworn to move further afield. But the party being thrown by my friend on that Saturday night gave them other ideas. Girls would be heading to the venue via a lonely road, and how could they pass that up? Also, Joe had been thinking about moving away from total strangers and towards women he... well, if not knew, then had at least seen or met before.

And so it was that they parked half a mile away and sneaked through fields and paths and trees, to set a booby trap and lurk by the bridge on Black Lane. And then along came a girl on a bike, zipping down the hill. Me.

Because Joe planned to attend the party, he had brought his own car and dressed for the occasion. The plan had been to snatch a girl, have their way, and then Drake would head off on foot while Joe attended the party.

It was, Joe said in hindsight, another example of sloppy work as a result of overconfidence. He hadn't thought things through. If the police found the body, they would crash that party and interrogate everyone. He might be called to provide an alibi for the three previous murders. Joe had fresh clothing in his car, but what if he missed a spot of blood on his skin or in his hair or in the car and a copper spotted it?

Such events never came to pass, as we well know. At the last moment, as I was seconds from their booby trap, Joe had a change of heart. Throughout his stalks with Drake, he'd always had a casual girlfriend, but there hadn't been a woman in his life for five weeks, and he was feeling lonely.

'Not this one,' he said.

'What? Why? She's perfect,' Drake said.

'I know. But no. I'm going to save her instead.'

'Eh? From what?'

Joe playfully slapped his pal's shoulder. 'From the Doll Slasher, you evil little maniac.'

I hit the electrical cable strung between the bridge posts and was yanked off my bike. Both men rushed forward and Drake slammed a rock into my head, stunning me. He then dragged the swimming cap over my head while Joe cable-tied my hands. Both men carried me to the bridge, and threw me over.

Drake came down the embankment, to stand over me as I lay across the train tracks. Joe remained above. All part of the plan.

'HEY.'

And with a thumbs up to Joe, Drake ran. He got in the car and vacated the area. By then, Joe was by my side and the police were on their way. The rest you know.

The last conversation Joe had with Drake was on the night Joe and I met at a restaurant. Drake was upset that Joe wanted a relationship with me. He didn't want to lose his kill partner. But Joe told him straight. 'I'm not interested anymore. I like this girl. I want to be with her. I have to cut you loose, my friend.' Their time apart had already dampened the deadly desires inside Joe, he claimed.

'But what am I supposed to do?' Drake asked.

'I am no longer in control, Drake. No more for me, but I can't stop you now. Go and fill your boots. You're free to stalk whoever, whenever. Just remember the pact, my friend.'

This, I guess, is what Joe meant when he said I saved lives.

Clearly, given Isla, Drake was happy to become a lone wolf. Whether there were other attacks by him before or after Isla, we will never know. Some women came forward years ago and are doing so now that the killer is trending again, claiming Drake attacked them, although he has made no admission or denial and we can only speculate. But Isla is concrete proof that Drake's bloodlust didn't require Joe as a reagent.

Once caught, Drake held up his end of their blood pact, perhaps because Joe played no part in the police finally arriving at Drake's door. I remember after Drake's arrest that Joe had vanished for a time, upset that he could have helped the poor, bullied kid known as Peanut, perhaps prevented his metamorphosis into a chilling brute. The truth, we now know, was out of fear that his former partner would announce to the world that he'd been a mere assistant to the real Slasher.

Joe fretted day after day, for months. But when Drake changed his plea to guilty after the first day of his trial, and still didn't mention an accomplice, Joe knew his terrible secret would survive. Drake's loyalty meant that for two decades the most violent of the killer duo remained free, and in my bed, where he gave me a daughter.

But blood pacts are supposed to go both ways. Think back to my visit with Drake at Orrell Prison. With each twiddle and tap and wave and spin of the pencil in his hands, Drake was communicating with Joe using their code. Silently, he told the story of Isla Greaves, long ago buried, and now in dire need of relocating because earth-moving machines were about to uncover her.

'Ignorance is the night of the mind, but a night without moon or star'. That Confucius quote was not a silly line employed to make Drake sound clever in front of me. It was a threat, aimed at Joe, and one that required real, audible words to stress its absolute importance.

It's not wise to ignore what I ask of you today. I did for you. Now you do for me.

Joe has admitted his crimes, so there was no trial. Now, a year and a half after that terrible night, he's settled into prison and the story has faded away. The republication of this book may spark more interest, but I want my story told.

Soon after the news broke, Marcie jetted off for Plettenberg Bay, as planned. Before she left, she told me she has a girlfriend. I am very happy for her, but a little surprised it turned out to be one of her friends I'd met a handful of times already.

I also relocated – Birmingham, where I am a little more anonymous. Jenny's son, Christian, and his wife had headed off for six months to trek the Kalalau Trail in Hawaii, so Jenny was left alone. She offered me a room at the large house and a job helping out on the riding range. I soon got my own flat down there, but the job became permanent once Christian returned. I still work there.

Best of all, Marcie is still in Africa, having extended her stay. I would rather suffer the pain of missing her than see her return to this country and wallow in rumour and abuse. I still create pottery, but my hands aren't as steady these days and the quality isn't great, so my work is given away rather than sold. I also dyed my hair blonde again for the first time since I was a teenager.

I just fancied a change, but others have alternative ideas. Marcie thinks it's a midlife crisis thing. Jenny's gone all psychoanalytic and believes I'm trying to eradicate the dark period of my life. The media claimed I was trying to hide my identity.

And as for Drake? Three months after the story faded, Drake was back in the headlines again. Hopefully for the final time. Again, it involved a death, but, thankfully, this time not a victim.

Isla's mother did not want the Crown Prosecution Service to charge Drake with her child's murder, to avoid another trial, and she got her way. But not in the manner she expected. Or exactly as she expected, dare I say? After all, she could rightly blame Drake for taking away two of her children. It came about because of a jar of coffee.

Coffee is valuable currency in prison and some inmates will do anything for it. A man called Jackson, serving a whole life term for killing his girlfriend and young son, earned his jar of coffee one afternoon in April 2020.

Once the story of Drake's murder of Isla Greaves made its rounds, he was moved into segregation for his own safety. His new neighbours were fellow vulnerable prisoners also convicted of sex crimes and crimes against children. Although he was in solitary confinement, he was able to mingle with these prisoners during yard association.

On that April afternoon, Jackson approached Drake with a knife someone had smuggled into the prison. There was a rumour that Isla's cousin, serving seven years in another prison for the one-punch kill of a man in a pub, had the clout to make this happen. It wasn't the only item someone managed to get to Jackson. When the prison guards finally pulled Jackson off Drake's stabbed, bloodied body, the serial killer's head was wrapped in a pink rubber swim cap.

He was spared the prolonged, painful torture of nature, did I hear you say? Drake never did have bowel cancer, it was later determined.

The CPS could not charge a man who was unable to defend himself. The murder of ten-year-old Isla Greaves is, and forever will be, officially unsolved. But the Greaves family will probably feel justice has been done.

Hands up those who disagree?

According to some inmates, Drake's final, painful moments on this earth were spent apologising for Isla. If so, it was hollow remorse at the end of a striking blade, the equivalent of a drowning man clutching at straws. Joe's penitence was far more sincere, right? He clearly felt ashamed of the monster he'd become, right?

I certainly believed that for the two years between his confession and this very morning. I had a dream the night before that gave me a different attitude. Did the beast in Joe die when he met me? Or had my husband – yes, we are still officially married – always been proud of his infamy, and had simply entombed his inner animal inside a bland persona for twenty years? Was his confession nothing but bragging?

The dream was not my original one, which I haven't had in two years. And I'm not sure this was a dream as such, more of a memory. I replayed that long ago night when the Slasher was still active and my car broke down on a dark, desolate road. When Joe came to rescue me, I said to him:

'I'm so stupid. I kept thinking the next man along was going to be the Slasher.'

'You're not stupid,' was my future husband's reply. Oh, how I now know he wasn't just uttering generic, soothing words, but playing a game. He got a thrill from blatantly telling me I wasn't stupid, because no claim, no matter how outlandish, is stupid if it's correct.

The next man along WAS the Slasher.

THE END

ACKNOWLEDGEMENTS

I've laid out a thanks buffet for the following people.

Coronation chicken scones for the Bloodhound Books and Open Road Media brass, including Fred Freeman, and Heather Fitt.

Sausage & fennel seed slices for she who oversaw the production process of this book, Tara Lyons. Check out her own fiction at Amazon and various other online bookshops.

Chorizo pastry slices are reserved for Betsy Reavley, who green-lit the novel. She's also an author and you should have a look at her thrillers.

Chicken wing dippers go to Ian Skewis, for editing this book. With teriyaki sauce, no less, because he had to work on the novel twice due to an embarrassing author mistake. Check out his author website here: www.ianskewis.com

Cheese and pesto whirls for Hannah Deuce, publicity master.

Good old sausage rolls for Helen Smith, fundraiser and dispatcher for Yorkshire Ambulance Service. She took time out from her fine work to help with research on a couple of novels.

Mini Victoria sponges are for pre-publications readers: Aileen Davis, Anne Mosedale, Carol Flynn, Deb Day, Gill Newens, June King, Louise Gordon, Lynda Checkley, Maggie Steel, Marcie Whitecotton-Carroll, Pamela DeWolfe-Morton, Rebecca Ashworth, Rebecca Charlesworth, Sheena Lowe, Sheree Thorpe, Susan Burns.

A NOTE FROM THE PUBLISHER

Thank you for reading this book. If you enjoyed it please do consider leaving a review on Amazon to help others find it too.

We hate typos. All of our books have been rigorously edited and proofread, but sometimes mistakes do slip through. If you have spotted a typo, please do let us know and we can get it amended within hours.

info@bloodhoundbooks.com